Licence Renewed

The whole thing was deadly, and Bond knew that M's worst fears were proved. This was no ordinary little plan but a full-scale, worldwide conspiracy of great danger. As for the contract killing, he could not even start to think how that fitted in. The weapon would be an air rifle, undoubtedly firing a capsule containing some quick-acting poison. The word palace had been mentioned, and the victim was a woman. Bond immediately thought of royalty. The Queen, even . . .

He was just returning the headset to the closet, packed away in the case, when he heard the click of the door bolts again. Surely Mary-Jane would not have the nerve to return to his room for a second visit. The handle was turning, and for the second time that night Bond moved quickly to the door and yanked it open.

There was a little squeal as Lavender Peacock half fell into the room, and James Bond's arms . . .

Also by the same author

James Bond Titles
For Special Services
Icebreaker
Role of Honour
No Deals, Mr Bond
Nobody Lives Forever
Scorpius
Win, Lose or Die
Brokenclaw
The Man from Barbarossa
Death is Forever
Never Send Flowers
Sea Fire
Licence to Kill (based on the film written by
Michael G. Wilson and Richard Maibaum)

Other Thrillers
The Dancing Dodo
The Nostradamus Traitor
The Quiet Dogs
The Werewolf Trace
The Garden of Weapons
Maestro

About the author

John Gardner was educated in Berkshire and at St John's College, Cambridge. He has had many fascinating occupations and was, variously, a Royal Marine officer, a stage magician, theatre critic, reviewer and journalist. As well as his James Bond novels, most recently *Death is Forever* and *Seafire*, Gardner's other fiction includes the acclaimed Herbie Kruger novels, most recently *Maestro*.

Ian Fleming's

JAMES BOND

in

John Gardner's

Licence Renewed

CORONET BOOKS

Hodder and Stoughton

First published in 1981 by Jonathan Cape Ltd.
and Hodder and Stoughton Ltd.
First published in paperback in 1982 by Hodder and Stoughton
A division of Hodder Headline PLC

A Coronet Paperback

10 9 8 7 6 5

A CIP catalogue record for this title
is available from the British Library.

ISBN 0 340 26873 5

Printed and bound in Great Britain by
Cox & Wyman Ltd, Reading, Berkshire

Hodder and Stoughton
A division of Hodder Headline PLC
338 Euston Road
London NW1 3BH

CONTENTS

	Acknowledgments	9
1	Passenger for Flight 154	11
2	Thoughts in a Surrey Lane	14
3	The Opposition	25
4	Dossier on a Laird	35
5	The Road to Ascot	45
6	Pearls Before Swine	60
7	King of the Castle	74
8	Virgin on the Rocks	82
9	All Mod Cons	92
10	Dilly-Dilly	104
11	The Slingshot Syndrome	113
12	A Contract, Mr Bond	127
13	Nightride	142
14	High Frequency	158
15	Gone Away	169
16	Fête and Fate	182
17	Death in Many Fashions	192
18	A Watched Plot	205
19	Ultimatum	220
20	Warlock	236
21	Airstrike	249
22	Warlock's Castle	258
23	Quite a Lady	268

In memory of

Ian Lancaster Fleming

ACKNOWLEDGEMENTS

I would like, especially, to thank the Board of Directors of Glidrose Publications Ltd, the owners of the James Bond literary copyright, for asking me to undertake the somewhat daunting task of picking up where Mr Ian Fleming left off, and transporting 007 into the 1980s. In particular, my thanks to Mr Dennis Joss and Mr Peter Janson-Smith; also to H.R.F.K., who acted as the original 'Go-Between'.

We have become so used to James Bond gadgets which boggle the mind that I would like to point out to any unbelievers that all the 'hardware' used by Mr Bond in this story is genuine. Everything provided by Q Branch and carried by Bond – even the modifications to Mr Bond's Saab – is obtainable on either the open, or clandestine, markets. For assistance in seeking details about such equipment I am especially indebted to Communication Control Systems Ltd and, more particularly, to the delicious Ms Jo Ann O'Neill and the redoubtable Sidney.

As for the inventions of Anton Murik, Laird of Murcaldy, only time will tell.

1981   JOHN GARDNER

PASSENGER FOR FLIGHT
154

THE MAN WHO entered the airport washroom had light hair, cut neatly to collar length. Stocky, and around five feet three inches in height, he wore crumpled jeans, a T-shirt and sneakers. A trained observer would have particularly noted the piercing light blue eyes, above which thin brows arched in long curves that almost met above the slim nose.

The man's face was thin in comparison with his body, and the complexion a shade dark in contrast to the colour of the hair. He carried a small brown suitcase, and, on entering the washroom, walked straight towards one of the cubicles, stepping carefully past a dungareed cleaner who was mopping the tiled floor with a squeegee, though without enthusiasm.

Once inside, the man slid the bolt and placed the suitcase on the lavatory seat, opening it to remove a mirror which he hung on the door hook before starting to strip as far as his white undershorts.

Before removing the T-shirt, he slid his fingers expertly below the hairline at his temples, peeling back the wig to reveal close-cropped natural hair underneath.

With a finger and thumb he grasped the corner of his left eyebrow and pulled, as a nurse will quickly rip sticking plaster from a cut. The slim eyebrows disappeared — together with what seemed to be some of the flesh — leaving black, untrimmed, thick lines of natural hair in their place.

The man worked like a professional — with care and speed, as though he was trying to beat a clock. From the suitcase he took a canvas corset, wrapping it around his waist, pulling tightly at the lacing, giving the immediate twin effect of slimming the waistline, and an illusion of more height. Within a few seconds the latter illusion was strengthened. Carefully folding the jeans and T-shirt, the man pushed his socks into his abandoned sneakers, and pulled on a new pair of dark grey socks, followed by well-cut lightweight charcoal grey trousers and black slip-on shoes, into which were built what actors call 'lifts': adding a good two inches to his normal stature.

Adjusting the mirror on the door, he now donned a white silk shirt, and knotted a pearl grey tie into place, before opening an oblong plastic box that had been lying – held in place by the shoes on either side – directly beneath the corset, socks, trousers and shirt, in the suitcase.

The plastic box contained new components for the man's face. First, dark contact lenses, and fluid, to change those distinctive light blue eyes to a deep, almost jet, black. Next, he inserted small, shaped foam rubber pads into his cheeks which fattened the face. While they were in place he would not be able to eat or drink, but that mattered little compared with achieving the desired effect.

The pièce de résistance was a tailor-made short beard and moustache, sculpted from real hair on to an invisible, adhesive, Latex frame – genuine bristles overhanging the flexible frame which, when he set it correctly in place on his chin and lower lip, gave the impression of complete reality, even at very close range. The beard had been made specially, in New York, by an expert who dubiously claimed distant kinship with the famous nineteenth-century Wagnerian singer, Ludwig Leichner, inventor of theatrical greasepaint.

The man smiled at the unfamiliar face now looking back at him from the mirror, completing the new picture with a pair of steel-framed, clear-glass lensed, spectacles. Leichner's unproven relative apart, the unrecognisable person looking out from the mirror was a make-up expert and disguise artist in his own right. It was part of his stock-in-trade – probably the least lethal part – and he had studied under top men and women in Hollywood, as well as being almost encyclopaedic in the personal knowledge he had culled from all the famous. works, such as Lacy's *Art of Acting*, the anonymous *Practical Guide to the Art of Making Up*, by 'Haresfoot and Rouge', and the other standard works by Leman Rede, C. H. Fox, and the great S. J. A. Fitzgerald.

Now he closed the oblong box, removed a jacket, which matched the trousers, from the case, filled his pockets with an assortment of items – wallet, passport, travel documents, handkerchief, loose change and notes – and took a final look at himself in the mirror. He then packed everything with extreme care, clipped a gold digital watch around his left wrist and removed a final item from a pocket in the lid – a tightly fitting cover, which, when slipped into place over the suitcase, gave it an outer skin: changing the colour from brown to a glossy black. Lastly, he closed up, slid the new skin around the case, and spun the numbered safety locks.

Taking a final look around, the man checked his pockets and left the cubicle, completely unrecognisable as the person who had entered. He walked straight to the exit, then out, across the concourse, to the check-in desk.

Inside the washroom, the man who had been engaged in swabbing the tiled floor, leaned his squeegee against the wall and left. He also headed across the concourse, passing close to the check-in desk, and going to a door marked Private, which he unlocked with a personal key. Inside the small room there was a table, chair and telephone.

As the man with a new face was preparing to board Aer Lingus flight EI 154 from Dublin to London, Heathrow, the insignificant-looking cleaner was speaking rapidly into the telephone. The time was shortly before eight forty-five a.m.

THOUGHTS IN A SURREY LANE

JAMES BOND CHANGED down into third gear, drifted the Saab 900 Turbo into a tight left-hand turn, clinging to the grass verge, then put on a fraction more power to bring the car out of the bend.

He was driving through a complicated series of country lanes – backdoubles as London cabbies would call them – following a short cut through the hedges, rolling fields and cathedral arches of trees threading the byways of Surrey. It was a cross-country route that would, finally, take him on to the Guildford by-pass and a straight run, on good roads, into London.

Bond was travelling much too fast. A glance at the head-up display of digital instruments, reflected in the wind-shield of this personalised Saab, told him the machine was touching seventy miles per hour. Decidedly dangerous for this kind of secondary road. The motor howled as he changed down again, then accelerated through a series of S-bends. Gently common sense took over, and Bond applied a touch to the brakes, reducing speed to a more realistic pace. He still, however, remained hot and angry.

Already that evening he had made the same journey, in the opposite direction, to his recently acquired and newly decorated country cottage. Now on this beautiful Friday evening in early June, he was driving at breakneck speed back to London.

The week-end had been planned for some time, and, as the builders and decorators had just moved out, this was to

have been his first free week-end at the cottage. Further-
more, he had planned to spend it with a girl friend of long
standing – an agile, superbly nubile blonde he had known
– as Bill Tanner, M's Chief-of-Staff put it – 'on and off for
years'. The fact that she lived only six miles or so from the
cottage had greatly influenced Bond's purchase. On that
Friday, he had completed a mound of paperwork in record
time, not even leaving the office for lunch, so that he could
get out of the hot chaos of London traffic in good time,
before the normal Friday evening snarl-up began.

The countryside was at its best; the mixed fragrance of a
perfect summer filtering into the car, bringing with it a
sense of well-being and contentment – something rare for
Bond these days.

James Bond was not a superstitious man, but, as he
neared the cottage that evening, he had noticed there
seemed to be more magpies than usual. They flew low,
rolling and fluttering across the roads and lanes like black
and white dice in a game of craps. Bond thought of the old
adage, 'One for sorrow, two for joy'. There were a lot of
single magpies swooping near the car.

On reaching the cottage, Bond put a bottle of Dom
Perignon '55 on ice, knowing that it would either be magnificent or the most expensive wine vinegar he had ever
tasted.

He then went into the downstairs spare room, discarded
the somewhat conservative business suit, and showered,
first under a scalding spray, then with ice cold water, which
seemed to cut into him like needles. After drying himself
with a rough towel, Bond rubbed a small amount of Guer-
lain's Imperial Cologne into his skin before putting on a
pair of lightweight worsted navy slacks, and a white Sea
Island cotton shirt. He slipped into comfortable soft leather
sandals and was just clipping the old and valued gold Rolex
Oyster Perpetual on to his wrist when the telephone rang.

It was more of a purr than a ring. The red 'phone. His
heart sank. Both here, at the cottage, and in his London flat

off the King's Road, James Bond was required to have two telephones: one for normal use, though unlisted; and a second, red instrument — a flat, angled piece of equipment, without dial or number punches. Called, in his trade, a 'wiretap trap', this secure, sterile, unbuggable 'phone was linked directly to the building overlooking Regent's Park, known as the headquarters of Transworld Export Ltd.

Before he had even put a hand to the 'phone, Bond experienced his first flash of mild annoyance. The only reason for a call from headquarters on a Friday evening could be some kind of emergency: or a state of readiness created by M for Bond's benefit. Bond's annoyance was, possibly, heightened by the fact that, of late, many emergencies had meant sitting in a control or communications room for days at a time; or going through a complex briefing which ended with orders to abort the planned mission. Times had changed, and Bond did not like some of the political restraints placed on the Secret Service, for which he had worked with fidelity for longer than he cared to remember.

He picked up the red 'phone.

'James?' As Bond expected, it was Bill Tanner's voice on the line.

Bond grunted a surly affirmative.

'M wants you here,' Tanner said, in a voice flat as a billiards table.

'Now?'

'His actual words are not for the telephone, but he indicated that sooner than now would be more acceptable.'

'On a Friday evening?' Bond mused, the irritation building quickly inside his head as he saw an idyllic week-end filtering away, like an excellent bottle of wine being poured down the drain.

'Now,' repeated the Chief-of-Staff, closing the line.

As he reached the Guildford by-pass, Bond remembered the sound of disappointment in his girl friend's voice when he had telephoned to say the week-end was off. He supposed that should be some consolation – not that there was much to console Bond these days. There had even been times, recently, when he had seriously considered resigning – to use the jargon, 'go private'. Argot changes. At one time the phrase would have meant defection; but not any more.

'Changing world; changing times, James,' M had said to him a couple of years ago, when breaking the news that the élite Double-O status – which meant being licensed to kill in the line of duty – was being abolished. 'Fools of politicians have no idea of our requirements. Have us punching time clocks before long.'

This was during the so-called Realignment Purge, often referred to in the Service as the SNAFU Slaughter, similar to the C.I.A.'s famous Hallowe'en Massacre, in which large numbers of faithful members of the American service had been dismissed, literally overnight. Similar things had happened in Britain, with financial horns being pulled in, and what a pompous Whitehall directive called 'a more realistic logic being enforced upon the Secret and Security Services'.

'Trying to draw our fangs, James,' M had continued on that depressing day. Then, with one of those rare smiles which seemed to light up the deep grey eyes, M grunted that Whitehall had taken on the wrong man while he was still in charge. 'As far as I'm concerned, 007, you will remain 007. I shall take full responsibility for you; and you will, as ever, accept orders and assignments only from me. There are moments when this country needs a trouble-shooter – a blunt instrument – and by heaven it's going to have one. They can issue their pieces of bumf and abolish the Double-O section. We can simply change its name. It will now be the Special Section, and *you* are it. Understand, 007?'

'Of course, sir.' Bond remembered smiling. In spite of M's brusque and often uncompromising attitude, Bond loved him as a father. To 007, M *was* the Service, and the Service was Bond's life. After all, what M suggested was

exactly what the Russians had done with his old enemies
SMERSH — *Smyert Shpionam*, Death to Spies. They still existed,
the dark core at the heart of the K.G.B., having gone
through a whole gamut of metamorphoses, becoming the
O.K.R., then the Thirteenth Department of Line F, and
now, Department Viktor. Yet their work and basic organisation remained the same—political murder; kidnap;
sabotage; assassination; the quick disposal of enemy
agents, either after interrogation or as acts of war on the
secret battlefield.

Bond had left M's office on that occasion in an elated
mood. Yet, in the few years that had passed since, he had
performed only four missions in which his Double-O prefix
had played any part. A portion of his work was to kill
people. It was not a facet of life he enjoyed, but he did it
very well in the course of duty. There was certainly no
pathological hankering after that kind of work. It was the
active life that Bond missed; the continual challenge of a
new problem, a difficult decision in the field, the sense of
purpose and of serving his country. Sometimes he wondered if he was falling under the spell of that malaise which
seemed, on occasions, to grip Britain by the throat — political and economic lethargy, combined with a short-term
view of the world's problems.

Bond's four most recent missions had been quick, cut
and dried, undercover operations; and, while it would be
wrong to say that James Bond yearned for the danger, his
life now seemed, at times, to lack real purpose.

He still kept in the peak of condition: each morning going
through a rigorous workout of press-ups, leg-raising, arm
and breathing exercises. There was a 'refresher' on combat
and silent kills once a month, at the firm's training estab-
lishment; the weekly small arms shoot in the sophisticated
electronic range far below the Regent's Park headquarters;
and the monthly all-weapons shoot at the Maidstone Police
Range. Twice a year he disappeared for a fortnight to the
SAS headquarters in Herefordshire.

Bond had even managed to alter his lifestyle, very slightly, adapting to the changing pressures of the 1970s and early 1980s: drastically cutting back – for most of the time – on his alcohol intake, and arranging with Morelands of Grosvenor Street for a new special blend of cigarettes, with a tar content slightly lower than any currently available on the market. At this moment twenty of these cigarettes, each one with the distinctive three gold rings just below the filter, lay in the gunmetal case, snug in Bond's breast pocket.

For the rest, the last few years for Bond had been the grind of an executive officer to M: planning paperwork, interrogating, de-briefing, analysis, dirty tricks and bugging operations, with his fair share of Duty Officer watches to stand. His only extra joys during this period had come from the purchase of the cottage and the new car.

He had fancied a small country retreat for some time, and found the right place five miles out of Haslemere, and a good mile from the nearest village. It fitted Bond's requirements perfectly and was bought within twenty-four hours of first viewing. A month later the builders and decorators had moved in with very precise instructions from the new owner.

The car was a different matter. With fuel costs running high, and the inevitability that they would continue to do so, Bond had allowed the beloved old Mark II Continental Bentley to go the way of its predecessor, the 4·5-litre Bentley.

Some eyebrows were raised at his choice of a foreign car, when all the pressure was on to buy British, but Bond shrugged it off by pointing to the fact that it was a British specialist firm which carried out the particularly complex and sophisticated personalisation – such as the head-up digital instrument display, the cruise control system, and several other pieces of magic, made possible by British know-how and the mighty micro-chip.

He did not mention the month during which the car had

been taken over by the multinational Communication Control Systems (C.C.S.) company, who added some of their own standard refinements – security devices that would make Q Branch's mouths water. Bond reasoned that it was his car, and he, not Q Branch – which was under severe financial restraint anyway – would decide what features should be incorporated. On several occasions he had seen Major Boothroyd, the Armourer, nosing around the Saab; and it was now commonplace for him to catch members of Q Branch – the 'gee-whizz' technicians of the Service – taking a close look. None of them ever mentioned the things they could not fail to notice – such as the bullet-proof glass, steel-reinforced ram bumpers and heavy-duty tyres, self-sealing even after being hit by bullets. There were other niceties, though, which nobody in Q Branch could detect without bringing out specialist gear.

The Saab now suited Bond's purposes, and was easily convertible from petrol to gas, if the fuel situation became even more critical; the consumption was low in relation to speed; while the turbo gave that extra dynamic thrust always needed in a tricky situation.

Only a few people knew about the cottage, so there were no raised eyebrows or jokes about Bond having a country seat.

The London Friday evening rush was almost over by the time he reached Roehampton; so the Saab was in Bond's personal parking slot, in the underground garage of the headquarters building, before seven-thirty.

Bond would have put money on M having some inane and boring job waiting for him, and even made a mental wager with himself as the lift sped him silently to the ninth floor, at the top of the building, where M's suite of offices was located.

Miss Moneypenny, M's P.A., looked up with a worried smile as Bond entered the outer office. This was the first sign that something important might be on the cards.

'Hallo, Penny,' Bond greeted her breezily, shrugging off

the slough of irritation over the lost week-end. 'Not out with one of your young men? It's wicked Friday night, you know.'

Miss Moneypenny cocked her head towards the door of M's office as she spoke: 'And he's been wickedly waiting for you. Keeping me here into the bargain.' She smiled. 'Besides, the only man who could lure me out on the town seemed to be otherwise engaged.'

'Oh Penny, if only . . .' Bond grinned. There had been a special bantering relationship between them for years, yet Bond had never fully realised how much the able and neat Moneypenny doted on him.

'Tell Commander Bond to come straight in,' M's voice snapped metallically from the intercom box on Miss Moneypenny's desk.

Bond lifted a quizzical eyebrow and moved towards the door. Lowering his voice, he said, 'Did anyone ever tell you that Janet Reger started her business with you in mind, Penny?'

Miss Moneypenny was still blushing as Bond disappeared into M's office and closed the door. A red warning light blinked on above the door as it clicked shut. She stared into space for a moment, her head filled with the after-image of the man who had just entered M's inner sanctum: the bronzed good-looking face, with rather long dark eyebrows above the wide, level blue eyes; the three-inch scar which just showed down his right cheek; the long, very straight nose, and the fine, though cruel, mouth. Minute flecks of grey had just started to show in the dark hair, which still retained its boyish black comma above the right eye. As yet, no plumpness had appeared around the jowls, and the line of the jaw was as straight and firm as ever. It was the face of an attractive buccaneer, Miss Moneypenny thought, shaking herself out of a slightly improper reverie, and wondering if she should have warned James Bond that M was not alone in his office.

As James Bond opened the door to M's office, another door was opening, some five hundred miles to the north of London.

The man who had left Dublin so skilfully disguised, early that morning, looked up, rising from his chair and extending a hand in greeting.

The room in which he had been waiting was a familiar place to him now, after so many visits: book-lined, with a large military desk, comfortable leather chairs, the impressive cabinet containing, literally, priceless antique weapons — a pair of chased silver flint-lock pistols, a matched set of American Kentucky hand guns, lavishly inlaid, a French wheel-lock with mother-of-pearl and gold wire stock decoration, a pair of cutlass pistols, and an Allen pepper-box with six revolving barrels. The artist of disguise knew the pieces and lusted after them on each viewing. The whole place had that air of solidity which comes with what is known as 'old money'.

The person who entered the room was its owner, playing host now to the man from Dublin. They shook hands, almost gravely, the guest waiting in silence until his patron had moved to the large upright chair behind the desk. He did not speak until he was seated.

'It's good to see you again, Franco.'

'Good also to see you. But I enjoy working for you; this always makes a difference.' The man called Franco paused, searching for words. 'You know, after all this time, I never know how to address you — your title, or scientific . . . ?' He made a small gesture with his hands.

The other man chuckled, his bulldog face creasing into a smile. 'Why not Warlock?'

They both laughed. 'Appropriate,' Franco nodded. 'Operation Meltdown, with you — its creative and directive force — Warlock.'

The man behind the desk laid his hands flat on the leather top. 'So be it.' He nodded his head in a quick, birdlike, manner. 'You had no trouble?'

'Nothing at all. Clean as your proverbial English whistle. The chopper was on time; there were no tails. By now you should know I always have care.'

'Good.' The birdlike pecking nod again. 'Then I trust, my friend, that this will be your last visit here.'

Franco gave a quirky little grin. 'Perhaps. But maybe not quite my last. There is the question of payment.'

The man behind the desk opened his hands, fingers splayed, palms upward. 'I mean, of course, your last visit until after Meltdown is completed. Yes, of course there is the question of picking up your share. But first, location and the small detail. That's one of the things we have to discuss; one of the reasons you will be here for a slightly longer period this time, Franco.'

'Naturally.' Franco's voice took on a cold edge and the word came out in four syllables, spoken curiously like the slow, cautious footsteps of a man testing an ice bridge across a deep crevasse.

'There is much to talk about. Europe, I presume, is completely arranged?'

'Everyone ready, yes.'

'And the States?'

'Ready and waiting for the final instructions.'

'The men . . . ?'

Franco leaned forward. 'These *people*, as I've already told you, have been waiting for a long time. They always were the least of my worries. Each of them is dedicated, ready to give his or her life for his separate cause. To all purposes, they consider themselves martyrs already. But the various organisations that have provided the personnel for your operation – organisations outlawed by most Western governments, and regarded as terrorists – are anxious. They want assurances that they will receive their share of the money.'

'Which, I trust, you have given them, Franco.' From behind the desk the bulldog face had ceased to beam. 'Our commitment was clear. I seem to recall that we spoke of

this, at great length, over a year ago. I provide the plan,
the — how do you say it these days? — the know-how. I also
arrange the means. You are the go-between, the contact
man. Now, we have more interesting things to talk about.'

- 3 -

THE OPPOSITION

BOND BECAME MORE alert when he reached the far side of M's door. He was prepared for his old chief to be seated in his usual concentrated position behind the large glass-topped desk; but he was not expecting to find two extra men in the room.

'Come in, Bond.' M addressed him with a small, econo-mic, movement of the hand. 'Gentlemen,' he glanced to-wards his visitors, 'allow me to introduce Commander James Bond. I think he's the man to fit the bill.'

Bond warily acknowledged the other men. He knew well enough who they were, though it would not do to show it openly.

M allowed the pause to lie for just the right length of time, as though testing Bond's discretion, before complet-ing the introductions. 'Commander, this is Sir Richard Duggan, Director-General of M.I.5; and Deputy Assistant Commissioner David Ross, head of the Special Branch of the Metropolitan Police.'

Bond reached out and, in turn, shook hands with the men, noting they both possessed firm dry handshakes. They also looked him straight in the eyes. These were two features Bond had long since come either to admire or guard against – depending on what side he suspected the owners of such attributes to be working.

It was certainly a puzzling situation. M.I.5, and its executive arm, the Special Branch, constituted what was known officially as the British Security Service – respon-sible for counter-espionage and anti-terrorist activities on British sovereign territory.

To Bond's service they were always jokingly known as 'The Opposition', and there had always been a keen rivalry between the two organisations: a rivalry which had sometimes led to grave misunderstandings; even open hostility.

It was certainly most unusual for the heads of 'The Opposition' to come calling on M, who saw them regularly anyway – at least once a week at the Joint Intelligence Committee meeting.

M motioned Bond into a leather chair and looked – a shade too benignly, Bond thought – first at his two visitors, then at Bond. 'Our friends from M.I.5 have a small problem, Commander,' he began, and Bond noted with caution that M was treating him with almost military correctness. 'It is an interesting situation, and I feel you might be able to help; especially as it has all the marks of moving out of M.I.5's jurisdiction, and into our own area.' He tapped his pipe into the copper ashtray on the desk. For the first time, Bond noticed his chief had a file lying directly in front of him. It was thick and marked with the red Most Secret: Classified tags. Two small circles, on the top right hand corner of the white binding, denoted that the file concerned both European and Middle East connections; while a small sticker bore the words, which Bond could easily read upside down, 'Not for Brotherhood', which meant it contained information not to be circulated to the American service, the C.I.A.

The fact of the file was enough to alert Bond. M would have had it photostated on a blow-up, direct from its stored microfilm, especially for this kind of meeting. It would be shredded once those instructed to read it had done so.

'I think,' M said, looking at the Director-General of M.I.5, 'it would be best if the two of you put Commander Bond in the picture. Then we can take it on from there.'

Sir Richard Duggan nodded, and leaned down to open his briefcase, removing a file and placing a matt ten-by-eight photograph on the desk in front of Bond. 'Know the face?' he asked.

Bond nodded. 'Franco – to the Press, public, and most of us. Code Foxtrot to those in the field – ourselves, G.S.G. 9, Gigene, Squad R, Blue Light, C.11 and C.13.' Bond was referring to the German, French, Italian and American anti-terrorist squads, together with C.11 and C.13, of Scotland Yard, who often worked closely with Special Branch (C.11 staffs the Anti-Terrorist Squad, in conjunction with C.1).

The head of M.I.5 was not, however, going to let Bond get off so lightly. Did the Commander know anything else about Code Foxtrot – Franco?

Again Bond nodded. 'Of course. International terrorist. Wanted in most European countries and some in the Middle East. There is a request for him to be held in the United States; though, as far as we know, he has not operated from, or in, that country. His full name is Franco Oliveiro Quesocriado; born Madrid 1948 of mixed parentage – Spanish father and an English mother. I believe her name was something quite ordinary, like Jones, Smith or Evans . . .'

'Leonard actually,' said D.A.C. Ross quietly. 'Mary Leonard.'

'Sorry,' Bond smiled at him, and the policeman returned the smile. He had the look of a modern copper, Bond thought. Almost certainly one of the university intake – quiet, with a watchfulness buried deep in his eyes, and the sense of a coiled spring held back by the retaining pin of both caution and calmness. A very tough and sharp baby if roused, was Bond's instant assessment.

He turned back to Sir Richard Duggan, asking if they wanted him to continue.

'Naturally.' Richard Duggan was a very different breed, and Bond already knew his pedigree – that was, after all, part of his job. Duggan was old school Home Office. Eton and Oxford, then a career in politics, which lasted only a short time before the Home Office snapped him up. Tall, slim and good-looking, with thick light-coloured hair, which his enemies claimed was tinted, Duggan looked the part – young and rich, authoritative and in control. The youthfulness, Bond also knew, was an illusion, and the luck of a good facial bone structure.

As the head of M.I.5 drawled, 'Naturally,' Bond's eyes momentarily met those of M, and caught the tiny stir of humour. Sir Richard Duggan was not one of M's favourite people.

Bond shrugged. 'Franco,' he continued, 'first came to our attention in connection with a hijacking of two British passenger jets – the airline was B.O.A.C. at the time – in the late 1960s. He appears to have no direct political affiliations, and has operated as a planner who sometimes takes part in terrorist actions, with groups like the former Baader-Meinhof gang, and is still connected with the so-called Red Army Faction. He has links with the P.L.O., I.R.A., and a whole network of terrorist groups.' Bond took out his gunmetal cigarette case, glancing at M for permission to smoke, and receiving a curt nod.

'He would, I think, be best described as an anti-capitalist.' Bond lit his cigarette and gave a small quick smile. 'The paradox has always been that, for an anti-capitalist, he appears to be exceptionally well-off. There is evidence that he has personally paid for, and provided, arms for a number of terrorist acts. He has certainly committed murder, in connection with two political kidnappings – not to mention those who have died in bomb attacks inspired directly by him. A very dangerous and most wanted man, Sir Richard.'

Both Duggan and Ross nodded in harmony, Ross muttering something about Bond knowing his man. Duggan voiced his opinion in a louder voice, saying Bond might well have to know his man even better. He then delved into his briefcase again, bringing out five more matt photographs, which he placed in a row on M's desk, in front of Bond. Each photograph carried a small sticker attached to the bottom right-hand corner. Each sticker bore a date.

Bond immediately noted the dates, before looking at the photographs. The most recent was today's. The other four were marked April 4th and 23rd; May 12th and 25th. The pictures were obviously blow-ups from a videotape recording, and he studied each one with great care. The man portrayed was dressed differently in each photograph; and, indeed, looked different – plump, in jeans and denim jacket, with long hair and a moustache; clean-shaven, but with shoulder-length blond hair and dark glasses, wearing a rumpled roll-neck sweater and slacks; grey-haired and gaunt in loud check, hung around with cameras, and clutching an American passport as though he expected it to be torn from his hand at any moment; clean-shaven again, but with dark hair, fashionably cut, clad elegantly in slacks and an expensive, fur-collared wind-cheater.

Today's photograph showed him with close-cropped hair, neat beard and spectacles. He wore a business suit.

The disguises were all excellent, yet Bond had no hesitation. 'Franco,' he said aloud, like an order.

'Of course.' Duggan sounded a little patronising, going on to point out that all the photographs had been taken at Heathrow.

'Five times in the past three months, and he hasn't been picked up?' Bond's brow creased.

Deputy Assistant Commissioner David Ross inhaled, and took over the explanation. At a meeting earlier in the year, it had been decided that certain major 'most wanted' terrorists like Franco should be kept under close surveillance if they appeared to arrive alone in the country. 'Big fish, little fish,' he grinned, as though it explained everything. 'When the surveillance teams at Heathrow spotted him in April – the first time – there was, naturally, a full-scale alert.'

'Naturally.' Bond did a fair imitation of Sir Richard Duggan's condescending drawl. M busied himself loading his pipe, gently kneading the tobacco into the bowl, and keeping his eyes well down.

Ross looked a little shamefaced. 'Afraid we lost him the first time. Not ready for him. Lost him in London.'

Something stirred in Bond's memory. There had been an increase in police activity early in April, and he recalled signals coming in with instructions about being more than normally alert: watching for packages and letters, stepping up embassy security – the usual stuff on a Terrorist Red, as the police and security services called it.

Ross was still talking. 'We checked all his possible contacts, and waited. He wasn't detected leaving the country.'

'But, of course, he did,' Duggan chimed in.

Ross nodded. 'As you can all see, he was back again, entering through Heathrow, later in the month. That time we established he moved straight out of London, almost certainly heading north.'

'You lost him again,' Bond stated. Ross gave a sharp affirmative before saying they had better luck during the first May visit.

'Followed him as far as Glasgow. Then he slipped the leash. But on the last trip we kept him in our sights all the way. He ended up in a village called Murcaldy, inland from Applecross, at the foot of the north-west Highlands.'

'And we're sure who it was he visited there,' Duggan smiled. 'Just as we're certain he's gone to the same place this time. I have two officers breathing down his neck. He came in from Dublin this morning – and we were tipped off from there. He went straight to King's Cross and took the first train to Edinburgh – rings the changes, you know. He'll have reached his destination by now. We expect further reports any time.'

A silence fell over the four men, broken only by the scraping of M's match as he lit his pipe. Bond was the first to speak. 'And he's visiting . . . ?' allowing the question to hang in the air like M's pipe smoke.

Duggan cleared his throat. 'Most of the land, including the village of Murcaldy, is owned by one family – the Muriks. For at least three centuries, possibly longer, the

Lairds of Murcaldy have been Muriks. It's almost a feudal set-up. Murik Castle, which dates back to the sixteenth century, has had many modernisations over the years; and there is the Murik estate – farms; hunting and fishing rights. The present Laird is also a celebrity in other fields – Dr Anton Murik, director of many companies, and a nuclear physicist of both renown and eccentricity.'

'Recently resigned, under some sort of cloud, from the International Atomic Energy Research Commission,' added Ross. 'And, as you'll see, there's grave doubt regarding his claim to be the Laird of Murcaldy.'

Bond chuckled, 'Well, Anton isn't exactly a well-known Scottish name. But where do I come in?' He already had a fair idea, but it would not do to jump the gun.

Duggan's face did not change: the granite good looks appeared flawed at close quarters. There was none of the usual smoothness about him as he spoke again. 'Franco has now almost certainly made four visits to Dr Murik. This will be his fifth. An international terrorist and a nuclear physicist of some eminence: put those together and you have a rather alarming situation. On each occasion, Franco has left the country again: probably – and we can only guess – via a Scottish port or airport. We're banking on the possibility that his business with Murik will take some time to conclude; but our hands are tied from the moment he leaves Britain. Our visit today is to ask the help of your service in tracing his movements outside this country.'

This time it was Bond's turn to nod, 'And you want me to dash off up to Scotland, make contact, and follow him out?'

Duggan deferred to M. 'Only if that is – ah – convenient. But I really don't think there's much time left on this trip. Anton Murik owns a string of race horses, which he has under training in England. Two are running at Ascot this coming week – one in the Gold Cup. It's his one passion, apart from nuclear physics. Franco will either be gone by the middle of the week, or up at the Castle awaiting Murik's return from Ascot.'

Bond stretched out his long legs and thought that if there really was a sinister connection between Franco and Murik, the timing indicated this would not be Franco's last visit. But you could never tell.

Duggan was on his feet. 'I've passed on all information to M.' He indicated the file – which Bond had taken to be one of M's dossiers – on the desk, as he gathered up the photographs and swept them into his briefcase. 'Also how to contact my people in the field, and all that. We have come to you for assistance, in the interests of the country. It is time to work in harness, and I must now leave the final decision here with you.'

M puffed on his pipe. 'I'll brief Commander Bond about everything,' he said pleasantly. 'Be in touch with you later this evening, Duggan. We'll do all we can – in *everybody's* interests.'

The two officers took leave of M and Bond quite cordially, and, as soon as the door closed behind them, M spoke – 'What do you think, 007?'

James Bond's heart leaped, and he felt a new urgency coursing through his veins. It was a long time since M had addressed him as 007, and it signified that he could well be off into the real unknown again. He could almost smell the possibilities.

'Well, what *do* you think?' M repeated.

Bond lit another cigarette and looked up at the ceiling before he spoke. 'I should imagine you'll want me on the way to Scotland tonight.' M's eyes betrayed nothing as Bond continued. 'Not a healthy mix – an international terrorist and a renowned nuclear physicist. Been one of the nightmares for some time, hasn't it, sir? That some group would get hold of not only the materials but the means to construct a really lethal nuclear device? We suspect some of them have the materials – look at that fellow Achmed Yastaff I took out for you. At least four of the ships he arranged to go missing were carrying materials . . .'

M snorted, 'Don't be a fool, 007. Easiest thing in the

world to construct a crude device. Yes, they've almost
certainly got the materials – and don't ask me who I mean
by "they". You've got to think logically on this one. If any
of the existing terrorist organisations wanted to use some
crude bomb to blackmail a government, they could do so.
But for a man like Franco to be consorting with an old devil
such as the Laird of Murcaldy – well, that's a very different
matter, and it could mean one of two things.'

'Yes . . . ?' Bond leant forward.

'First,' M ticked off the index finger of his left hand with
that of his right, the pipe jammed into the corner of his
mouth, held tightly between his teeth as he spoke. 'First, it
could mean that Franco is setting up a very sophisticated
operation, and is soliciting Anton Murik's specialist help
and knowledge. Second' – the fingers moved – 'it could be
the other way around: that Dr Anton Murik is seeking
Franco's aid on a little adventure of his own. Either of those
possibilities is going to take more than five short visits from
Franco.'

'And Anton Murik is capable of either of these things?'
Bond's brow furrowed. He could read absolutely nothing in
M's weatherbeaten face, and that was always a danger
signal. There was far more to all this than the information
brought to them by 'The Opposition'.

'Not only capable of it, but also a most likely candidate.'
M opened a drawer in his desk and dropped another file on
top of the one provided by M.I.5. 'We've had our eye on Dr
Anton Murik, Laird of Murcaldy, for some time now.' He
tapped the two files. 'What Ross told you is a slight understatement – the business about Murik resigning from the
International Atomic Energy Commission under some sort
of cloud. *They* don't have all the facts. We do. Murik resigned, 007, under a damned great storm. In fact the man
was kicked out, and didn't take kindly to it. He is a man of
some brilliance, and very large resources.'

M took the pipe from his mouth, looking Bond straight in
the eyes. 'Even his title – Laird of Murcaldy – is more than

highly suspect, as Ross mentioned. No, I don't intend to send you scooting off to Scotland, 007. It's my job to see that you're properly briefed, and given good support and cover. The hell with "The Opposition" and their surveillance team. I want to get you as close to Murik as possible. On the inside; and before we get to that, there's a great deal you should know about the so-called Laird of Murcaldy.'

4

DOSSIER ON A LAIRD

IT WAS OBVIOUSLY going to be a long evening, and Bond thought he should not surprise May, his able and devoted housekeeper, by returning suddenly and late to the flat off the King's Road.

Before M could launch into the details of the dossiers which lay, full of secrets, in front of them, Bond asked permission to leave the office for a moment.

M gave one of his irritated old-fashioned looks, but grudgingly nodded his consent for Bond to make a telephone call from the privacy of his own office.

In the end, it was easier for Bond to dial his own number on Miss Moneypenny's extension. May had given up trying to fathom her employer's working hours long ago, and merely asked if he fancied anything special to eat when he did get in. Bond said he would not be averse to a nice pair of Arbroath Smokies – should she have some tucked away. May, being a strict conservative in matters of kitchen equipment, would never in a thousand years have allowed a freezer in her domain. Bond agreed with her, though it was sometimes nice to be able to have delicacies within reach, so they had compromised. With tact, Bond had talked her round to allowing him to buy a large Bosch refrigerator with a spacious freezing compartment, which May christened the ice box. She thought, now, that there might be a pair of Smokies in 'the ice box', adding, 'So I'll see what I can do, Mr James; but mind you don't get back too late.' May had a habit of treating Bond, when the mood was on her, as a nanny will treat her small charges.

The fact that Bond was only out of his office for a few

minutes mollified M, who had refilled his pipe and was poring over the dossiers. Caustically he asked if 007 had managed to arrange matters so that they were not interrupted again.

'Yes, sir,' Bond replied calmly. 'I'm quite ready for the Laird of Murcaldy, Rob Roy and even Bonnie Prince Charlie, if you wish.'

'It's not a matter for levity, 007,' M spoke sharply. 'The Murik family is a noble line. There was a Laird of Murcaldy at Dunbar, and another at Culloden Moor. However, it is possible that the true line died out with the present Laird's grandfather. It has yet to be proven, or even properly tested, but it is a matter which disturbs the Lord Lyon King of Arms greatly.' He shuffled through some of the first dossier. 'Anton Murik's grandfather was well-known as an adventurer – a traveller. In the year 1890 he was missing for more than three months in central Europe – searching, it is said, for his brother who had been disinherited for some offence. Their parents were dead, and the village folk believed that Angus Murik – that was his name – planned to return with his brother, shepherding the black sheep back into the fold. When he did return it was with a wife: a foreign woman, the records say. She was with child, and there are also written documents suggesting that the prodigal Laird was not Angus at all, but the brother, Hamish. It is also suggested that the child, who became Anton's father, was born out of wedlock, for there are no records of a marriage having actually taken place.'

Bond grunted, 'But surely that would only weaken the line, not destroy it altogether.'

'Normally, yes,' M continued. 'But Anton was also born in strange circumstances. His father was a wild lad who, at the age of eighteen, also began to travel. He did not return at all. There is a letter, extant, saying that he had married an English woman of good family in Palermo. But shortly after that a young woman arrived at Murik Castle, in an advanced state of pregnancy, with the news that her husband, the heir to the title, had been killed by bandits during an expedition in Sicily.'

'When was this?' It sounded a confused and odd story to Bond.

'Nineteen-twenty,' M nodded, as though reading Bond's thoughts. 'Yes, and there *are* newspaper reports of some "English" gentleman having been killed in Sicily. The newspapers, however, claim that this gentleman's wife also perished at the hands of the bandits; though the young woman insisted it was her maid who died. The graves, at Caltanissetta, are so marked; but diaries, and some memories, say that the girl who presented herself as wife of the Laird-presumptive was far from being an English lady of good breeding. It's difficult to sort out fact from fiction, or even bigotry. What is certain is the fact that some of the older people on the Murik estate maintain Anton is not the true Laird – though, knowing which side their bread is buttered, they only whisper it privately, and will not commit themselves to either strangers or authority.'

'But the baby was baptised Anton and took the title?'

'Baptised Anton Angus, yes; and took the title Laird of Murcaldy, yes,' M said with a slight curl of the lip.

'So, whatever else, we must treat him as a Scottish Laird. I presume he is also a bona fide nuclear scientist? We have to take that part seriously?'

'We take him very seriously indeed,' M looked grave, repeating, 'Very seriously. There is no doubt at all that Anton Murik is a man of great intellect and influence. Just take a glance at the background précis.' He passed the relevant sheet from the dossier across to Bond, who took it in with a quick sweep of the eyes:

Anton Angus Murik. Born Murik Castle, Murcaldy, Ross and Cromarty, Scotland, December 18th, 1920. Educated Harrow and St John's College, Cambridge. First Class Honours in Physics followed by a Fellowship, then a Doctorate. So good that he was reserved for work

under Professor Lindemann – later Lord Cherwell –
scientific adviser to Winston Churchill; also worked on
Manhattan Project (the making and testing of the first
atomic bomb); Committee for the Peaceful use of Atomic
Energy; International Atomic Energy Commission . . .

Murik had resigned from this last position just two years
ago. There followed a lengthy and impressive list of companies with which Murik was associated. Bond's eyebrows
gradually rose higher as he read the list. Among other
things, Anton Murik was Chairman of Micro-Modulators
Ltd, Eldon Electronics Ltd, Micro Sea Scale Ltd and
Aldan Aerospace, Inc. In addition he sat on countless
boards, all of which had some direct application to nuclear
power or electronics. Bond also saw that the firms included
some specialist contractors with great knowledge of design
and building in the field of nuclear reactors.

'You spot the odd man out?' M asked from behind a
cloud of pipe smoke.

Bond looked down the list again. Yes, there tucked away
among all the electronics, nuclear companies and aerospace conglomerates, was a strange entry, Roussillon
Fashions. Bond read out the entry.

'Yes. Damned dressmaking firm,' M snorted.

James Bond smiled to himself. 'I think a little more than
just a dressmaker, sir. Roussillon is one of the world's
leading fashion houses. They have branches in London,
Paris, Rome, New York; you name it. Ask any woman with
dress sense. I suppose Roussillon would come among the
top five fashion houses in the world.'

M grunted, 'And charge top prices as well, I've no doubt.
Well, Anton Murik has a majority holding in that firm.'

'Don't suppose he just likes dressing up in high-class
ladies' clothes or something like that?' Bond grinned.

'Don't be flippant, 007. You have to look at the financial
aspect.'

'Well, he must be a multi-millionaire,' Bond said, almost

to himself. He was rarely impressed by such things, but, even from the list in front of him, it was obvious that Dr Anton Murik wielded considerable power. 'How in heaven's name did a man with these qualifications manage to get himself thrown out of the International Atomic Energy Commission, sir?'

M did not hesitate. 'For one thing he's unscrupulous in business matters. Sailed very close to the wind in some dealings with those companies you see listed. At least two of the chairmanships were gained by stepping almost literally, over the bodies of other men.'

'Most good businessmen are inclined to be ruthless . . .' Bond began; but M held up a hand.

'There was another matter,' he said. 'Anton Murik is a bit of a fanatic, and he tends to take the view of most of those people you see protesting against the use of nuclear power and the dangers of the disposal of nuclear waste. He mounted a stiff campaign against the use of the major types of nuclear reactor already in service, or planned to go into service. Worldwide. You see, 007, the man claims to have designed the ultimate in reactors – one which not only provides the power but safely disposes of the waste, and cannot go wrong. Calls it the Murik Ultra-Safe Reactor.'

'And his colleagues didn't buy it?'

' "Didn't buy" is an understatement. His colleagues say there are grave flaws in the Ultra-Safe design. Some even go as far as claiming the whole thing is potentially a hundred times more dangerous than the current families – the fast-breeders, B.W.R.s, P.W.R.s, gas/graphites and liquid metal fast-breeders. Murik wanted funds from the Commission to prove them wrong, and build his own reactor.'

'So they cut off the money.'

M said they did exactly that, and Bond laughed again, remarking that a little thing like money should not make much difference to a multi-millionaire. 'Surely Murik could go out and build his own – in his back garden: it seems big enough.'

M sighed. 'We're talking in billions of dollars; billions of pounds sterling, James. Anton Murik argued. There were, apparently, some terrific rows, and suggestions that the man's far from stable,' he touched his forehead with an index finger. 'That's really why this whole business of contact with a fellow like Franco worries me. It is also why I will on no account allow you to go charging into the field without preparation. Could be wrong, of course, but I really don't think a week or so is going to make that much difference. Especially if I can turn you into the ideal penetration agent – establish you within the Murik entourage: and to that end,' M began to leaf through his own dossier again, 'I think you'd better meet Anton Murik and his household.' He drew several photographs from the bulky depths of the file.

'You're going to officially deny Duggan's request, then?' Bond's mind had become completely concentrated on the job in hand by now. Having been inactive for a long time made little difference to him. The job was like swimming or driving; once the rudiments had been mastered, professionalism – when something big turned up – came back like the flicking of a switch. Whatever plot was being hatched – either by Franco or Dr Anton Murik – Bond would not, now, rest until every end was tied up; no matter how dangerous or arduous, or even plain dull, it turned out to be.

M grunted. 'Duggan's got two good people in the field. They've already had four tries at keeping tabs on Franco – plenty of practice. That should, eventually, make them perfect. I have confidence that they'll discover his port of exit this time. We'll put a tail on Franco when the moment comes. Your job's too important . . .' he must have seen the quizzical look on Bond's face, 'and don't tell me that I'm putting you in on M.I.5's territory. I know that, and so do you, but my bones tell me it won't be for long. The action's going to move out of Scotland as soon as whatever it is they're cooking comes to the boil. Now for the pretty pictures.'

First, he explained the obvious. With the castle and huge estate, the Laird of Murcaldy had immediate access to manpower. 'He's got gamekeepers, wardens, and every imaginable kind of servant up there, from drivers to guards: so, as far as the Laird's concerned, he has no real security problem. There is a central core of family, though. First, the doctor himself.'

The photograph showed a pugnacious face, not unlike that of the late Lord Beaverbrook, but without the crescents of humour bracketing the mouth. A bulldog of a man, with cold eyes that were fixed on somebody, or something — certainly not the camera — slightly to his right. The line of the mouth was hard, uncompromising; and the ears, which lay very flat against the head, gave him an odd, symmetrical outline. Photographs can be deceptive — Bond knew that well enough — but this man, captured by a swift click and the activation of a shutter, could have been a son of the Manse. He had that slightly puritanical look about him — a stickler for discipline; one who knew his own mind and would have his own way, no matter what lay in his path. Bond felt vaguely uneasy. He would not admit to anything so grave as fear when confronted by a photograph, but the picture said clearly that the Laird of Murcaldy was a force: a power.

The next print showed a woman, probably in her early forties, very fine-looking, with sharp, classic features, and dark, upswept hair. Her eyes were large, but not — Bond thought — innocent. Even in this image they seemed to contain a wealth of worldly knowledge; and the mouth, while generous, was not out of proportion, the edges of the lips tilting slightly upwards, in some ways softening the features.

'Miss Mary-Jane Mashkin,' said M, as though it explained everything.

Bond gave his chief a look of query, the comma of hair connecting with his right eyebrow as though to form a question mark.

'His *éminence grise*, some say.' M puffed at his pipe, as
though slightly embarrassed. 'Certainly Murik's mistress.
Was his secretary for ten years. Murik's strong right arm
and personal adviser. She's a trained physicist. Cambridge
University, the same as the Laird, though not his standard
it seems. Acts as hostess for him; lives at Murik Castle.
Travels with him, eats . . . and all the rest of it.'

Bond reflected that he could have been wrong about the
puritanism, but then amended his thoughts. It was quite
possible for Anton Murik to have strong moral feelings
about what everybody else did while excepting himself
from similar restrictions. It happened all the time: like the
people who campaigned against certain television programmes and films, yet imagined they were themselves
immune to moral danger.

'I should think he takes her advice in a lot of matters; but
I doubt he would be swayed by her on very large issues.' M
pushed a third photograph towards Bond.

This time it was another woman, much younger, and
certainly, if the picture was really accurate, a stunning girl.
Blonde hair fell around the sides of her face in a smooth,
thick sheen; while the face itself was reminiscent of Lauren
Bacall as a young woman. This one had the same high
cheek bones, the promise of some smoulder in the dark
eyes, and a mouth made striking by the sensuality of her
lower lip. Above the eyes, her brows were shaped naturally,
in a kind of elongated circumflex. Bond allowed himself to
relax in an almost inaudible low whistle.

M cut short this reflex reaction. 'Anton Murik's ward.
Miss Lavender Peacock. The relationship is not known.
She became his ward in 1970, all legal – daughter of some
second cousin, the court report says. Father and mother
both killed in an air crash. There's a little money – several
thousand – which comes to Miss Peacock when she reaches
her twenty-seventh birthday. That is next year.'

Bond observed that Lavender Peacock was quite a girl,

though he somehow thought he recognised her – not just from her resemblance to the young Bacall.

'Possible, 007. The girl's kept on a tight rein, though. In some matters the Laird is very old-fashioned. Lavender Peacock is treated like a fragile piece of china. Private tutors when she was a kid, trips abroad only when accompanied by Murik and trusted watchdogs. The Mashkin woman's toted her around a bit, and you may have seen her picture in connection with that dressmaking business. From time to time the Laird allows her to model – but only at very special functions, and always with the watchdogs around.'

'Watchdogs?' Bond picked on the expression.

M rose and strode to the window, looking out across the park, now hazy as the sun dropped slowly and the lights began to come on over the city. 'Watchdogs?' M queried. 'Oh yes, mainly women around the Mashkin lady and the dressmaking firm.' He did not turn back towards Bond. 'Murik always has a few young Scottish toughs around. A kind of bodyguard: you know what these people are like. Not just for the ward, but the whole family. There's one in particular: sort of chief heavy. We haven't got a photograph of him, but I've had a description and that certainly matches his name. He's called Caber.'

There was a long silence. At last Bond took a deep breath. He had been looking at the triptych of photographs in front of him. 'So you want me to ingratiate myself with this little lot; find out why Franco's paying so much attention; and generally make myself indispensable?'

'I think that's the way to go.' M turned from the window. 'We have to play the game long, 007. Very long indeed. I have great reservations about Dr Anton Murik. He'd kill without a second thought if it meant the success of some plan with which he's obsessed; and we all know he's obsessed, at this moment, with the business of his Ultra-Safe Nuclear Reactor. Maybe there's some hairbrained scheme of investing in one of Franco's endeavours, and raking in a

rich profit – a quick return: enough money to prove the
Atomic Energy Commission wrong. Who knows? It'll be
your job to find out, James. Your job, and my responsibility.'

'Suggestions on how to do it would be welcome,' Bond
began, but, as M was about to reply, the red telephone
purred on his desk.

For a few minutes, Bond sat silently listening to M's side
of a conversation with Sir Richard Duggan. When the call
was completed, M sat back with a thin smile. 'That settled
it then. I've told M.I.5 that you're ready to move in and
follow up any information they care to give. Duggan's left
details of his surveillance people here,' he tapped the M.I.5
file with his knuckles. 'All the usual cloak and dagger stuff
they seem to like.'

'And Franco?'

'Is definitely at Castle Murik. They've confirmed. Don't
worry, James, if he leaves suddenly I'll put someone on his
back to cover you with M.I.5.'

'Talking of cover . . .' Bond started.

'I was coming to that. How you get into the family circle,
eh? Well, I think you go under your own name, but with a
slightly different passport. We can drum it all up here. A
mercenary, I think. You heard what Ross said about
Murik's second passion in life – racing. Well, as you know,
he's got horses running at Ascot next week. In fact the one
he's entered in the Gold Cup has only been in the first three
once in its life. Name of China Blue. Our friend, the Laird
of Murcaldy, merely seems to like watching them train and
run – enjoys all the business of race tracks and trainers.'

'Just for the kicks,' Bond stated, and M looked at him
curiously for a moment.

'I suppose so,' M replied at last. 'But Murik's visit to
Ascot next week should give us the opportunity. Unless
there's any sudden change of plan, I think you should be
able to make contact on Gold Cup day. That'll give us time
to see you're well briefed and properly equipped, eh?'

5

THE ROAD TO ASCOT

APART FROM THE great golf tournaments, James Bond did not care much for those events which still constitute what the gossip columnists – and the drones who pay lip-service and provide morsels for them – call 'the Season'. He was not naturally drawn to Wimbledon, the Henley Regatta, or, indeed, to Royal Ascot. The fact that Bond was a staunch monarchist did not prevent the grave misgivings he felt when turning the Saab in the direction of Ascot on Gold Cup day.

Life had been very full since the Friday evening of the previous week, when M had taken the decision to place Bond within the heart of the Laird of Murcaldy's world.

Inside the building overlooking Regent's Park, people did not ask questions when a sudden personal disappearance, or a flurry of activity, altered the pattern of days. Though Bond was occasionally spotted, hurrying to or from meetings, he did not go near his office.

In fact, Bond worked a full seventeen-hour day during this time of preparation. To begin with, there were long briefings with M, in his big office, recently redecorated and now dominated by Cooper's painting of Admiral Jervis's fleet triumphing over the Spanish off Cape St Vincent in 1797 – the picture having been lent to the Service by the National Maritime Museum.

During the following weeks, Bond was to recall the battle scene, with its background of lowering skies and the British men-o'-war, trailing ensigns and streamers, ploughing through choppy seas, tinted with the glow of fire and smoke of action.

It was under this painting that M quietly took Bond through all the logical possibilities of the situation ahead; revealed the extent to which Anton Murik had recently invested in businesses all connected, one way or another, with nuclear energy; together with his worst private fears about possible plots now being hatched by the Laird of Murcaldy.

'The devil of it is, James,' M told him one evening, 'this fellow Murik has a finger in a dozen market places – in Europe, the Middle East, and even America.' As yet, M had not alerted the C.I.A., but was resigned to the fact that this would be necessary if Bond found himself forced – by the job he hoped to secure with Anton Murik – to operate within the jealously guarded spheres of American influence.

Primarily, the idea was to put Bond into the Murik ménage as a walking listening device. It was natural, then, for him to spend much time with Q Branch, the experts of 'gee-whizz' technology. In the past, he had often found himself bored by the earnest young men who inhabited the workshops and testing areas of Q Branch; but times were changing. Within the last year, everyone at headquarters had been brightened and delighted by the appearance of a new face among the senior executives of Q Branch: a tall, elegant, leggy young woman with sleek and shining straw-coloured hair which she wore in an immaculate, if severe, French pleat. This, together with her large spectacles, gave her a commanding manner and a paradoxical personality combining warm nubility with cool efficiency.

Within a week of her arrival, Q Branch had accorded its new executive the nickname of Q'ute, for even in so short a time she had become the target of many seductive attempts by unmarried officers of all ages. Bond had noticed her, and heard the reports. Word was that the colder side of Q'ute's personality was uppermost in her off-duty hours. Now 007 found himself working close to the girl, for she had been detailed to arrange the equipment he would take into the field, and brief him on its uses.

Throughout this period, James Bond remained professionally distant. Q'ute was a desirable girl, but, like so many of the ladies working within the security services these days, she remained friendly yet at pains to make it plain that she was her own woman and therefore Bond's equal. Only later was 007 to learn that she had done a year in the field before taking the two-year technical course which provided her with promotion to executive status in Q Branch.

At forty-eight hours' notice, Q'ute's team had put together a set of what she called 'personalised matching luggage'. This consisted of a leather suitcase together with a similarly designed, steel-strengthened briefcase. Both items contained cunningly devised compartments, secret and well-nigh undetectable, built to house a whole range of electronic sound-stealing equipment; some sabotage gear, and a few useful survival items. These included a highly sophisticated bugging and listening device; a VL 22H counter-surveillance receiver; a pen alarm, set to a frequency which linked it to a long-range modification of the SAS 900 Alert System. If triggered, the pen alarm would provide Bond with instant signal communication to the Regent's Park headquarters building in order to summon help. The pen also contained micro facilities so that it operated as a homer; therefore, when activated, headquarters could keep track of their man in the field — a personal alarm system in the breast pocket.

As a back-up, there was a small ultrasonic transmitter; while, among the sabotage material, Bond was to carry an exact replica of his own Dunhill cigarette lighter — the facsimile having special properties of its own. There was also a so-called 'security blanket' flashlight, which generates a high-intensity beam strong enough to disorientate any victim caught in its burst of light; and—almost as an afterthought—Q'ute made him sign for a pair of TH70 Nitefinder goggles. Bond did not think it wise to mention that these lightweight goggles were part of the standard fittings Communication Control Systems, Inc. had provided for the Saab. He had tested them himself — on an old, disused, airfield during a particularly dark night — driving the Saab without lights, at high speed, while wearing the Nitefinder set strapped to his head. Through the small projecting lenses, the surrounding countryside and cracked runway down which he took the car could be seen with the same clarity he would have experienced on a summer evening just before twilight.

As well as the time spent with M and Q'ute, Bond found himself in for some long hours with Major Boothroyd, the Service Armourer, discussing weaponry. On M's instructions, 007 was to go armed — something not undertaken lightly these days.

During the years when he had made a special reputation for himself in the old Double-O Section, Bond had used many hand weapons: ranging from the ·25 Beretta — which the Armourer sarcastically dismissed as 'a lady's gun' — to the ·38 Colt Police Positive; the Colt ·45 automatic; ·38 Smith & Wesson Centennial Airweight; and his favourite, the Walther PPK 7·65mm. carried in the famous Berns-Martin triple draw holster.

By now, however, the PPK had been withdrawn from use, following its nasty habit of jamming at crucial moments. The weapon did this once too often, on the night of March 20th, 1974, when a would-be kidnapper with a history of mental illness attempted to abduct Princess Anne and her husband, Captain Mark Phillips. The royal couple's bodyguard, Inspector James Beaton, was wounded, and, in attempting to return fire, his Walther jammed. That, then, was the end of this particular hand gun as far as the British police and security services were concerned.

Since then, Bond had done most of his range work with either the Colt ·45 — which was far too heavy and difficult to use in covert field operations — or the old standby ·38

Cobra: Colt's long-term favourite snub-nosed revolver for undercover use. Bond, naturally, did not disclose the fact that he carried an unauthorised Ruger Super Blackhawk ·44 Magnum in a secret compartment in the Saab.

Now, minds had to be clear, and decisions taken regarding Bond's field armament; so a lengthy, time-consuming, and sometimes caustic battle ensued between Bond and the Armourer concerning the relative merits of weapons.

They had been through the basic arguments a thousand times already: a revolver is always more reliable than an automatic pistol, simply because there is less to go wrong. The revolver, however, has the double drawback of taking longer to reload, usually carrying only six rounds of ammunition in its cylinder. Also – unless you go for the bigger, bulky weapon – muzzle velocity, and, therefore, stopping power, is lower.

The automatic pistol, on the other hand, gives you much easier loading facilities (the quick removal and substitution of a magazine from, and into, the butt), allows a larger number of rounds per magazine, and has, in the main, a more effective stopping power. Yet there is more to go wrong in the way of working parts.

Eventually it was Bond who had the last word – with a few grumbles from Major Boothroyd – settling on an old, but well-tried and true friend: the early Browning 9mm. originally manufactured by Fabrique Nationale-De Guerre in Belgium from Browning patents. In spite of its age this Browning has accurate stopping power. For Bond, the appeal lay in its reliability – eight inches overall and with a barrel length of five inches. A flat, lethal weapon, the early Browning is really a design similar to the ·32 Colt and weighs about thirty-two ounces, having a magazine capacity of seven 9mm. Browning Long cartridges, with the facility to carry one extra round in the breech.

Bond was happy with the weapon, knew its limitations, and had no hesitation in putting aside thoughts of more exotic hand guns of modern manufacture.

Unused weapons of all makes, types and sizes, were contained in the Armourer's amazing treasure trove of a store; and he produced one of the old Brownings, still in its original box, thick with grease and wrapped in yellow waxed paper. No mean feat, as this particular gun has long since ceased to be manufactured.

The Armourer knew 007 well enough not to have the pistol touched by any member of his staff; calling Bond down to the gunsmith's room, so that the weapon could be cleaned off, stripped, checked and thoroughly tested by the man who was to use it. If Bond had been scheduled to make a parachute jump, both the Armourer and Q Branch would have seen to it that 007 packed his own 'chute. In turn, it was the only way Bond would have it done. The same applied to weapons.

Late one afternoon Bond found himself down in the empty gunsmith's room, with the run of the place, plus the underground range, while he went through the exacting chore upon which his life might depend.

He was, therefore, surprised when, just as he started to clean the grease from the Browning, the door opened to reveal Q'ute, dressed in brown velvet and looking exceptionally desirable. Major Boothroyd, she told Bond, had suggested that she come down to watch the cleaning and preparation of the weapon.

'Why should he do that?' Bond hardly glanced up at the girl, conscious for the first time that her cool manner constituted a direct challenge. He had worked hard over the past days: now a sensual snake stirred in the back of his mind. Q'ute would make a relaxing partner for the evening.

Q'ute swung herself on to the workbench, after making certain she had chosen a clean patch of wood. 'The Armourer's giving me a weapons' course, when I'm off duty,' she told him. For the first time, Bond noticed Q'ute's voice had a throaty quality to it. 'I'm not very good with hand guns, and he says you are. He mentioned that the weapon was of an old type as well. Just thought it would be a good idea, if you didn't mind.'

Bond's strong, firm hands moved expertly, even lovingly, over the pistol as he silently chanted the stripping routine.

'Well, do you?' Q'ute asked.

'Do I what?'

'Mind me watching?'

'Not at all.' He glanced up at the girl, whose pretty face, behind the large spectacles, remained impassive. 'Always best to handle weapons with care and gentleness,' he smiled, as the movements of his hands over the mechanism became increasingly erotic.

'With care, of course,' Q'ute's voice took on a slight edge of sarcasm. Now she repeated, parrot-fashion, from the Service training manual, ' "Weapons of all description should be treated with great care and respect." Don't you carry it a bit too far, Commander Bond?'

Hell, he thought. Q'ute was a good nickname for her. Bond even slowed down the movements of his hands, allowing the process of stripping to become more obvious as he silently repeated the instructions:

Grasp head of recoil spring guide; push towards muzzle to release the head of the guide from the barrel. Draw out barrel from breech end. Remove stocks, giving access to lockwork. Dismount slide assembly, starting with firing pin and continue normally . . .

'Oh come on, Commander Bond. I do know something about weapons. Anyway, nobody believes all that stuff about guns being phallic symbols any more.' She tossed her head, giving a little laugh. 'Stop playing strip the lady with that piece of hardware, if you're doing it for my benefit. I don't go for those paperback books with pictures of girls sitting on large guns, or even astride them.'

'What do you go for then, Q'ute?' Bond chuckled.

'My name's Ann Reilly,' she snapped, 'not that damn

silly nickname they all use around here.' She looked at him, straight in the eyes, for a full twenty seconds. 'As for what I like and dislike – go for, as you put it – maybe one day you'll find out.' She did not smile. 'I'm more interested in the way that automatic works, why you chose it, and how you got that white mark on your hand.'

Bond glanced up sharply, his eyes suddenly losing their humour and turning to ice in a way that almost frightened Q'ute. 'Someone tried to be clever a long time ago,' he said slowly. In the back of his mind, he remembered, quite clearly, all the circumstances which had led to the plastic surgery, that showed now only as a white blemish, after the Cyrillic letter Щ – standing for SH – had been carved into the back of his hand in an attempt by SMERSH to brand him as a spy. It was long ago, and very far away now; but clear as yesterday. He detected the break he had made in Q'ute's guard with his sharp cruelty. So long ago, he thought: the business with Le Chiffre at Royale-les-Eaux, and a woman called Vesper – about the same age as this girl sitting on the workbench, showing off her shapely knees and calves – lying dead from an overdose, her body under the sheets like a stone effigy in a tomb.

The coldness in Bond's mien faded. He smiled at Q'ute, again looking down at his hand. 'A small accident – carelessness on my part. Needed a bit of surgery, that's all.' Then he went back to removing the packing grease from the Browning. All thoughts of dallying with the Q Branch executive called Ann Reilly were gone. She was relatively young and still learning the ways of the secret world, in spite of her electronic efficiency, he decided.

As though to break the mood, she asked, in a small voice, 'What's it like to kill somebody? They say you've had to kill a lot of people during your time in the Service.'

'Then they shouldn't talk so much.' It was Bond's turn to snap. He was reassembling the gun now. 'The need-to-know system operates in the Service. You, of all people, should know better than to ask questions like that.'

'But I *do* need to know.' Calmer now, but showing a streak of stubbornness that Bond had detected in her eyes before this. 'After all, I deal with some of the important "gee-whizz" stuff. You must also know what that covers – secret death: undetectable. People die in this business. I should know about the end product.'

Bond completed the reassembly, ran the mechanism back and forth a couple of times, then picked up one of the magazines containing seven Browning Long 9mm. rounds that would shatter a piece of five-inch pine board at twenty feet.

Looking at the slim magazine, he thought of its lethal purpose, and what each of the little jacketed pieces of metal within would do to a man or woman. Yes, he thought, Q'ute – Ann Reilly – had a right to know. 'Give me a hand;' he nodded towards a box on the workbench. 'Bring along a couple of spare magazines. We have to test this little toy on the range, then work's over for the night.'

She picked up the magazines and slid down from her perch as she repeated the question. 'How does it feel to kill a person?'

'While it's happening, you don't think much about it,' Bond answered flatly. 'It's a reflex. You do it and you don't hesitate. If you're wise, and want to go on living, you don't think about it afterwards either. I've known men who've had breakdowns – go for early retirement on half pension – for thinking about it afterwards. There's nothing to tell, my dear Q'u . . . Ann. I try not to remember. That way I remain detached from its reality.'

'And is that why you clean off your pistol in front of someone like me – stripping it as though it were a woman?'

He did not reply to that, and she followed Bond quietly through the corridor that led to the range.

It took Bond nearly an hour, and six extra magazines, before he was completely happy with the Browning. When they finished on the range, he went back to the gunsmith's room, with Q'ute in his wake, and stripped the gun down for cleaning after firing. As he completed this last chore, Bond looked up at her. 'Well, you've seen all there is to see. Show's over. You can go home now.'

'You no longer require my services then?'

She was smiling. Bond had not expected that. 'Well,' he said cautiously. 'If you'd care for dinner . . .'

'I'd love it,' she grinned.

Bond took her in the Saab. They went into Kensington, to the Trattoo in Abingdon Road, where Carlo was pleased to see his old customer. Bond had not been there for some time and was treated with great respect, ordering for the pair of them—a simple meal: the *zuppa di verdura* followed by *fegato Bacchus*, washed down with a light, young, Bardolino (a '79, for Bardolino should always be drunk young and cool, even though it is red, rather as the French imbibe their rosé wines young, Bond explained). Afterwards, Carlo made them plain crêpes with lemon and sugar, and they had coffee up in the bar, where Alan Clare was at the small piano.

Ann Reilly was enchanted, saying that she could sit and listen to the liquid ease of Clare's playing for ever. But the restaurant soon started to fill up. A couple of actors came in, a well-known movie director with crinkled grey hair, and a famous zany comedian. For Ann, Alan played one last piece – her request, the sentimental oldie from *Casablanca*: 'As Time Goes By'.

Bond headed the Saab back towards Chelsea, at Ann Reilly's bidding. Between giving him directions, she laughed a lot, and said she had not enjoyed an evening like this for a long time. Finally they pulled up in front of the Georgian terraced house where Q'ute said she had the whole of the second floor as her apartment.

'Like to come in and see my gadgets?' she asked. Bond could not see the smile in the darkness of the car, but knew it was there.

'Well, that's different,' he chuckled. 'I still stick to the etchings.'

She had the passenger door open. 'Oh, but I have gadgets,' she laughed again. 'I'm a senior executive of Q Branch, remember. I like to take my work home with me.'

Bond locked the doors, followed her up the steps and into the small elevator which had been installed during what estate agents call 'extensive modernisation'.

From the small entrance hall of Q'ute's apartment Bond could see the kitchen and bathroom. She opened the main door and they passed into the remainder of the apartment – one huge room – the walls hung with two large matching gilt-framed mirrors, a genuine Hockney and an equally genuine Bratby, of a well-known composer whose musicals had been at their peak fifteen to twenty years ago. The furnishings were mainly late 1960s Biba, and the lighting was to match – Swedish in design, and mounted on battens angled into the corners of the room.

'Ah, period décor,' said Bond with a grin.

Ann Reilly smiled back. 'All is not as it seems,' she giggled, and for a moment Bond wondered if she was not used to drinking: perhaps the wine had gone to her head. Then he saw her hand move to a small console of buttons by the light switches. Her fingers stabbed at the buttons, and in the next few seconds Bond could only think of transformation scenes at childhood pantomimes.

The lights dimmed and the room became bathed in a soft red glow which came from the skirting boards. The large, circular, smoked glass table which formed a focal point at the centre of the room seemed to sink into the carpet, and from it there came the sound of splashing water as it gleamed with light to become a small pond with a fountain playing at its centre. The Hockney, Bratby, and both of the mirrors appeared to cloud over, then clear, changed into paintings of a nature that almost shocked Bond by their explicitness.

He sniffed the air: a musky scent had risen around him, while the sound of piano music gently rose in volume – a slow, sensual blues solo, so close and natural that Bond peered about him, thinking the girl was actually sitting at an instrument somewhere. The scent and music began to claw at his senses. Then he took a step back, his eyes moving to the wall on his right. The wall had started to open up, and, from behind it, a large, high, waterbed slid soundlessly into the room – above it a mirrored canopy hanging from crimson silk ropes.

Ann Reilly had disappeared. For a second, Bond was disorientated, his back to the wall, head and eyes moving over the extraordinary sight. Then he saw her, behind the fountain, a small light, dim but growing to illuminate her as she stood naked but for a thin, translucent nightdress; her hair undone and falling to her waist – hair and the thin material moving and blowing as though caught in a silent zephyr.

Then, as suddenly as it all happened, the room started to change again. The lighting returned to normal, the table rose from the fountain, the Hockney, Bratby, and mirrors were there once more, and Q'ute slowly faded from view. Only the bed stayed in place.

There was a chuckle from behind him, and Bond turned to find Q'ute, still in her brown velvet, and with her hair smooth and pleated, as she leaned against the wall laughing. 'You like it?' she asked.

Bond frowned. 'But . . .?'

'Oh come on, James. The transformation's easy: micro and electronics; *son et lumière*. I built it all myself.'

'But you . . .?'

'Yes,' she frowned, 'that's the most expensive bit, but I put most of that together as well; and the model *is* me. Hologram. Very effective, yes? Complete 3D. Come on, I'll show you the gubbins . . .'

She was about to move away when Bond caught hold of her, pulled her close and into a wild kiss. She slid her hands to his shoulders, gently pushing him away. 'Let's see.' She cocked an eyebrow at him. 'I thought you'd have got the idea. You said the place was period décor – 1960s. All I've

done – and I've spent many happy hours getting it right –
is add in a 1960s' fantasy: music, lights, the waterbed,
scent, and an available bird with very few clothes on. I
thought you of all people, James Bond, would have got the
message. Fantasies should change with the times. Surely
we're all more realistic these days. Particularly about
relationships. The word is, I think, maturity.'

Yes, thought Bond, Q'ute *was* a good name for Ann
Reilly, as she scurried around showing off the electronics of
her fantasy room. 'It might be an illusion', he said, 'but it
still has a lethal effect.'

She turned towards him, 'Well, James, the bed's still
there. It usually is. Have some coffee and let's get to know
one another.'

In his own flat the next morning, Bond was awake before
six-thirty. The biter bit, he thought, with a wry smile. If
ever a man's bluff had been called, it was by the ingenious
Q'ute. In good humour he exercised, took a hot bath,
followed by a cold shower; shaved, dressed and was in his
dining room when the faithful May came in with his copy of
The Times and his normal breakfast – the favourite meal:
two large cups of black coffee, from De Bry, without sugar;
a single 'perfectly boiled' brown egg (Bond still affected to
dislike anything but brown eggs, and kept his opinion
regarding three and one-third minutes constituting the
perfect boiling time); then two slices of wholewheat toast
with Jersey butter and Tiptree 'Little Scarlet' strawberry
jam, Cooper's Vintage Oxford Marmalade or Norwegian
heather honey.

Governments could come and go; crises could erupt;
inflation may spiral, but – when in London – Bond's
breakfast routine rarely changed. In this he was the worst
thing a man in his profession could be: a man of habit, who
enjoyed the day starting in one particular manner, eating
from the dark blue egg cup with a gold ring around the top,
which matched the rest of his Minton china, and happy to

see the Queen Anne silver coffee pot and accessories on his table. Faddish as this quirk certainly was, Bond would have been outraged if anyone told him it smacked of snobbery. For James Bond, snobbery was for others, in all walks of life. A man has a right to certain pleasurable idiosyncrasies – more than a right, if they settled his mind and stomach for the day ahead.

Following the Q'ute incident, Bond hardly took any time off during the preparation for what he now thought of as an assignation with Anton Murik on Gold Cup day.

On most evenings lately he had gone straight back to his flat and a book which he kept between his copies of *Scarne's Complete Guide to Gambling* and an 1895 edition of the classic *Sharps and Flats – A complete revelation of the secrets of cheating at games of chance and skill* by John Nevil Maskelyne. The book he read avidly each night had been published privately around the turn of the century. Bond had come across it in Paris several years before, and had it rebound in board and calf by a printer often employed by the Service. It was written by a man using the pseudonym Cutpurse and titled *The Skills, Arts and Secrets of the Dip*. It was, in fact, a comprehensive treatise on the ancient arts of the pickpocket and lightfingered body-thief.

Using furniture, old coats – even a standard lamp – Bond practised various moves in which he was already well skilled. His discussions with M, as to how he should introduce himself to the Laird of Murcaldy and his entourage, had formulated a plan that called for the cleverest possible use of some of the tricks described by Cutpurse. Bond knew that to practise some of these dodges, it was necessary to keep in constant trim – like a card sharp, or even a practitioner of the harmless, entertaining, business of legerdemain. He therefore began anew, re-learning the bump, the buzz, the two-fingered lift, the palm-dip (usually used on breast pockets), the jog – in which a small billfold is literally jogged from a man's hip pocket – or the thumb-hitch.

A pickpocket seldom works alone. Gangs of from three to ten are the normal rule, so Bond's own plan was to be made doubly difficult: first he had to do the thing by himself; second, the normal picking of pockets did not apply. He was slowly working up his skill to the most difficult move in the book – the necklace flimp: flimp being a word that went back to the early nineteenth century, when flimping referred, normally, to the removal of a person's fob watch. Towards the end of the period Bond was spending several hours a night perfecting the moves of the necklace flimp. All he could hope for was that M's information, given to him during those long hours of briefing under the Cooper painting of Admiral Jervis's victory, would prove accurate.

Now, a signpost read 'Ascot 4 miles', and Bond joined a queue of Bentleys, Rolls-Royces, Daimlers and the like, all heading towards the race course. He sat calmly at the wheel; his Browning in its holster, locked away in the glove compartment; Q'ute's personalised luggage in the boot of the car, and himself in shirtsleeves, the grey morning coat neatly folded on the rear seat, with the matching topper beside it. Before leaving, Bond had reflected that he would not have put it past Q'ute to arrange some kind of device inside a top hat. She had been very affable, promising any assistance in the field – 'Just let me know, and I'll be out with whatever you need, 007,' she had said with only the trace of a wink.

Bond allowed her a small twitch of the eyebrow.

Now he looked like any other man out to cut a dash in the Royal Enclosure. In fact his mind was focused on one thing only – Dr Anton Murik, Laird of Murcaldy, and his association with the terrorist, Franco.

The careful, if quickly planned, run-up to the assignment was over. James Bond was on his own, and would only call up help if the situation demanded it.

As he approached the race course, Bond felt slightly elated, though a small twist in his guts told him the scent of danger, maybe even disaster, was in the air.

6

PEARLS BEFORE SWINE

There was only one part of any race course that James Bond really enjoyed – the down-market public area. Alongside the track itself life was colourful: the characters always appearing more alive and real – the day-trip couples out for a quick flutter; tipsters with their sharp patter, and the ebullient, on-course bookies, each with his lookout man watching a partner; the tick-tack sign language being passed across the heads of the punters, relaying changes in the betting odds. Here there was laughter, enjoyment and the buzz of pleasure.

For the first couple of races that day, Bond – immaculate in morning suit and topper – strolled in the public crowd, as though reluctant to take his rightful place in the Royal Enclosure, the pass for which (provided by M) was pinned to the lapel of his morning coat.

He even stayed down near the rails to watch the arrival of Her Majesty, Prince Philip and the Queen Mother – stirred, as ever, by the inspiring sight of tradition as the members of the Royal Family were conveyed down the course in their open carriages: a blaze of colour, with liveried coachmen and postillions – like a ceremony from another age.

His first action, on arrival, had been to check the position of Anton Murik's box in the Grand– or Tattersalls–Stand (another fact gleaned from one of M's expert sources). The Murik box was third along from the left on the second tier.

Leaning against the rails, Bond scanned the tiered boxes with binoculars provided by Q Branch—field glasses of a particular powerful nature, with Zeiss lenses, made especially for the Service by Bausch & Lomb. The Murik box was empty, but there were signs that it would soon be inhabited. Bond would have to keep his eye on the paddock prior to the Gold Cup; but, before that event, there was an overwhelming desire to have a wager on his target's horse. Dr Anton Murik's entry did not stand much chance. That was patently obvious from the odds being offered.

For the Gold Cup, the Queen's horse was favourite, with Lester Piggott up; and odds at only five-to-four on. Other contenders were very well-tried four-year-olds, most of them with exceptional records. In particular, Francis' Folly, Desmond's Delight and Soft Centre were being heavily tipped. The other ten runners seemed to be there merely for the ride; and the Laird of Murcaldy's China Blue — by Blue Light out of Geisha Girl — appeared to have little opportunity of coming anywhere near the leaders. Bond's race card showed that in his last three outings, the horse had achieved only one placing, the card reading 0–3–0.

The harsh facts were borne out by the betting odds, which stood at twenty-five-to-one. Bond gave a sardonic smile, knowing that M would be furious when he put in his expenses. If you're going to plunge rashly with the firm's money, he thought, do it with a little style. With this in his head, Bond approached a bookmaker whose board showed him to be Honest Tone Snare, and placed a bet of one hundred and ten pounds to win on China Blue. One hundred and ten pounds may be a negligible sum, but, to the Service accountants, even five pounds was a matter of arguable moment.

'You got money to burn, Guv?' Honest Tone gave Bond a toothy grin.

'One hundred and ten to win,' Bond repeated placidly.

'Well, you know yer own mind, Guv; but I reckon you've either got money to burn or you know something the rest of us don't.' Honest Tone took the money in return for a ticket that, if China Blue should — by some chance of fate — win, would yield Bond something in the region of two and a half

thousand pounds: taking into account the eight per cent
betting tax – hence the extra ten pounds stake.

Once in the Royal Enclosure, Bond felt his dislike for this
side of the race meeting descend on him like a dark, depressing cloud. As much as he liked the female form, he was
repelled by the idea of so many women, young and old,
parading in fashionable dresses and outlandish hats. That
was not what racing was about, he considered.

Some of them, he acknowledged, would be there for the
sheer pleasure of the day, which had turned out to be warm
and cloudless. Yet a fair majority attended only to be seen,
attract the attention of the gossip columnists, and out-do
one another with bizarre headgear. Maybe this aversion
was a sign of maturity. A depressing thought; and to quell
it, Bond headed for the main bar where he consumed two
rounds of smoked salmon sandwiches and a small bottle of
Dom Perignon.

On M's personal instructions, he had come into the
Enclosure unarmed – the Browning still snug in the car. In
case of trouble, Bond carried only the small pen emergency
contact device, and the replica Dunhill cigarette lighter –
which contained more dangerous possibilities than Messrs
Dunhill would have approved.

Casually he strolled around the Enclosure, finally settling himself under the shade of the trees which surrounded
the paddock. Safe in his pocket was M's other piece of
cover – a well-forged owner's pass that would get him
inside the paddock, and close to the target. He did not have
to wait long. The horses were already entering the paddock, from the end farthest from the stands. Bond watched.
Within a few minutes he identified China Blue.

The horse looked an unpromising proposition by any
standards. The coat was dull and the animal had about him
an odd, lack-lustre look – as though it would take dynamite
rather than a jockey to make him perform anything more
than a sedate canter on this warm afternoon. Bond gave the
animal a good looking over and decided that it was just an

unpromising-looking horse. This did not mean that the animal could not show unusual form. Stranger things had happened. Looking at the horse being led round by the stable-boy, Bond had one of those sudden instincts – the kind which so often saves lives in his profession – that he would win his money. There was more to China Blue than the eye could tell.

How? He had no idea. Frauds on race courses in England are rare these days. Anton Murik would certainly not resort to unsophisticated risks like doping or substitution, when competing against the kind of stock running in the Ascot Gold Cup. Yet Bond knew at that moment that China Blue would almost certainly win.

Suddenly the short hairs on the back of his neck tingled, and he experienced a shiver of suspense. A man and two women were approaching China Blue – the trainer turning towards them, hat in hand and a deferential smile of welcome on his face. Bond was getting his first view of Dr Anton Murik.

He shifted position, moving closer to the paddock entrance.

It *was* Anton Murik; the face of the man he had seen in the photograph. What the picture had not captured was the high mane of white hair sweeping back from the bulldog face. It came as a shock, until Bond remembered the photograph had been cut off just above the forehead. Also, no still photograph could ever capture the walk or manner. The Laird of Murcaldy was barely five feet tall, and walked, not as Bond had imagined, with the stride of a Scottish chieftain, but in a series of darting steps. His movements – hands, head, fingers and neck – were of the same quick precision. In a phrase, Dr Anton Murik, Laird of Murcaldy, was possessed with the movements of a grounded bird.

The features, and authoritative way he appeared to address his trainer, however, made up for any other physical deficiency. Even at this distance, the man clearly had a power that overrode physical peculiarities or eccentricities.

A born leader, Bond thought; sometimes the best of men, or the worst; for born leaders usually knew of their power early in life, when they chose either their good or evil angel as a guide to success.

The two women with Murik were easily recognisable. Oddly, Bond considered, they were identically dressed, except in the matter of colour. Each wore a classic, V-necked, mid-calf length dress in a knitted bouclé. Over the dress was a short, sleeveless gilet.

The elder of the women — obviously Mary-Jane Mashkin — wore the ensemble in navy, with white trimming, and a neat, short-brimmed hat in white.

The ward, Lavender Peacock, was taller, more slender, and just as stunning as her photograph. Her identical clothes were in white, with navy trimmings and hat. Bond wondered if their outfits were originals from Murik's Roussillon Fashions.

The younger girl was laughing, turning towards Murik, the gilet flaring away from her to reveal firm and impertinent breasts, under the dress, in splendid proportion to the rest of her body. The sight was breathtaking, and Bond could see why the Laird of Murcaldy kept her on what M referred to as a tight rein. Lavender Peacock looked like a spirited, healthy and agile girl. To Bond's experienced eye, she also had the nervous tension of a young woman unused, and straining at the leash. Left to her own devices, Lavender Peacock might well carve a path of broken hearts — even broken marriages — through Scottish and English society, in a matter of months.

Bond narrowed his eyes, straining and never taking them off the girl. She talked animatedly, constantly glancing at Murik. Concern seemed to pass over her face each time she looked at the Laird, but Bond only took this in as a kind of side issue. He was looking for something more. Something essential to the whole scheme of insinuating himself into the Laird of Murcaldy's immediate circle. Something M had revealed to him in great detail during their hours of planning.

It was there. No doubt. The triple, heavy rope of match-ing pearls clearly visible around Lavender's neck. From this distance, under the shade of the paddock trees, it was, of course, impossible to tell if they were the real thing: but they would, undoubtedly, be taken as such. The real thing certainly existed – £500,000 worth of *mohar* pearls, graded and strung on three short ropes, all held by a decorated box clasp and safety chain at the back of the neck.

The pearls had been kept in trust for Lavender until her twenty-first birthday, having originally been a wedding present from her father to her mother, during whose life-time they had been kept mainly in a bank vault.

Lavender – M told Bond – had broken this habit, against Anton Murik's advice, and now wore them on every possible occasion. In the confines of M's office, Bond wondered, aloud, if the Laird of Murcaldy did, in fact, allow the pearls to be worn. Substitution would, for a man of his resourcefulness, be relatively easy. M had snappily told him this was not the point. The Peacock pearls were known to be worn in public. They certainly seemed to be around Lavender's neck this afternoon.

Bond thought they could not be around a prettier neck. If he had been taken with the photograph of the girl, he was certainly dazzled by the real thing. Murik had turned away and was talking to the two women, while the trainer leaned close to the jockey, giving him last instructions. In the background China Blue looked as docile as ever: as spirited as a wooden rocking horse.

It was time for Bond to move. The entrance to the paddock was busy, with people passing in and out. Already he had noticed that the Ascot race course officials were only giving cursory glances at proffered owners' passes. Within the next few minutes, Anton Murik and his party would be coming through this entrance – which doubled as the main exit – out into the Royal Enclosure, through which they would presumably pass on their way to the Tattersalls

Stand. The whole of the present operation's future depended upon timing, and Bond's skill. With the binocular case over his right shoulder, race card held open, firmly, in his left hand, he made his way into the paddock, flicking the owner's pass quickly in front of the official who seemed most preoccupied.

Horses were being mounted, and two had already begun to walk towards the exit that would take them down on to the course. Bond circled China Blue and the group around him; staying back, seeming to keep his eyes on another horse near by.

At last, with a final call of good luck from the assembled party, China Blue's jockey swung into the saddle. Murik, the Mashkin woman, the trainer and Lavender moved back, pausing for a second as the horse walked away, urged forward by the jockey, who, Bond noticed, looked very relaxed and confident.

Murik's party began to move slowly towards the exit through which Bond had just come. It was now becoming crowded with owners, their families and select friends leaving to view the race. Carefully Bond stepped close to Murik's party. The Laird himself was talking to the trainer, with Mary-Jane Mashkin standing to one side. Lavender Peacock was to their rear. Bond sidled between her and the Laird with his two companions, staying behind them just long enough for others to press around him, therefore putting several people between Murik's group and Lavender Peacock, so that she would be reasonably far behind them when they reached the exit.

Bond sidestepped again, allowing himself to be overtaken until he could push himself in just behind Lavender Peacock. They were five or six paces from the exit, now jammed with people trying to get through as quickly and politely as possible. Bond was directly behind the girl, his eyes fixed on the box clasp and safety chain at the back of her neck. It was clearly visible, and, as he was pushed even closer, hemmed in by the crowd, Bond caught the smell of the girl's scent — Mille de Patou, he thought: the limited edition, and the most expensive scent on the market. So exclusive that you received a certificate with your purchase.

There were enough people around, and Bond was well screened. Allowing himself to be jostled slightly, he now pushed his shoulders forward for added protection, and bumped full into Lavender Peacock's back.

The next complicated moves took only a fraction of a second, just as he had practised and planned them during the past few days. Keeping the left hand, which was clutching the open race card, low down by his side, Bond's right hand moved upwards to the nape of the girl's neck. The inside of his first and second fingertips grasped the box clasp which held the pearls, lifting them away, so that no strain would be felt by their owner. At the same time, his thumb passed through the safety chain, breaking it off with a deft twist. Now the box clasp fell into position, held tightly by the thumb and forefinger. He pressed hard, tilting, and felt the clasp give way.

The box clasp is constructed, as its name implies, as two metal boxes — in this case decorated by tiny pearls — which fit one inside the other. When released by pressure they fall apart, but there is an added safety feature. The inner box contains a small hook, which slips around a bar in the outer box. Using the thumb and first two fingers, Bond controlled both boxes, slipping the hook from its bar. He then withdrew his hand, glancing down and dropping his race card. Silently the pearls fell to the turf. His aim and timing were perfect. The race card followed the pearls, falling flat and open on top of them. Lavender Peacock did not feel a thing, though Bond caused a minor clogging of the exit as he bent to retrieve his card, lifting the pearls with it, so that they were securely held inside the card.

Relaxed now, and holding the card and pearls, hidden behind the tail of his morning coat, Bond sauntered towards the Tattersalls Stand, following Anton Murik's party, at a discreet distance, as they moved towards the Tattersalls Stand – just as he hoped they would. Lavender had caught up with them, and Bond prayed she would not discover her loss before reaching the Murik box.

Bond slowed considerably, allowing the Laird's party to get well ahead. He knew there was still the vague possibility that some plainclothes policeman had spotted his moves. Any moment one of two things could happen – a cry from Lavender, announcing the pearls were missing; or the firm hand on his shoulder that would mean, in criminal parlance, that he was having his 'collar felt'. If the latter occurred it would be no use telling them to ring M. Precious time would have been lost.

Murik's party had now disappeared into the stand. Nothing happened, and Bond entered the side door, climbing the stairs to the second tier about two minutes after the Laird's group entered. On reaching the corridor running behind the boxes, Bond transferred the pearls to his right hand and advanced on the Laird of Murcaldy's box.

They all had their backs to him as he knocked and stepped inside. Nobody noticed, for they seemed intent upon watching the runners canter down to the starting line. Bond coughed. 'Excuse me,' he said. The group turned.

Anton Murik seemed a little put out. The women looked interested.

Bond smiled and held out the pearls. 'I believe someone has been casting pearls before this particular swine,' he said, calmly. 'I found these on the floor outside. Looks like the chain's broken. Do they belong to . . . ?'

With a little cry, Lavender Peacock's hand flew to her throat. 'Oh my God,' she breathed, the voice low and full of melody, even in this moment of stress.

' "My God" is right,' Murik's voice was almost unnaturally low for his stature, and there was barely a hint of any Scottish accent. 'Thank you very much. I've told my ward often enough that she should not wear such precious baubles in public. Now, perhaps, she'll believe me.'

Lavender had gone chalk white and was fumbling out towards Bond's hand and the pearls. 'I don't know how to — ' she began.

Murik broke in, 'The least we can do, sir, is to ask you to stay and watch the race from here.' Bond was looking into dark slate eyes, the colour of cooling lava, and with as much life. This gaze would, no doubt, put the fear of God into some people, Bond thought: even himself, under certain circumstances. 'Let me introduce you. I am Anton Murik; my ward, Lavender Peacock, and an old friend, Mary-Jane Mashkin.'

Bond shook hands, in turn; introducing himself. 'My name is Bond,' he said. 'James Bond.'

Only one thing surprised him. When she spoke, Mary-Jane Mashkin betrayed in her accent that she was undoubtedly American — something that had not appeared on any of the files in M's office. Originally Southern, Bond thought, but well overlaid with the nasalities of the East Coast.

'You'll stay for the race, then?' Murik asked, speaking quickly.

'Oh yes. Please.' Lavender appeared to have recovered her poise.

Mary-Jane Mashkin smiled. She was a handsome woman, and the smile was much warmer than the subdued malevolence of Anton Murik. 'You must stay. Anton has a horse running.'

'Thank you.' Bond moved closer within the box, trying to place himself between Murik and his ward. 'May I ask which horse?'

Murik had his glasses up, scanning the course, peering towards the starting gate. 'China Blue. He's down there all right.' He lowered his glasses, and for a second there was movement within the lava-flow eyes. 'He'll win, Mr Bond.'

'I sincerely hope so. What a coincidence,' Bond laughed, reaching for his own binocular case. 'I have a small bet on your horse. Didn't notice who owned him.'

'Really?' There was a faint trace of appreciation in Murik's voice. Then he gave a small smile. 'Your money's safe. I shall have repaid you in part for finding Lavender's pearls. What made you choose China Blue?'

'Liked the name.' Bond tried to look ingenuous. 'Had an aunt with a cat by that name once. Pedigree Siamese.'

'They're under starter's orders.' Lavender sounded breathless. They turned their glasses towards the far distance, and the start of the Ascot Gold Cup—two and a half flat miles.

A roar went up from the crowd below them. Bond just had time to refocus his glasses. The horses were off.

Within half a mile a pattern seemed to emerge. The Queen's horse was bunched with the other favourites—Francis' Folly and Desmond's Delight, with Soft Centre clinging to the group, way out in front of three other horses which stood back a good ten lengths; while the rest of the field straggled out behind.

Bond kept his glasses trained on the three horses behind the little bunch of four leaders who seemed set to provide the winners. Among this trio was the distinctive yellow and black of Murik's colours on China Blue.

There was a strange tension and silence in the box, contrasting with the excited noise drifting up from the crowds lining the course. The pace was being kept up hard; and the leading bunch did not appear to be drawing away from the three horses some distance behind them. The Queen's horse was ahead, but almost at the half-way mark Desmond's Delight began to challenge, taking the lead so that these two horses, almost imperceptibly, started to pull away, with Francis' Folly and Soft Centre only half a length behind them, running as one animal.

As the field passed the half-way mark, Bond shifted his glasses. Two of the trio following the lead bunch seemed to be dropping back, and it took Bond a second to realise this was an optical illusion. He was aware of Anton Murik muttering something under his breath. China Blue was suddenly being hard ridden, closing the distance between himself and the third and fourth runners among the leaders.

'Blue! Come on, Blue,' Lavender called softly. Glancing along the box rail, Bond saw Mary-Jane Mashkin standing, taut, with her hands clenched.

The crowd was intent on the four horses battling for position at the front of the field. They were past the three-quarter mark by the time people realised the serious challenge China Blue presented as he came up, very fast, on the outside.

The racing China Blue could have been a different animal from the horse Bond had watched in the paddock. He moved with mechanical precision in a steady striding gallop; and now he was reaching a speed far in excess of any of the lead horses. By the time they reached the straight final three furlongs, China Blue was there, scudding past Francis' Folly and Soft Centre—well up and gaining on Desmond's Delight, who had again taken second place to the Queen's horse.

A great burst of sound swept like a wind over the course as China Blue suddenly leaped forward in a tremendous surge of speed, outstripping both Desmond's Delight and the Queen's horse, to come loping home a good length in front of the pair who had made the running from the start.

Lavender was jumping up and down, excitedly clapping her hands. 'He did it. Uncle Anton, he did it.'

Mary-Jane Mashkin laughed — a deep, throaty sound — but Dr Anton Murik merely smiled. 'Of course he did it.' Bond saw that Murik's smile did not light up his eyes. 'Well, Mr Bond, my horse has won for you. I'm pleased.'

'Not as pleased as I am,' said Bond, quickly, as though blurting out something he would rather have kept hidden. It was just enough to interest Murik — the hint of a man rather in need of hard cash.

'Ah,' the Laird of Murcaldy nodded. 'Well, perhaps we'll meet again.' He fumbled in his waistcoat pocket, producing a business card. 'If you're ever in Scotland, look me up. I'd be glad to provide some hospitality.'

Bond looked down at the card bearing Anton Murik's address and again feigned surprise. 'Another coincidence,' he said, smoothly.

'Really?' Murik was ready to go. After all, he had just won the Ascot Gold Cup and wanted his moment of triumph. 'Why another coincidence?'

'I leave for Scotland tonight. I'll be in your area in a couple of days.'

The slate eyes grew even cooler. 'Business or pleasure?'

'Pleasure mostly. But I'm always open for business.' He tried to make it sound desperate.

'What kind of business, Mr Bond?'

Bond hesitated slightly, timing the pause. 'The contracting business.'

'And what do you contract?'

Bond looked at him levelly. 'Myself as a rule. I'm a soldier. A mercenary – up to the highest bidder. There, that'll be the end of our acquaintance, I expect. We're a dying breed.' He gave a short laugh at his grim little joke. 'People don't take too kindly to mercenaries these days.'

Anton Murik's hand closed around Bond's forearm, pulling him to one side, away from the two women. 'I am not averse to your profession, Mr Bond. In fact I have been known to employ mercenaries in a way – gamekeepers, people on my estates. Who knows, I may even have a place for a man like yourself. To me, you look tough enough. Come to Murik Castle. On Monday we have a little annual fun. Most of the land and the nearby village – Murcaldy – is mine. So each year we hold our own version of the Highland Games. You know the kind of thing – the caber, the hammer, shot-putting, a little dancing, wrestling. You will enjoy it.' This last sentence was almost an order.

Bond nodded, as Murik turned towards the ladies. 'We must go down, greet China Blue, and accept our just rewards. Mary-Jane, Lavender, you will be seeing Mr Bond again soon. He's kindly consented to come and stay – for the Games.'

As they left the box, Bond was aware of a mildly sardonic look in Mary-Jane Mashkin's eyes.

'Thank you again – for the pearls, I mean, Mr Bond,' Lavender said. 'I look forward to seeing you soon.' There was something odd about the way she phrased the parting sentence, as though she meant what she said but was hinting some warning. Lavender, Bond thought, appeared at first meeting to be a woman with some hidden fear below the charming, easy and poised exterior.

The Laird of Murcaldy did not even look at Bond again – leaving the box in his quick, birdlike manner without a word or backward glance.

Bond stood, looking after them for a moment, wondering about Murik's personal version of the Highland Games, and the part he might be expected to play in them. Then he went down to collect his winnings from a suitably impressed Honest Tone Snare, before making a short doubletalk telephone call to Bill Tanner; and another to the Central Hotel in Glasgow, booking himself a room for the following morning: stressing that he would need to use it immediately on arrival, which he hoped, would be in the early hours.

The Laird of Murcaldy would doubtless be flying his party back to Scotland. Bond did not want to be far behind them. Neither did he wish to arrive at Murik Castle without rest and time for reflection.

Slipping the leather strap of his glasses' case over one shoulder, James Bond walked as casually as he could towards the car park.

7

KING OF THE CASTLE

DURING THE FURIOUS night drive north Bond had plenty of time to puzzle over Anton Murik's win with China Blue. Horses for courses, he thought. But that horse had not looked fit enough for any course. How, then, had it romped home at Ascot? The only possible explanation lay in the old trick of having China Blue pulled back by his jockey in earlier races – not displaying his true form until the strategic moment. But perhaps the real answer would be found, with the others he sought, at Murik Castle.

The journey to Glasgow was without incident. Bond went flat-out on the motorway sections, managing to avoid police speed traps, and stopping to refuel at a couple of all-night motorway service areas.

He was parked, settled into his room at the Central Hotel, and eating a breakfast of porridge, scrambled eggs, toast and coffee, by nine in the morning. He then hung out the 'Do not disturb' sign and slept like a baby, not waking until seven that evening.

After a lengthy study of the Ordnance Survey maps to plan the route, Bond went down and dined in the hotel's Malmaison Restaurant – named after Napoleon and Josephine's retreat, and one of the best French restaurants in Scotland. Bond, however, had no desire for rich food that evening, and settled for a simple meal of smoked salmon followed by a fillet steak with a green salad. He drank only Perrier water. He was determined to do most of the journey by night – travelling like one crossing a desert in secrecy.

He was on the road, with the bill paid, by ten thirty, heading north on the A82, which took him right alongside the waters of Loch Lomond. Early on the following morning, Bond stopped for a day's rest, at a village just short of Loch Garry – having switched to the A87 that would eventually lead him as far as the coastal lochs, and those narrow roads with frequent passing places, around the western seaboard.

He reached a wooded area just to the east of Loch Carron early the next morning, and having parked the Saab well out of sight among trees, remained at rest through a day of pale blue skies and the scent of pine and heather, knowing that as soon as dusk set in, the village of Murcaldy, and from there Murik Castle, would only be a matter of seventy or eighty minutes' drive. He had brought pies and some fruit, together with more Perrier water, not wanting to chance anything stronger at this stage of the operation.

Having concentrated on making the journey in good and safe time, Bond so far had not been able to savour the views or delight in the beauties of Scotland. Indeed, there had been no opportunity while doing most of his travelling by night. So now he lay back, adjusted the driving seat, dozing and eating as the sun slid across the sky and began to settle behind the trees and hills.

While there was still light, Bond began to make his emergency preparations, unlocking the boot and transferring a packet of cigarettes from Q Branch's prepared briefcase to his pocket. Only six of the cigarettes were of any use to a smoker, the remainder being cut short to hide an easily accessible compartment into which four pre-set electronic microbugs nestled comfortably. If Bond was to be a walking surveillance unit within the Murik household, he might well need assistance; and the small receiver for these bugs – complete with tape and minute headset – remained in one of Q'ute's ingenious hiding places in the luggage.

He also made certain that the pen alarm was still in his pocket, and that the fake Dunhill lighter – dangerous to the point of immobilising any grown man for the best part of an hour – was well separate from his own, real lighter.

The rest of his weaponry remained locked away in the safety compartments of the car. The only other tools he required were to hand – the Bausch & Lomb field glasses and the strap-on Nitefinder headset.

As the last traces of daylight vanished and the first stars began to show in the wide sky, Bond started the Saab, turning the car in the direction of Applecross, skirting Loch Carron in the knowledge that his destination was not far away and there was cause for him to be alert. He made good time, and seventy minutes later the Saab was crossing the small bridge at Murcaldy, leading directly into the one village street with its quaint, neat rows of cottages, the two shops, inn and kirk.

Murcaldy was situated on a small river at one end of a wide glen, the sides of which, Bond could see by the now risen and bright moon, were devoid of trees. Ahead, at the far end of the glen and above the village, the castle stood against the sky like a large outcrop of rock.

The village appeared to be deserted except for occasional lights from the cottages, and Bond calculated that it took him less than forty-five seconds to travel through this little cluster of buildings. At the far end, near the kirk, the narrow road divided, a signpost pointing its two fingers in a V. Murik Castle lay directly ahead, up the glen; the other sign showed an equally narrow track leading back towards the road to Shieldaig, though Bond considered the track would eventually meet yet another narrow road, with its inevitable passing places, before one was really on the main A896 to that small town. The track thus marked, however, would have to follow the line of the glen to the east, so would probably lead him to a vantage point from which he could gain a view of the castle.

Pausing for a second, Bond slipped the infra-red Nitefinder kit over his head so that the little protruding glasses sat comfortably on his nose. Immediately the moonlit night became as clear as day, making the drive along the dry track a simple matter. He switched off the headlights and began to move steadily forward. The track dipped behind the eastern side of the glen, but the upper storeys of the castle were still visible above the skyline.

Both village and castle had been built with an eye to strategy, and Bond had little doubt that his passage through Murcaldy had already been noted. He wondered if it had also been reported to the Laird.

At last Bond reached a point which he considered to be parallel to the castle. Stopping the car, he picked up the binoculars and, with the Nitefinder headset still in place, got out and surveyed the area. To his right he could clearly see low mounds of earth, just off the track and running for about a hundred yards, as though somebody had been doing some fresh digging.

He paused, thinking he should investigate, but decided the castle must be his first concern. Turning left, Bond walked off the track and made his way silently towards the rolling eastern slope of the glen.

The air was sweet with night scents and clear air. Bond moved as quietly as possible, almost knee-deep in gorse, bracken and heather. Far away a dog barked, and there came the call of some predatory night bird beginning its long dark hunt.

On reaching the top of the rise, Bond stretched himself out and looked around. He could see clearly down the glen to the village, but it was impossible to gain any vantage point above the castle, which lay about a mile away in a direct line, having been built on a wide plateau. Far away behind the castle he could just make out the jutting peak of Beinn Bhan breasting itself almost three thousand feet above sea level.

Taking up the binoculars, Bond adjusted them against the Nitefinders and began to focus on the Murik Castle. He could see that half-way along the glen the track from the village became a metalled road, which ended at a pair of wide gates. These appeared to be the only means of access to the castle, which otherwise was surrounded by high

granite walls, some apparently original, other sections built
by later hands. Indeed, most of the present castle seemed to
have undergone vast reconstruction. To the rear Bond
could just make out what could well be the ruins of the
original keep; but the remainder looked more like a great
Gothic-style heap, beloved of Victorians – all gables and
turrets.

Three cars stood in front of what was obviously the main
door – a wide structure with a pillared portico. The castle
seemed to be set in the midst of large formal gardens, and
the whole aspect produced a half-sinister, half-Disneyland
quality. Craning forward, Bond could just make out the
edge of a vast lawn to the right of his view. He thought he
could glimpse the corner of a marquee. For tomorrow's
Games, he presumed. Well, Dr Anton Murik certainly had
a castle and, no doubt, acted like a king in it.

Bond was just about to get to his feet, return to the car,
drive back and present himself at King Murik's court,
when he realised, too late, that he was not alone.

They had come upon him with the craft and experience
of professional hunters, materialising from the ground like
spirits of the night. But these were not spirits – particularly
their leader who now loomed huge above him.

'Spyin' on Murik Castle, eh?' the giant accused him in a
broad Scots accent.

'Now wait a minute . . .' Bond began, raising a hand to
remove the Nitefinder kit; but, as he moved, so two hands,
the size of large hams, grasped him by the lapels, and he
was lifted bodily into the air.

'Ye'll come guy quiet wi' us. Right?' the giant said.

Bond was in no mood for going quietly with anybody. He
brought his head down hard, catching the big man on the
forward part of his nose bridge. The man grunted, letting
go of Bond, who could see the butt had been well placed. A
small trickle of blood had begun to flow from the man's
nostrils.

'I'll kill ye for – ' The man was stopped by another voice

from behind them.

'Caber? Hamish? Malcolm? What is it?'

Bond instantly recognised the slight nasal twang of Mary-Jane Mashkin. 'It's Bond,' he shouted. 'You remember, Miss Mashkin. We met at Ascot. James Bond.'

She appeared, like the others, suddenly as though from the ground. 'My God, Mr Bond, what're you doing here?' She peered at the giant. 'And what's happened to *you*, Caber?'

'Yon man gied me a butt to the neb,' he muttered, surly.

Mary-Jane Mashkin laughed. 'A brave man, doing something like that to Caber.'

'I fear your man thought I was a poacher. He – well, he lifted me up, and became generally aggressive. I'm sorry. Am I trespassing?'

Caber muttered something which sounded belligerent, as Mary-Jane Mashkin spoke again, 'Not really. This track is a right-of-way through the Laird's land. We've been, doing a little night hunting, and looking at the digging.' She inclined her head towards the other side of the track where Bond had seen the low earth piles. 'We've just started working on a new drainage system. Just as well you didn't wander that way. You could've stumbled into a pretty deep pit. They've dug down a good fifteen feet, and it's over twelve feet wide.' She paused, coming closer to him so that he caught the scent of Madame Rochas in his nostrils. 'You didn't say why you were here, Mr Bond.'

'Lost,' Bond raised his hands in a gesture of innocence. He had already slipped the Nitefinder set from his head, as though it was the most natural thing to be wearing. 'Lost and looking for the castle.'

'Which I guess you found.'

'Found, and was observing.'

She put a hand on his arm, 'Then I think you'd better take a closer look, don't you? I presume you were coming to visit.'

'Quite,' Bond nodded. In the darkness the men shuffled

and Mary-Jane Mashkin gave some quick orders. There was, apparently, a Land Rover up the track a little way. 'I'll guide Mr Bond down and you follow,' she told Caber, who had calmly relieved Bond of the Nitefinder set.

'You should have taken the track straight ahead at the village,' she said when they were settled in the Saab and moving.

'I gathered that.'

The Land Rover was close behind as they swept up to the gates. A figure appeared to open up for them, and Mary-Jane Mashkin told Bond they kept the gates closed at night, and on special locks. 'You can never tell. Even in an out-of-the-way place like this, where we know everybody, some stranger might . . .'

'Come in and ravage you all?' Bond grinned.

'Could be fun,' she laughed. 'Anyhow, it's nice to know we have a guest like yourself, Mr Bond – or can I call you James?'

'No need for formality here, I suppose,' said Bond as they came up to the main door with its great pillared porchway.

Behind them, Caber and the men called Hamish and Malcolm were climbing down from the Land Rover. Mary-Jane Mashkin called out for Hamish to inform the Laird, then turned to Bond, 'If you let Caber have your keys he'll take your luggage in, James.'

But Bond had carefully locked the door. 'I think the luggage can wait.' He made a courteous gesture towards the door of the castle. 'After being taken for a poacher, or a spy, the Laird might not want me . . .' He stopped, for the small, birdlike figure of Dr Anton Murik was emerging from the castle. He peered forward for a moment. Then his face lit up.

'Why, it's Mr Bond. You've come as promised – Good heavens, what happened to your nose, Caber?'

The big man was still dabbing blood away with his handkerchief. 'My fault, I'm afraid,' said Bond. 'Sorry, Caber, but you were a little over-enthusiastic.'

'I thocht yon man was some kindo' spy, or a poacher, Laird. I didna ken he was a visitor. Mind, he acted strange.'

'Get him to bring your luggage in, Mr Bond,' Murik smiled, and Bond repeated that it could wait. He had no desire for Caber to be messing about with the car.

'Fine,' beamed Murik. 'No need to lock anything here. We'll collect the bags later. Come in and have a dram,' and, with a sharp order to Caber and his henchman to look after the Saab, Murik ushered Bond through the gloomy porchway.

Mary-Jane Mashkin had already gone ahead, and as they crossed the threshold, Murik gave a small cackle of laughter. 'May have made an enemy there, Bond. Caber doesn't take kindly to being bested. You gave him a little nose bleed as well. Not good. Have to be careful.'

8

VIRGIN ON THE ROCKS

LATER BOND CONSIDERED that, in all probability, he had expected the Victorian Gothic gloom of the porchway to be reflected in the interior of Murik Castle – Landseer and deer antlers. He was, therefore, greatly surprised by the dazzling sight that met his eyes.

From the brooding exterior he was suddenly transported into another world. The hall, with its vast circular staircase and surrounding gallery, was decorated in shimmering white, the doors being picked out in black, and the matching white carpet underfoot giving Bond the impression that he was sinking into a soft, well-kept lawn.

The lower part of the walls was decorated, with elegant sparseness, by a series of highly polished, mint-condition halberds, *ronchas*, bat's wing *corsèques*, war forks and other thrusting weapons of the fifteenth and sixteenth centuries, which gleamed under the light thrown from a huge steel candelabra of intricate modern design. The arrangement was in no way cluttered or overdressed.

Murik spread out an arm, 'The raw materials of war,' he said. 'I'm a bit of a collector, though the best pieces are kept in other parts of the house – except, possibly, these.' He pointed to a gilded console table on which rested a glass case covering an open pistol box – a pair of duelling pistols, with tell-tale octagonal barrels, the case fitted out with all necessary accessories, brass powder measure and the like. 'Last known English duel,' Murik said proudly. 'Monro and Fawcett, 1843.' He indicated the nearest pistol. 'Monro's weapon. Did the killing.'

Bond stepped back to view the hallway again. There

were other illuminations, placed strategically over modern
pictures which hung higher up the walls. He recognised at
least two from Picasso's Blue Period, and what looked like
the original of Matisse's 'Pink Nude'.

Bond caught the smile on Murik's face. 'You're a collector of other things too,' he said. 'That looks like the — '

'Original? Yes,' Murik made a little swooping movement.

'But I thought — '

'That it was in the Baltimore Museum of Art?' The Laird
nodded. 'Yes, well, you know the art world. After all there
is a da Vinci "Virgin of the Rocks" in the Louvre and in
London. The same goes for the de Champaigne "Riche-
lieu". Come now, Mr Bond. You would like a drink.' He
raised his voice for Mary-Jane Mashkin, who appeared as
though on cue at the top of the stairs.

'Had to do a quick change.' She smiled, making a regal
descent and extending a hand which appeared to drip with
expensive rings. 'Nice to see you, Mr Bond. It was kind of
dark outside.' She raised her voice. 'Lavender, where are
you? We have a guest. The nice Mr Bond is here. The one
who was so helpful with your necklace.' She crossed the hall
to Bond's right, opening a pair of double doors.

'You will excuse me.' Murik gave his birdlike nod. 'The
ladies will take care of you. I must talk to Caber. I hope he
did not treat you too roughly; though you seem to have
given him good measure.'

'Come.' Mary-Jane Mashkin ushered Bond towards the
drawing room, in the doorway of which Lavender Peacock
now stood.

'Mr Bond, how nice.' Lavender looked even more like a
young Bacall, and somehow seemed almost relieved to see
Bond, her eyes shining with undisguised pleasure.

Both women were dressed in evening clothes, Mary-Jane
having done her quick change into a sombre black, probably by Givenchy. Lavender glowed in flowing white which
was, to Bond's experienced eye, undoubtedly a Saint

Laurent. They motioned him towards the room.

'After you, ladies.' As they turned, Bond detected a tiny noise on the balustraded gallery above them. Glancing up quickly, he was just in time to see a figure slipping into a doorway on the landing. It was only a fleeting glimpse, but there was little doubt in Bond's mind concerning the identity of the man. He had studied too many pictures and silhouettes of him in the past few days. Franco was still at Murik Castle.

The room in which Bond now found himself was long and wide, with a high, ornate ceiling, decorated in the same bold style as the hall. The walls were a delicate shell pink, the furnishings designed for comfort, and mainly in leather and glass. The wall opposite the doorway had been transformed into one huge picture window. Even in this light, Bond recognised the tint of the glass, similar to that in the Oval Office of the White House, but in a pink shade and not the green of that elegant seat of power. One would be able to see out of this huge window; but, from the outside, the human eye would only be able to note light, without detail. It was undoubtedly bulletproof.

'Well now, a drink, Mr Bond.' Mary-Jane stood by a glass cabinet. 'What will you take after all our exertions?' She made it sound coquettish.

Bond had an overwhelming urge to ask for a Virgin on the Rocks, but chose Talisker. 'When in Scotland . . .' he explained. 'A small one. I'm not a great drinker – a little champagne sometimes, and a well-made vodka martini. But here – well . . .'

Mary-Jane Mashkin smiled knowingly, opening the cabinet and taking out the fine malt whisky. 'There.' She held out the glass of amber liquid which glowed like a precious stone in the light.

Lavender had seated herself on a deep leather sofa. 'Well, it's certainly nice to have someone else staying here, Mr Bond. Especially for the Games.' She looked him straight in the eyes as she said it; as though trying to pass a message. Yet, as he looked quizzically at her, Bond saw the eyes alter, the steady look faltering, her gaze shifting over his shoulder.

'They're looking after you, then, Mr Bond?' Murik had come silently back into the room, and Bond turned to acknowledge his presence. 'I have verbally chastised Caber,' the Laird continued. 'He has no right to man-handle people – even if he does suspect them of poaching or spying.' The old, dangerous grey lava lurked in Anton Murik's eyes, and Bond saw that he was holding out the Nitefinder headset. 'An interesting toy, Mr Bond.'

'In my profession we use interesting toys,' Bond smiled, raising his hands. 'I have to admit to carrying out a re-connaissance of the castle. You invited me; but my training . . .'

Murik gave a small smile. 'I understand, Mr Bond. Probably more than you will ever know. I rather like your style.'

Lavender asked what the strange glasses and headset might be, and Bond told her briefly that they allowed you to see clearly in the dark. 'Very useful for night driving,' he added.

'Mr Bond,' Murik cut in, 'if you'll let one of my men have your car keys, I'll see your luggage is taken to the guest room.'

Bond did not like the idea, but he knew the only way to gain Anton Murik's confidence was to appear unruffled. After all, they would need a great deal of time and some very expert equipment to discover the secrets of both the car and baggage. He felt in his pockets and handed the keys to Murik. Almost at the same moment a burly man, whose tail coat and general demeanour proclaimed him as the butler, entered and stood in subservient silence. Anton Murik addressed him as Donal, telling him to get 'one of the lads to take Mr Bond's luggage to the East Guest Room and then park the car'.

Donal acknowledged the instructions without a word,

and departed with the car keys.

'There now, Mr Bond.' Anton Murik gestured to one of the comfortable leather chairs. 'Sit down. Rest yourself. As you see, we're old-fashioned enough to be formal here. We dress for dinner. But, as you've arrived late, and unprepared, we'll forgive you.'

'If the ladies don't mind.' Bond turned to smile at Mary-Jane Mashkin and Lavender Peacock. The Mashkin woman returned his smile; Lavender gave him a broad, almost conspiratorial grin.

'Not at all, Mr Bond,' said Mary-Jane, and Lavender followed with a quick, 'Just this once, Mr Bond.'

James Bond nodded his thanks and took a seat. He had long ago ceased to worry about being the odd man out on formal occasions – except, of course, when it was some forewarned important function.

In the back of his mind, Lavender Peacock caused niggling concern. She was beautiful, obviously intelligent, and at ease when Dr Anton Murik was absent; but in her guardian's presence Lavender had about her a certain wariness that he could not readily define.

It should not surprise him, Bond realised. Anton Murik and his castle, with people like Caber and the butler creeping around, would be enough to make anyone wary. There was something eery about this large Gothic structure with its interior which stank of wealth, taste and gadgetry, all set far out in the middle of a beautiful nowhere.

Murik helped himself to a drink, and they chatted amiably – Murik mainly interested in Bond's journey north – until Donal, the butler, reappeared to confirm that Mr Bond's luggage had been taken to his room and that the car was parked next to the Laird's Rolls outside. As an afterthought, and a look of distinct disapproval at Bond's apparel, he announced that dinner was served.

Bond was led across the hall – automatically glancing up at the doorway through which he had seen Franco vanish – into the long dining-room, this time decorated in more traditional style, but still retaining light colours and the same stamp and flair which showed in the hall and drawing room. None of Murik's weapon collection was on view in either drawing or dining room.

They sat at a fine long mahogany table, polished and kept in magnificent condition, and ate with Georgian silver from an exquisite dinner service, every piece of which was rimmed in gold. The Lairds of Murcaldy had obviously lived well for many decades: the table silver and china would, Bond considered, have brought a small fortune in any reputable London auction room.

Murik's food matched the outer show: a fine lobster cocktail, prepared individually at each diner's elbow from freshly cooked and cooled crustaceans; a light consommé with a chicken base, followed by rare rib of beef which almost dissolved on the tongue; and, before the cheese board was circulated, there was one of Bond's favourite Scottish puddings, the delicious cream-crowdie – toasted oatmeal folded into thick whipped cream.

'The simplest things are best at table,' Anton Murik commented. 'You pay a fortune for that in the Edinburgh and Glasgow hotels, and yet it's merely an old farmhouse dish.'

Bond reflected on a fact he had noted so often in his travels: that the wealthy of today's world take their so-called 'simple' pleasures for granted.

He was not surprised when the port arrived and the ladies withdrew, leaving the two men to their own devices. The running of Murik Castle, it seemed, clung to the fashions of more gracious days. The servants – there had been two muscular young men waiting at table under Donal's eye – withdrew; as did the butler himself, after placing cigars, cutter and matches within the Laird's reach. Bond refused a cigar, asking permission to smoke his own cigarettes.

As he drew out the old and faithful gunmetal case, James Bond's thumb felt the rough section around the middle, where it had been skilfully repaired. The thought flashed through his head that this very case had once saved his life, by stopping a SMERSH assassin's bullet. The evidence was in the rough patch, invisible to the eye, on either side of the case. For a second he wondered if he would have need of any life-saving devices in this present encounter with the Laird of Murcaldy.

'So, you took up my offer, Mr Bond?' The eyes assumed the grey and menacing lava flow look as Anton Murik faced Bond across the table.

'To visit you, yes.' Bond watched as Murik expelled a great cloud of cigar smoke.

'Oh, I didn't just mean the visit.' He gave a throaty chuckle. 'I know men, Bond. I can scent them. You are a man of vigour who lives for danger. I smelled that the moment I met you. I also felt you have a similar facility – for scenting out possible dangers. Yes?'

Bond shrugged. It was not time to commit himself to anything.

'You must be good,' Murik continued. 'Only good mercenaries stay alive; and you did all the right things – reconnoitring my estate, I mean. There may well be a job for you. Just stay for a day or two and we shall see. Tomorrow I may even give you a small test. Again, we shall see.'

There was a moment's pause, and then Bond asked levelly, 'How did you do it?'

Murik arched his eyebrows in surprise. 'Do what?'

'Win the Gold Cup with China Blue?' Bond did not smile.

Murik spread out his hands. 'I have a good trainer. How else would I win such a prestigeous cup race? And I had the right horse.'

'How?' Bond asked again. 'China Blue's form made him the biggest outsider in the race. He even looked like a loser. Now I know that's easy enough to do, but you brought it off and there were no questions. You have him pulled in his other races?'

Slowly the Laird of Murcaldy shook his head. 'There was no need for that. China Blue won. Fair and square.' Then, as though suddenly making up his mind, he rose from the table. 'Come, I'll show you something.' He led the way to a door Bond had not noticed, in a corner on the far side of the dining room. He took out a bunch of keys on a thin gold chain, selected a key and unlocked the door.

They went down a cool, well-lit passage which terminated at yet another door, which Murik unlocked with a second key. A moment later they stood in a large book-lined room. There were three leather chairs facing a wide military desk and a cabinet containing some exquisite pieces of antique weaponry. On the wall above the desk hung the only painting in the room – a large and undeniable Turner.

'Genuine?' asked Bond.

'Naturally.' Murik moved behind the desk and motioned Bond into one of the chairs facing him. 'My inner sanctum,' he commented. 'You are honoured to be here at all. This is where I work and plan.'

Gently Bond drew the chair nearer to the desk. Murik was opening one of the drawers. He removed a small buff folder, opened it and passed two photographs to Bond. 'Tell me about these photographs, Mr Bond.'

Bond said they were pictures of China Blue.

'Almost correct.' Murik smiled again: a deep secretive smirk. 'They are brothers. You see – I will not bore you with the documents – just over four years ago I had a mare in foal, here on the estate. I happened to be in residence at the time, and was in at the birth, so to speak. Happily I have a vet who knows how to keep his mouth closed. It was a rare thing, Bond. Two identical foals. Absolutely identical. No expert could have told them apart, though it was obvious to the vet and myself that the second would always be the weaker of the two. That is usual in such cases.'

He paused for effect. 'I registered one only. They were from good racing stock. There is one China Blue – the one you saw running at Ascot – with tremendous stamina and the natural aptitude for racing. The other? Well, he races, but has no speed and little stamina. Though still, at four years, you would be hard put to tell the difference in build. Now, I've shared a secret with you. I am attempting to establish a trust between us. But if it ever leaks out, I promise you are a dead man.'

'Nobody's going to hear it from me.' As he spoke, Bond moved the chair even closer, taking out his gunmetal cigarette case and the package of cigarettes provided by Q'ute. The Laird of Murcaldy had just answered a prize question. The man was a cheat and a fraud. Franco was in the house, and, for Bond, that was enough. M had been right to send him: this was certainly no panic or fool's errand.

Quickly he removed a couple of the cigarettes from the packet and placed them in his case. At the same time Bond pressed on the side of the packet, expelling one of the small electronic micro-bugs into his hand. Murik was still chuckling as he picked up the photographs from the desk. As he leaned down to return them to the drawer, Bond slid his hand under the foot-well of the desk, pressing the adhesive side of the bug hard against the woodwork. Now the Laird of Murcaldy's inner sanctum was wired for sound.

Murik snapped the drawer closed and stood up. 'Now, Mr Bond, I suggest you say goodnight to the ladies and retire. Your cases are in your room, and tomorrow we must all take part in the Games. After that you may wish to stay; and I may wish to make you a proposition. It depends on many things.'

In the drawing room, Mary-Jane Mashkin and Lavender Peacock sat listening to Mozart through hidden speakers. Bond thought he glimpsed the look of friendly conspiracy on Lavender's face as they entered the room. Once again he experienced the feeling that she was trying to warn him of something as they shook hands, bidding each other goodnight.

The silent Donal had appeared, summoned surreptitiously by Murik, and was instructed to show Bond to the East Guest Room.

As he left, Bond caught Lavender's eyes in his, warm, friendly, but with a lonely message hidden within. Of one thing he was certain, she was a living virgin on the rocks— though he admitted to himself that he was being presumptuous about the first part of that statement.

He followed Donal up the stairs, anxious to get at the receiver in his case and set it up so that any further business transacted by Murik in his inner sanctum could be recorded and listened to at leisure.

Donal opened the door, intoning, 'The East Guest Room, sir,' and Bond stepped into an Aladdin's Cave for the passing visitor.

9

ALL MOD CONS

THE ROOM WAS DECORATED almost entirely in black, with
soft lighting hidden high up behind pelmets, where there
must once have been ornate old picture rails. It took Bond
a second to realise that there were two rooms and not one;
for half of each of the bedroom walls and a large section of
the ceiling was made of mirror – difficult to distinguish
against the black décor. This gave the illusion of more
space; it also had the unnerving effect of disorientation.
Donal spoke just as Bond confirmed, to himself, that an
archway led from the bedroom into a bathroom.

'You did not leave the keys to your luggage, sir;
otherwise I would have had your clothes unpacked and
pressed. Perhaps tomorrow?'

'Certainly,' Bond turned his back, speaking sharply.
'Goodnight, Donal.'

'Goodnight, sir.' The butler withdrew, and Bond heard
a very solid click as the door closed. He went over and
tried the handle, immediately realising he had been
correct in his identification of the sound. The door was
fitted with a remote-controlled electronic lock. He was
virtually a prisoner. At least, he thought, setting the
roomy briefcase on a side table, he would not be a prisoner
who would be secretly watched or overheard.

Unlocking the briefcase by turning the keys twice, he
pressed down hard on the catches, which lifted on small
hinges, revealing the real locking devices underneath:
three wheels of numbers on each side. Bond spun the
dials, and the briefcase opened. With this one they had
made little effort to hide the equipment inside, the top of

the case being a simple tray in which his toilet gear rested. Lifting out the tray, Bond uncovered the few pieces of hardware beneath.

The largest item was the one Bond required – the standard VL 22H counter-surveillance receiver, which looked something like a chunky walky-talky, but with headphones and a hand-held probe.

Bond plugged in the headset and probe, slipped the instrument's shoulder strap around his neck, adjusted everything and switched on. For the next ten minutes he carefully ran the probe over the entire room, covering every corner and fitment. The built-in verifier would quickly determine any type of bug, differentiate between various signals and even lead him to any television cameras hidden behind the large expanses of glass; or secret fibre-optic lenses, the size of pencil holes, in the wall. He followed a well-learned pattern, completing the sweep with great care. Nothing showed. The note in the earphones remained constant, and the needle in the VU unit did not waver.

Returning the counter-surveillance unit to its hiding place, he pulled out the larger piece of luggage. Checking the locks, he once more used his keys to open the lid, throwing the clothes out in a manner that would have made the sinister and fastidious Donal wince. When the case was empty, Bond returned to the locks, turning the keys a further three times in each. At the final click of the right lock, a minute panel slid back in the far left-hand corner of the case bottom, revealing a small numbered dial.

Bond spun the dial, selecting the code arranged between Q'ute and himself only a few days previously. Another click and he was able to slide a larger portion of the case bottom to one side, disclosing some of Q Branch's special hardware, packed neatly in velvet-lined trays. Removing the tiny receiver/recorder – based on the STR 440, and only eighty-four by fifty-five millimetres in size, complete with a specialised tape cassette and foam-padded minute headset – Bond switched on, set the control dial to the figure 1, and saw a small light glow like a red-hot pinhead. The bug placed in Murik's study was now active. A cassette lay ready attached to the machine. Now, any conversation or movement in Murik's room would be recorded on Bond's receiver. He looked around and decided that, for the moment at least, it was safe to leave the receiver on the long dressing table that took up the bulk of one wall. He put the small piece of apparatus carefully on the dressing table and started to unpack, first sliding the hidden compartment in the case back to its locked position.

Long experience had taught Bond to pack and unpack with speed and efficiency. In less than five minutes he had shirts, underwear, socks and other necessities packed neatly in the drawers which ran down the outer ends of the long dressing table, and his other clothes hung in the closets built into the walls on either side of the archway leading to the bathroom. He left one or two special items in the cases, which, after locking, he placed at the bottom of one of the closets. Only then did Bond allow himself an examination of the room, which had all the makings of an expensive movie set.

The centrepiece of the main room was a vast bed, made up with white silk sheets and pillows. The visible edges of the bed glowed with light, and the whole was partially enclosed by two high, padded semi-circular panels. Bond slid on to the bed, and found himself in what was almost another bedroom within the main room. The inside of the panels was softly lit; a large console took up the whole of one section to his left, while a television screen was set into one of the panelled sections which made up the semi-circle at the bed's foot.

After a few experiments with the console, Bond found that each section of the two semi-circles could be moved by remote control; that the bed could be slowly rotated;

and even raised or lowered at will. The console also had facilities for complete quadrophonic sound, television video-recording, the Ceefax system, a telephone and intercommunication sets. Behind him, in a rack sunk into the black padding of the panel was a whole range of music and video cassettes, plus a pair of expensive Koss headphones. Bond glanced briefly at the cassettes, seeing that Anton Murik appeared to provide for all tastes – from Bach to Bartok, the Beatles to the latest avant-garde rock bands; while the video cassettes were of movies only recently released in cinemas.

Bond recognised the bed as the famous and exclusive Slumberland 2002 Sleepcentre, with some modifications, made probably on Murik's own instructions. He noted that the console provided sound and light programmes marked 'Peace Mood', 'Wake', 'Sleep' and 'Love'. Something Q'ute would have appreciated, he thought with wry amusement.

It took a lot of will-power for Bond to leave the so-called Sleepcentre and investigate the bathroom which also had several intriguing gadgets, including a sunken whirlpool bath, and even a blood-warm lavatory seat. 'All mod cons,' he said aloud.

With a short chuckle, Bond returned to the bedroom. He would try out the communications system and complain that his door seemed to be jammed. As he headed towards the bed, a glance at the receiver on the dressing table showed the tape revolve for a second and then stop. The bug placed in Murik's study was picking up noises. Grabbing the receiver and headset, Bond dived into the Sleepcentre, slipping the 'phones over his ears.

Someone was in Murik's study. He heard a distinctive cough, then Murik's voice: 'Come in, the door's open. Close it and shoot the bolt. We don't want to be disturbed.'

The sounds came clearly through the headphones: the door closing, and then the rustle as someone sat down.

'I'm sorry about dinner,' Anton Murik said. 'It was unavoidable, and I didn't think it wise for you to show yourself to my visitor, even though he probably wouldn't recognise you from Adam.'

'The message was understood. Who is the man?' The other voice was heavily accented. Franco, Bond thought.

'Harmless, but could be useful. I can always do with a little intelligent muscle. Caber is good, but rarely puts his brain into gear before working. You have to give him orders like a dog.'

'This man . . .?'

'A mercenary out for hire. I shouldn't think he has many scruples. We met by accident at Ascot . . .'

'You have him checked out?'

'You think I'm that much of a fool? He says his name's Bond. I have the number and details of the car – very smart. It'll give us an address and by tomorrow night I shall know everything I need about Mr James Bond.'

Bond smiled, knowing that M had him very well covered. Any enquiries coming from passport number, driving licence, car registration, or other means, would be nicely blocked off. All Murik could learn would come from the cover dossier – the service record of one Major James Bond, a Guards officer who had probably served with the SAS, and performed certain dubious duties since leaving the armed forces – under a slight cloud – six years previously.

Murik was still speaking. '. . . but I smell the need for money. Mercenaries are good earners, if they live, yet they all have that tendency to spend as though tomorrow did not exist. Or they turn to crime.'

'You must keep sights on all strangers until they are proved.'

'Oh, I'm testing him. He'll give us some interesting sport.' The laugh was unpleasant. 'At least we'll see what he's made of. But, my dear Franco, you're leaving shortly, and I want to get things finalised.'

'Everything in my head. Clear as day. You know me well now, Warlock. The teams ready in England, France and Germany. No trouble. They are on call. Listening the whole time. There is only America, and my people wait there for me.'

'And you'll be in the States by tomorrow night?'

'Afternoon.'

There was a long pause and a rustling of paper before Murik spoke again. 'You're quite certain of your American people?'

'The same as the others.'

'Willing to expend themselves in the cause?'

'Absolutely. They expect death. I have said it is not likely for them to survive. This is good psychology. Yes?'

'I agree. Though as long as they do exactly as they're told, there'll be no risk. That's the beauty of it. First, the fact that we only need to place four men in each station – to secure themselves within the control rooms – and take orders from *me* alone. Second, that they refuse to maintain contact with anyone outside – no hostage-taking, nothing to distract them. Third, that I make it plain to the governments concerned that they have twenty-four hours only, from the moment of takeover. The twenty-four hours runs out . . . then *Boom*: England, France, Germany and the United States have big problems on their hands for many years to come – problems, if all the scientists are correct, that will not be confined to the four countries concerned. The death toll and damage could cover almost half of the world. This is the one time that governments will have no choice but to give in to blackmail.'

'Unless they do not believe you.'

'Oh, they'll believe me,' Murik chuckled. 'They'll believe me because of the facts. That's why it's all-important that your people go in at the same moment. Now, your Americans. How long will it take to brief them?'

There was another pause, as though Franco was trying
to make up his mind. 'Twenty-four hours. One day at the
most.'

'For both lots? For Indian Point Unit Three, and San
Onofre Unit One?'

'Both. No problems.'

'It's the San Onofre that's going to scare the wits out of
them.'

'Yes, I've studied papers. Still active, even though the
authorities know how close it is to a fault. A seismic
fault – is that how you say it?'

'Yes. America will press Europe. They just won't be
able to take the risk. As long as your American people
know what is expected and do only what I tell them. You
must stress – as you have done in Europe – that if they
obey orders, nobody can get at them for a minimum of
twenty-four hours. By that time Meltdown will all be
over anyway. So I see no reason why Meltdown cannot
go ahead at twelve noon British Summer Time on
Thursday, as planned.'

'There's one thing . . .'

'Yes?' Murik's voice, sharp.

'How are you to give the signals – pass on the instructions – without detection?'

A slight chuckle, subdued and humourless. 'Your
people have the receivers. You have a receiver, Franco.
Just use them, and let me worry about the rest.'

'But with radio signals of that strength – covering
Europe and the United States – they'll pinpoint you faster
than you can do your *Times* crossword; which is fast.'

'I told you, Franco. Let me worry. All is arranged, and
I shall be quite safe. Nobody'll have the slightest idea
where any instructions are coming from. Now, Franco, we
are on schedule for Thursday, which is ideal. If you can
really finish everything in America within twenty-four
hours, it means you will be in a position to carry out the
other assignment for me on Wednesday night. You think

you can make that location?'

'There is time enough. Better I should do it than someone else . . .'

Even with the headphones on, Bond was suddenly distracted by a click from the door. His head whipped around, and he saw the handle turn a fraction. In one movement he grabbed the 'phones from his head, stuffing the receiver under the pillow before launching himself out of the Sleepcentre towards the door.

His hand shot out, grasping the door and pulling it sharply towards him.

'It's okay,' whispered Mary-Jane Mashkin, 'only me.' She slipped inside, the door swung to heavily, and Bond heard the locks thud into place again. His heart sank. Mary-Jane Mashkin was a handsome woman, but not Bond's fancy at all. Yet here she was, dressed a shade too obviously in a heavy silk Reger nightdress and wrap, her dark hair hanging around her face; a flush to her cheeks. 'I thought I should come and see that you're comfortable,' she murmured coyly. 'Have you got everything you need?'

Bond indicated the door. When Donal had closed it, Bond had realised there was some kind of automatic locking system. The noise following Mary-Jane's entrance had confirmed his fear. 'How do you get through that system? It's electronic, isn't it?' he asked.

She pushed herself towards him, smiling in a faraway manner. 'Some of the rooms – like this – have electronic locks for safety. The doors can always be opened from the outside; and all *you* have to do is dial "one" on the 'phone. That puts you through to the switchboard. They'll open it up for you. If Anton agrees, of course.'

Bond backed away. 'And that's what you'll do? To get out, I mean.'

'Oh, James. Are you telling me to leave?'

'I . . .'

She slid her arms around his neck. 'I thought you needed company. It must be lonely up here.'

Bond's mind scrabbled around for the right actions and words. There was something decidedly wrong here. A carefully orchestrated seduction scene by this American woman: an intellectual, mistress to Anton Murik, and almost certainly in on whatever villainy was being planned at this moment by the doctor and Franco.

'James,' she whispered, her lips so close that he could feel her breath, 'wouldn't you like me to stay for a while?' Mary-Jane Mashkin, fully dressed, made up, and with her hair beautifully coiffured, seemed a handsome and attractive woman. Now, close to, with her body unfettered from corset or girdle, and the face cleaned off, she was a very different person.

'Look, Mary-Jane. It's a nice thought, but . . .' He wrenched himself free. 'What about the Laird?'

'What about him? It's you I've come to see.'

'But isn't this risky? After all, you're his . . . trusted confidante.'

'And I thought you were a man who was used to taking risks. The moment I set eyes on you, I . . . James, don't make me humiliate myself . . .'

She was a good actress, Bond would say that for her. The whole thing smelled of either a set-up or a special reconnaissance. Had he not just heard Anton Murik talk about testing him? Women involved with men like Murik did not offer themselves to others without good reason. Bond took the woman by the shoulders and looked her straight in the eyes. The situation was delicate. A false move now might undo all the good work which had got him into Murik Castle. 'Mary-Jane, don't think I'm not appreciative, but . . .'

Her lips tightened into a petulant grimace that changed her expression into one of acid, unpleasant hardness. A lip curled upwards. 'I've made a fool of myself. Men used to flock . . .'

'It isn't like that,' Bond began.

'No? I've been around, James Bond. You think I don't

know the signs by now?'

'But I'm Anton Murik's guest. A man can't abuse hospitality like . . .'

She laughed: a derisive single note. 'Since when did a man like you stand on that kind of ceremony?' She stood up. 'No, I just misread the signals; got my wires crossed. You should know by now, James, that a woman can always tell when a man finds her – well, I guess, unattractive.'

'I told you. It's not like that.'

'Well, I know it is. Just like that.'

She was at the door now, turning, her mood changing to one of anger. 'I could've saved you an awful lot of hassle, James. You could've avoided much unpleasantness with me on your side. But I could make you regret the last few minutes. You'll see, my friend.'

It all sounded very melodramatic, and Bond was becoming more and more convinced that Mary-Jane's presence in his room – her thrusting, unsophisticated attempt to seduce him – was an act designed for some other purpose. Her hand reached out to the door.

'Shouldn't I ring the switchboard?' he asked, trying to sound suitably subdued.

'No need. They have warning lights that go on and off when the bolts move; but I have arrangements with them. There's also a way out for the members of this household.' From the folds of her robe she produced a small oblong piece of metal the size of a credit card and slipped it into a tiny slot that Bond had not noticed, to the right of the lock. The bolts shot back, and Mary-Jane Mashkin opened the door. 'I'm sorry to have troubled you,' she said, and was gone in a rustle of black silk.

Bond sat down on the bed and looked at the door. Possible friend or eternal enemy? he wondered. The whole business had been so bizarre that he found it difficult to take seriously. Then he remembered the receiver and Murik's conversation with Franco.

The cassette was not turning when he retrieved the apparatus from under the pillow. He put the headphones over his ears and started to wind back the tape. The conversation had finished only a few minutes before. Now he rewound it to the point at which he had left them talking. The voices, through the 'phones, were as clear as though the two men were with him in the room.

'Now, Franco,' Murik was saying, 'we are on schedule for Thursday, which is ideal. If you can really finish everything in America within twenty-four hours, it means you will be in a position to carry out the other assignment for me on Wednesday night. You think you can make that location?'

'There is time enough. Better I should do it than someone else.'

'It would give me greater confidence to know that it is you.'

'And I shall be required to be in the appointed place at . . .'

'At the time we've already talked about. What I need to know, for my own peace of mind, is how you will do it. Will she suffer? What reaction should I expect?'

'No suffering, Warlock, I promise you. She feels nothing; and the onlookers, they imagine she has fainted. The weapon will be high-powered, an air rifle, and the projectile, it has a gelatine coating. She feels a little pinprick but no more. I shall use a . . .'

There was a thud in the earphones, and the conversation became blurred. It took Bond a few seconds to realise what had happened. Either the adhesive on the micro-bug under Murik's desk had given way or one of the men had accidentally dislodged it with his knee. Gently he wound the tape back, but the whole conversation was now muffled, and he could pick up only a few words. It was not even possible to separate the voices of the two men — '. . . very fast . . . cat-walk . . . below . . . neck . . . bare flesh . . . Warlock . . . steps . . . point . . . palace . . . Majorca

. . . coma . . . death . . . two hours . . . heart attack . . . time . . .' and so on. It meant little, except the obvious fact that someone – a woman – was being set up to be killed, probably just before this operation that Murik referred to as Meltdown.

The whole thing was deadly, and Bond knew that M's worst fears were proved. This was no ordinary little plan but a full-scale, worldwide conspiracy of great danger. As for the contract killing, he could not even start to think how that fitted in. The weapon would be an air rifle, undoubtedly firing a capsule containing some quick-acting poison. As for the place and target, it was anybody's guess. The word palace had been mentioned, and the victim was a woman. Bond immediately thought of royalty. The Queen, even. Then there was the word Majorca. A meeting place, perhaps? These were things he would have to pass on to M as soon as possible. It even crossed his mind, as he carefully packed away the receiver, to trigger the pen alarm now, inside the house. But that could prove more dangerous than helpful. Murik had him neatly stowed away, and the place was a fortress. Stay with it for the time being, Bond decided.

He was just returning the headset to the closet, packed away in the case, when he heard the click of the door bolts again. His stomach turned over. Surely Mary-Jane would not have the nerve – even at Murik's instigation – to return to his room for a second visit? The handle was turning, and for the second time that night Bond moved quickly to the door and yanked it open.

10

DILLY-DILLY

THERE WAS A LITTLE squeal as Lavender Peacock half fell into the room, and James Bond's arms. She quickly recovered, snatching at the door, but was too late to stop it closing behind her, with its ominous electronic click.

'Blast,' she said loudly, shaking out her long sheen of hair. 'Now I'm locked in with you.'

'I can think of worse fates,' Bond said, smiling, for Lavender was also dressed in her night clothes, making a distinctly more desirable picture than Mary-Jane Mashkin. 'Anyway,' he asked, 'haven't you got one of those neat little metal things that opens the door from inside?'

She leaned against the wall, pulling her wrap around her, one hand brushing back her hair. 'How do you know about those?' she started. Then: 'Oh Lord, has Mary-Jane been up here? I can smell her scent.'

'Miss Mashkin did play a scene of some ardour, but I fear she didn't go away contented.'

Lavender shook her head. 'She wouldn't expect that. I thought I might get here before they started to play tricks with you. Anton has a warped sense of humour. I've seen him put her on offer before now, just to test people. Have you got a cigarette?'

Bond took out his case and lit one for each of them. His mind had gone into a kind of overdrive. Quite suddenly he had recognised two of the things overheard in Murik's conversation with Franco, via the bug: two names that were familiar – Indian Point Unit Three and San Onofre Unit One. He was beginning to come to some conclusions.

Lavender inhaled deeply, then shook her head again. 'No, I haven't the privilege of being allowed to carry electronic keys. In this place I'm usually just as much a prisoner as yourself.' She gave a little smile. 'Don't doubt that you're a prisoner, Mr Bond.'

'James.'

'Okay; James.'

Bond gestured towards the bed, 'Make yourself comfortable now you're here, Lavender; and you might as well tell me why you *are* here.' He did not doubt that this might be yet another test.

She moved away from the wall, heading for one of the armchairs. 'I think I'd better sit over here. That bed's too much. Oh, and call me Dilly, would you? Not Lavender.'

'Dilly?'

'Silly old song – "Lavender blue, dilly-dilly" – but I prefer it to Lavender. You're honoured, incidentally. Only real friends call me Dilly. Nobody here would dream of it.'

Bond settled himself on the Sleepcentre, where he had a good view of his latest visitor. 'You still haven't told me why you're here, Dilly.'

She paused for a moment, taking another long pull at the cigarette. 'Well, I shouldn't be. Here, I mean. I suppose I'm taking a chance. Don't know if I should even trust you, James. But you've come out of the blue, and I've got to talk to someone.'

'Talk away.'

'There's something very strange going on. Mind you, that's not unusual for this place. My guardian is not like other men: but you know that already. I should ask you what you know about him, I suppose.'

Bond told her that he gathered Anton Murik was wealthy; that he was a nuclear physicist of some note; and had half promised him a job.

'I should be careful about the job.' She smiled – a knowing, somewhat foxy smile. 'Anton Murik hires people to do the dirty work. It's a terrible thing to say, but when he fires them, he does it in a literal sense,' she lifted her hand, holding the fingers as a child will play at using its hand as a gun. 'Bang!' she said.

Bond looked straight into her eyes. She was the kind of woman who had an immediate appeal for him. 'You sure you wouldn't be more comfortable over here?' There was a challenge in her eyes, and Bond thought he detected that familiar charge of static pass across the room between them.

'Probably *too* comfortable. No, James, I came to give you some advice. I said something strange is going on. It's more than that. It could even be something terrible, disastrous.'

'Yes? What sort of thing?'

'Don't ask what it is because I just don't know. All I can gather is that it has something to do with the Laird's plans for building a new kind of nuclear reactor. He left the International Atomic Research Commission because they wouldn't fund his idea. He calls it an Ultra-Safe Reactor. There's a mountain of money needed, and I think he plans to use you in some way. But first – apart from the danger of being involved with him – he's going to put you at risk. Tomorrow. I heard him talking to Mary-Jane.'

'Tomorrow? But he has his Games tomorrow.'

She stubbed her cigarette out in one of the large glass ashtrays. 'Quite. It probably has something to do with the Games. I really don't know.'

'I might get hurt then. It wouldn't be the first time.'

'No, but . . . Another cigarette?'

'Smoking damages your health, Dilly. It says so on the packets.'

'It's not just smoking that can damage you here, James. Give.'

He went over to her, lit her cigarette, then bent down and kissed her lightly on the forehead. She drew back fractionally, putting a hand up to his shoulder. 'That wasn't what I came for, James.'

'No?'

Firmly she moved her head. 'No. People've already got into a lot of trouble because of me. I just came as a kind of Cassandra, uttering warnings.'

'Just uttering warnings? I wonder, Dilly. You said you were taking a risk to trust me; that you were virtually a prisoner like me. I wonder if you came hoping that I'd get you away; that I'd take fright and run, carrying you off on the pommel of my saddle.'

'That's not on, I'm afraid. But I think you should get out, and I'm willing to help you.'

'So that I can ride back with the Fifth Cavalry and save you?'

'Maybe I'm beyond salvation.'

Bond squeezed her shoulder and went back to the bed. For a time they were silent. Did she, he asked himself, have any inkling of what was really going on? Already his mind had latched hard on to the locations of Indian Point Unit Three and San Onofre Unit One. He knew exactly what they were, and the possibilities of Murik's involvement with them carried things into a nightmare world.

He returned to Lavender's last words, 'Why beyond salvation, Dilly?'

'Because I am who I am – the Laird's ward, a distant relative, trapped in the outmoded traditions of this place, and by my guardian's intrigues.'

'Yet you're willing to get me out?'

'I think you should. Not just you, James. I'd probably say it to any stranger who came here and took the Laird's fancy.'

'I can't go yet, Dilly. You've whetted my appetite about what's going on here. If I find that it's something really dangerous, or even criminal, then I'll take you up on your offer. I'll let you give me a hand. If it comes to that, will you ride off for help with me?'

Once more she slowly shook her head. 'I was brought up here. It's all I know. Prisoner or not, there are certain responsibilities . . .'

Bond showed surprise. 'Brought up here? I thought you had only been his ward . . .' he stopped, realising he had already given away too much.

'Legally only for a short time. But I've lived here – well – for ever.'

'And you don't like it, and yet don't want to leave?'

She said that if she ran away now and something went wrong, things could be very bad for her. 'At least you can get out now, while the going's good.'

Bond said that was the last thing he wanted to do. Privately he also knew that it might be the only thing he *could* do. Triggering off the pen alarm from the castle roof – if he discovered the full extent of Murik's plans – might put a spoke into the Laird's wheel; but spokes can easily be mended. No, he told Lavender, if he discovered something really criminal going on, then he would get out and bring help. He added that he would be happier if she came as well, but she gave a stubborn shake of her head. Bond found it difficult to believe that a girl of her spirit would allow herself to remain in these circumstances. She really was a virgin on the rocks; or a damned good actress.

'Well, for your sake, I hope you find out something quickly.' Lavender rose, went over to the door, realised there was no way out, and turned to walk back to her chair. 'It'll break this week, I'm pretty certain. We're off to do a fashion show and if he is up to something, that could be perfect cover for him.'

Bond tried to sound surprised at the mention of the fashion show, and Lavender explained what he already knew, that Anton Murik owned the controlling interest in one of the world's leading fashion houses. 'Roussillon. I am lent out to them for major shows. A clothes' horse with legs, that's me, James; but I can tell you, those shows are the high spots of my year.'

'You slip the leash, eh?'

She almost blushed, and Bond slid from the bed,

walked over to her chair, sat on the arm and put a hand
across her shoulders, drawing her close. She looked up at
him, her eyes cold.

'James. No. I only cause trouble.'

'What kind of trouble?'

'The kind I wouldn't want to bring on you.' She
hesitated, indecisive for a moment. 'Okay. The first time
was years ago. A boy. Worked here on the estate. I was
about sixteen or seventeen. Mary-Jane Mashkin caught us
and sent for Anton. The boy – David – disappeared, and
his family were moved. I'm pretty certain Anton had him
killed.'

'And, if I touched you? What would he do to me?'

'You'd end up the same way. David was just the first.
After I began to model for Roussillon there was a guy in
Paris. I didn't know anyone had discovered, but he was
found in an alley with his throat cut. Yes, I think he would
kill you, James. He was once forced to buy someone off,
but that was in Rome – one of the modelling jaunts again.
The man was from a wealthy Italian family. One day
things were fine, the next I had a letter saying he had to go
away and wouldn't be seeing me any more. A year later I
heard my guardian talking to Mary-Jane. He said it had
cost almost a quarter of a million dollars, but it was
money well spent.'

Bond bent down and kissed her on the lips. 'I'm willing
to chance it, Dilly. You're . . .'

She pulled away again. 'I mean it, James.' Then she
smiled, putting a hand up to his cheek. 'Not that I . . .
Well, perhaps I'm being selfish. If something sinister
really *is* going on here, you're my one hope – if they don't
do for you at the Games tomorrow. I'll get you out, and
you can bring in the stormtroopers: rescue the damsel in
distress.'

'Some damsel,' Bond laughed. 'How do you get out of
this room, then? Or are we forced to spend the night
together in separate corners?'

Lavender said she would have to stay now – until early morning, at least, when Bond could ring down and get the locks taken off. 'You can say you want to go for a walk or something, when it's light. They'll let you do that because they can keep an eye on you then.' She giggled: 'We could bundle.'

'Aye, we could do that an' all,' Bond laughed, thinking of the old custom of courtship by sharing a bed, fully dressed, with a bolster to separate the couple.

'I'm for that. I'm bloody tired as well.' Lavender stood up. 'I hope there's a spare bolster in that mobile gin-palace the Laird's provided you with.'

They made do with pillows, and Bond found it a frustrating experience, being so near and yet so far from this delightful girl. When they were settled, she asked if he really would go for help if anything came to light.

'I'd be happier if you came as well. But I understand your wanting to stay. In the long run you'll be safer. But, yes, if there is something that means taking urgent action, I'll get the hell out as quickly as possible – with your help – and be back to bring your precious guardian to book.' Then, trying to make it sound like an afterthought, Bond asked if he was the only stranger in the castle.

She did not hesitate. 'There's someone else here, but he's become a regular visitor. Anton calls him Franco, and we're all under instructions not to talk about him. When you turned up he was pushed out of sight; but I think he's due to leave early in the morning.'

'You think he's got something to do with what's going on?'

'I'm certain of it. He spends a lot of time closeted with Anton when he's here.'

'How does he come and go?'

'In the helicopter. My guardian has a helicopter pad tucked away behind the old part of the castle.'

'Thank you, Dilly. You just hang on and we'll sort it out; and thanks for the warning,' he reached over the pillows and squeezed her hand.

'If we get out of here, James . . .'

'Yes?'

'Oh, nothing. There might be no need to get out at all. Sleep, eh?'

For a few moments Bond's mind was in a turmoil of anger, the eye of his personal hurricane centred on Anton Murik: cheat, fraud; a man willing, and ruthless enough, either to kill or buy off his ward's lovers. He was like some Victorian millionaire martinet. Slowly Bond pushed down the anger. It was no good becoming emotionally outraged. Coolness would be the only way to deal with Murik, and he would have to establish himself quickly to gain the man's trust and get him to fill in some of the details of Meltdown. Then he must get word out fast to M – who would have his own problems explaining the source of his information to M.I.5 and the Special Branch.

With this in mind, Bond set his own mental alarm, which seldom failed to work, and drifted into restful sleep, waking accurately at five in the morning, just before dawn.

He roused Lavender and asked about the electronic locks. She told him the door locks on rooms in the castle were made up of three cylindrical bolts, activated by an electro-magnet. When the locks went on, the bolts slid into tightly fitting housings. At the end of each housing the bolt completed an electric circuit, activating an 'on' light in the castle's switchboard room.

Would they notice the light flickering? Probably not, Lavender said. They had experienced cases of momentary malfunction: lights going out completely, then coming on again within a few seconds. She had only intended to stay for a minute of whispered warning on the previous night.

'And there's no way in which you can get hold of one of the inside keys – the oblong strips?'

She told him that was impossible. The castle gates were another matter; but the electronic keys were held only by

certain people, and there was never any chance with
them. Bond nodded. He now had to turn his mind to
gaining Murik's confidence.

He went into the bathroom and changed into slacks and
a sweatshirt, then dialled the castle switchboard to tell his
story about the door being jammed. A detached voice
asked why he wanted to leave his room, and he said it was
his habit to exercise each morning. The voice told him to
wait for a moment.

Within a minute they heard the locks fall back. Bond
tried the door, and it opened easily. He kissed Lavender
on the cheek, and to his surprise she reached up and
kissed him quickly but firmly on the mouth. Then she was
gone.

Within a few minutes he had checked the room to make
certain nothing incriminating was left lying around. With
a final cautious look, he left.

The first hint of dawn was touching the sides of the glen
as James Bond went along the corridor, down the stairs
and out into the castle grounds. As he emerged, the sound
of a helicopter came throbbing in from the west. He
waited until the machine – a small Bell JetRanger – came
up the glen, turned, hovered, and slowly dropped out of
sight behind what had once been the keep of the old castle.

Hunching his shoulders, Bond began to jog around the
house, heading for the wide lawns where, only last night,
he thought he had glimpsed a marquee set up for the day's
Games. He wanted to give his body the best possible
work-out. He knew all his reserves of stamina would be
needed that day.

11

THE SLINGSHOT
SYNDROME

LATER BOND WAS to learn that the four acres of beautifully kept grass which ran down the far side of Murik Castle — bordered with shrubs, gravel paths and topiary work — had been known as the Great Lawn for at least two centuries.

Even at this early hour the estate workmen were out and about, putting the finishing touches to two large marquees, a number of small tents and an oblong arena the size of a small landing strip.

As he jogged past, Bond reflected it would be somewhere in this arena that he would probably face whatever test Anton Murik had devised for him. He used the jogging as an opportunity first to get the lie of the land, and second to settle his mind and concentrate on the numerous problems he had to resolve.

It was obvious, from what he had overheard of the conversation between Murik and Franco the previous night, that they planned at least five terrorist attacks, in Europe and the United States. The two in America, he knew from the names, were connected with nuclear power stations. Logically, the ones in Europe would be similar targets. He also knew that the codename was Meltdown. If his suspicions were correct, Meltdown could mean only one terrifying thing. What intrigued Bond even more was the codename Anton Murik appeared to have adopted for himself—Warlock.

Jogging around the castle, Bond slowly made up his mind. In spite of what he had said to Lavender, there were

two clear choices. Either he could get out now and alert M
with the information already in his possession, or stay, face
the test and glean the full details of the plot. If he could
make a good showing, it was possible that Murik would put
more trust in him; maybe even reveal everything. That this
final course of action was dangerous, Bond did not doubt;
yet it was the path he had to take.

Again he thought about Murik's conversation with
Franco the night before. Meltdown, the Laird had said,
would begin at twelve noon British Summer Time on
Thursday. That would be noon in England, one in the
afternoon in France and Germany, seven in the morning at
the place they called Indian Point Unit Three, and four in
the morning at San Onofre Unit One. The operation was to
be held strictly to twenty-four hours, and it involved the
blackmailing of governments. For the time being he put the
other problem, the contract killing by Franco, to one side.
In time all things would be made clear.

After eleven circuits Bond returned to his room in the
castle. Things now appeared to be stirring throughout the
building. The morning noises of a house coming alive.

Bond could smell his own sweat from the harsh exercise,
but as he opened the door to his room, his nostrils caught
another scent. Somebody else had been there during his
absence.

Quickly he checked the cases. They were out of align-
ment, but the locks showed no sign of having been forced or
tampered with in any way. Murik was checking him out –
on the spot as well as through his own, possibly dubious,
outside sources. Bond made a mental note to look at the
Saab at the earliest opportunity – not that anyone would
easily be able to penetrate its secrets. The car certainly
looked all right as he had jogged past it, parked between
Murik's gleaming Rolls and a wicked black B.M.W. M1,
which was probably Mary-Jane Mashkin's speed.

Returning to his toning up, Bond ran through his usual
morning press-ups, sit-ups and leg raising. Then he cleared

a space in the room and started that magic, dance-like series of elegant, deadly, movements which make up the first *kata* – or formal exercises – of Uechi's style of karate: the *Sanchin* which you see men and women performing in parks and gardens, during the early morning or evening, in the East. Bond's body moved in a smooth, prearranged pattern as he went twice through the routine. By the time he had completed the physical and mental exercises, Bond's body was soaked in perspiration. He stripped off, padded through to the bathroom and showered – first under scalding water, then with an ice-cold spray.

After a good rub down and shave, he changed into light-weight slacks with a matching beige shirt and cord anorak. He slipped his feet into comfortable Adidas sports shoes. Normally he would have preferred the soft moccasins, but, as a possible confrontation was imminent, Bond thought it best to choose reliable athletic shoes that would not slide or let him down.

He filled the gunmetal cigarette case – making a resolution that he would not smoke until after the test, whatever it might be – and put it in the jacket, together with his Dunhill lighter. The pen alarm was clipped into the inside of the jacket, while Q'ute's version of the Dunhill was deposited in his right-hand trouser pocket.

Quietly he left the room. Passing through the hall, Bond heard voices from the dining room. Breakfast was obviously in progress, but first he had to take a quick look at the Saab.

The car was locked. Perhaps they had not got around to running a full check on it. Certainly, once he was inside, he saw that nothing seemed to have been moved or touched. Slipping the keys into the ignition, Bond started the motor. It fired straight away, and he allowed it to idle for a few seconds. When he switched off, Bond found Donal standing on one side of the car, and the man he recognised from last night as Hamish on the other.

Removing the keys, he put on the wheel lock and acti-

vated a switch under the dashboard, then climbed out with
a curt 'Yes?' to Donal.

'Breakfast is being served in the dining room, Mr Bond.'
The butler's face showed no emotion, and Bond assumed
the man had about as much sensitivity as a block of stone.
He replied that he was just going in. Not looking at either of
the men, Bond locked the driver's door and stalked into the
house.

Lavender and Mary-Jane were both seated at the table
when he entered the room, where a sideboard almost
groaned with dishes reflecting the old-style expensive life
lived by the Laird in his castle. Bond by-passed the eggs –
fried and scrambled – bacon, kippers, kedgeree and other
delights; choosing only two pieces of dry toast and a large
cup of black coffee. Breakfast was his favourite meal, but on
this occasion he knew it would be unwise to fill his stomach.

Both Mary-Jane and Lavender greeted him with seeming pleasure, and Bond had only just seated himself when
Anton Murik came in, dressed, as befitted a Scottish laird,
in kilt and tweed jacket, his pugnacious face all smiles. He
also seemed pleased to see Bond, and the talk was easy,
Lavender giving no sign of what had passed between them
during the night. All three appeared to be excited about the
Murcaldy Games, Murik himself particularly bouncy and
full of good humour – 'It's my favourite day of the year, Mr
Bond. Even tried to get back here for it whenever I was out
of the country. Landowners and people like myself have a
responsibility to tradition. Traditional values mean anything to you, Mr Bond?'

'Everything.' Bond looked straight into the lava of the
eyes. 'I've served my country and abide by its traditions.'

'Even when it lets you down, Mr Bond? Or should I call
you Major Bond?' Murik let out a small cackle of laughter.

So the Laird had swallowed the bait: followed up the one
clue available – the Saab registration – and got the facts
back, as M had arranged. Bond tried to look puzzled.

'We'll talk later, James Bond.' Again the laugh. 'If

you're able to talk. I think your breath may be taken away
by the Games. It's quite a show.'

'Quite a show,' echoed Mary-Jane, smiling. She had said
little during breakfast, but appeared unable to take her eyes
off Bond – an experience which he found disconcerting, for
the look she gave him lay half-way between one of feminine
interest, and that of a Roman empress sizing up a gladiator.
There was no hint of the malice she had shown on leaving
his room the previous night.

Bond remarked that things seemed to be starting outside. He was rewarded by Murik, who launched into a
complete and lengthy programme of events that would take
place throughout the day. 'Almost dawn to dusk. I must get
going. After all, the Laird is the host. You will excuse me, I
trust.' He turned at the door. 'Oh, Mr Bond, I would
particularly like to see you at the wrestling. My man Caber
is Champion of Glen Murcaldy – that's the equivalent to
being the Laird's Champion around here – a singular honour. He takes challengers at noon sharp. Please be there.'

Bond had no time to answer, for the man was gone,
almost with a hop, skip and jump. So that was it: a bout
with the giant Caber. Bond turned to the ladies, trying to be
gallant, asking them if he could be their escort. Lavender
said yes, of course; but Mary-Jane gave her enigmatic
smile, remarking that she would have to accompany the
Laird. He would, she said, have to 'make do' with Lavender. Bond could not decide if the remark was meant to
sound belittling, but Lavender hardly seemed to notice,
rising and asking Bond if he would give her a few minutes to
get ready.

'The child doesn't get much company.' Mary-Jane slid
an arm through Bond's, in a surprisingly familiar manner.
'There aren't many of the right sort around here, and she's
impressionable.'

'You make her sound very young and unsophisticated.'
Bond spoke quietly.

'In many ways she is. I've tried – for Anton's sake of

course — but I fear unless a good and understanding man arrives in the area, she'll have to go to London or Paris. She *needs* a good course in sophistication.' She giggled, 'Perhaps if you please the Laird he'll present her to you as a prize.'

Bond gave her a cool, humourless, look.

'Oh come on, I was only joking.' She laughed again.

'Look,' said Bond, trying to change the subject, 'I wonder — do you have a library? I realised last night that I came without any reading matter.'

'Of course. I'll take you there before I go out to join the Laird. But what a pity, James, that you won't allow other things to occupy your nights. No hard feeling about *last* night, by the way.'

'None for my part,' said Bond, puzzled by her friendliness.

'Pity,' she giggled. Then her expression changed, and he glimpsed the face behind the mask. 'For my part there are a lot of feelings. I said you could avoid trouble, but you refused, James, and you'll be sorry. I have suggested a small test at the Games. Anton agrees. In fact he thought it amusing. You will be matched with Caber at the wrestling, and Caber has his blood up. Given his head, he'd kill you.' Another laugh. 'And just for giving him a bloody nose. How vain men are. But come, I'll show you the library. You may need it, and a lot of bed-rest, when Caber's finished with you.'

The library backed on to the drawing room, and was decorated in light colours. Three of the high walls were covered with books, and there were library steps on fitted rollers for each wall. The fourth wall contained three large, bay windows, each provided with a padded surrounding seat.

It took Bond a few moments to get his bearings and work out how the books were graded — moving the high steps along each wall until he found what he wanted. First, he quickly chose a book to cover his story — snatching one of his old favourites, Eric Ambler's *The Mask of Dimitrios*, from its place among the novels. Then he made for his real quarry: a thick, beautifully bound copy of *Webster's Dictionary*, which he dragged out and placed on a large lectern.

Thumbing the volume to the letter W, Bond ran his finger down the lines of words until he came to Warlock. Rapidly he scanned the entry. It gave the usual definition 1: 'One given to black magic: SORCERER, WIZARD. 2: CON-JURER.' Then Bond's eyes slid up to the derivations, and his heart skipped a beat. 'Old English – *wǣrloga* one that breaks faith, scoundrel, the Devil.'

One that breaks faith? Bond wondered. Could that be it? Was Murik having his own unholy joke in choosing War-lock as his name for the direction of a terrorist operation he had planned? Was he, in turn, scheming to break faith with the international terrorists he had hired through Franco? A man so obsessed by his own brilliance as a nuclear physicist, and feeling snubbed and cheated of his triumph, might well be forced to such lengths.

He was replacing the heavy copy of *Webster*, when a sound made him whirl around, his hand moving naturally to the hip, where he would normally be carrying a pistol, in the field; realising a fraction of a second later that there was no weapon there.

Lavender stood just inside the library door, wearing a pink creation which gave her a cool, poised look. In one hand she carried a large matching hat. As Bond approached, he saw she was pale under the smoothly applied make-up.

She put her finger to her lips. 'James, he's putting you up against Caber in the wrestling.'

Bond grinned. 'I know, the Mashkin told me with great relish, Dilly.'

'It's not funny. He's asked me to take you out there. He wants us to mingle. Caber knows, and he's after you. The business last night: apparently some of the lads have been pulling his leg. Did you really nearly break his nose?'

'Gave it a butt in the right place. Made it bleed a bit.'

'He'll pound all hell out of you, James. I've seen him in action. He's a rough fighter – knows a lot of tricks. He's got the weight and tremendous strength as well. Making Caber look stupid with a nosebleed could drive him wild with anger.'

'Let me worry about Caber, Dilly darling.' Bond took hold of her hand and squeezed it. 'If you get no other message from me, can you come to my room tonight?'

'I can try.'

'With a way to let me through the main gates?'

'You're going to run?'

'Only if I've got the full story, and it's bad enough to take some definite action. I'll do my damnedest to have enough on your guardian and his crew to bring the law – or worse – into this place. If not, then we'll just have to do some more bundling.'

'You'll be lucky if you're not just a bundle yourself by the end of the morning.'

'I told you – just work out a way for me to get through the gates, and leave Caber to me. If not tonight, then tomorrow night will have to do. Okay?'

She replied with a worried nod; and he could feel her body trembling close to his as they went out through the hall and into the sunlight.

The band of a well-known Scottish regiment was playing on the Great Lawn and already the Games were in full swing. Bond thought the village of Murcaldy would be a ghost hamlet today; and certainly there were many people who had obviously made more lengthy journeys to the Murcaldy Games. Murik did not stint his guests on this occasion: there was free food and drink for all, and plenty of entertainment. Bond was cynical enough to wonder what price the local people had to pay in service – and silence – to the Laird for this one day of blatantly feudal fun.

Groups of men and women in Highland costume were preparing to dance, while brawny young men were at the far end of the arena indulging in the incredible sports of tossing the caber and hammer throwing.

Several people doffed their bonnets or bowed to Lavender, showing great respect. Bond also noticed that they glanced at him with undisguised suspicion. Out of long habit and caution, he tried to pick out the more dangerous of the Laird's private army – the big young men with watchful eyes, quiet and careful, silent and alert as loyal *mafiosi*. Of one thing he was sure: there were a lot of them. For the next couple of hours he remained with Lavender, watching with interest the traditional sports and dancing.

Eventually a crowd started to gather around an area at the castle end of the arena, and Bond allowed himself to be led towards it by Lavender, who whispered that this was where her guardian wanted him.

Mats had been laid down, and he saw the little figure of Murik talking to a group of men on the far side, his mane of hair slightly ruffled, but a smile permanently set on the bulldog face. He spotted Bond and waved cheerfully before making his way towards the pair.

'Well, Mr Bond. My champion is almost ready to take on all comers. Do you feel like facing up to him?'

Bond smiled, pretending the Laird was joking. 'I mean it, Bond.' The trickling deadly lava was back, deep in the eyes. 'I want to see what you're made of. If you do well, there may be much in it for you. Can I announce you as the first competitor?'

Now Bond laughed aloud. 'I hardly think I'm his weight, Laird. He'd lay me out with one finger.'

Anton Murik's face was set, grim as a tombstone. 'That's not the point, Bond. I want to see what stuff you're made of – if you've got the guts to go into a wrestling bout with someone as dangerous as Caber. It's not a question of beating him, but standing up to the man, even avoiding him. Guts, Mr Bond, that's what I'm looking for. Guts.'

Bond smiled once more, 'Oh, well,' he spoke casually, 'that puts a different complexion on it. Yes, Laird, I'll take a bout with your champion.'

He heard Lavender's sudden quick intake of breath as Murik gave a tough little grin: 'Good man. Good man,' and disappeared over the mats to the far side of the arena.

In a moment he was back, this time in the centre of the mats, holding up his arms for silence. A hush came over the crowd. The pipes and drums played on in the distance, but for a man of his size the Laird of Murcaldy had a strong, carrying voice. 'Friends,' he shouted. 'As you all know, it's time for the unquestioned Champion of Murcaldy – Champion of the Laird of Murcaldy – to offer himself to anyone who wishes to challenge his right. Give your hands to my Champion, Caber.'

Caber emerged from the crowd, among which he had been sitting, hidden from public view.

Bond had only really caught a glimpse of the man on the previous night. Now he seemed even larger and more formidable – well over normal height, his chest roughly the size of a standard barrel, and the biceps standing out like miniature rugby footballs. Yet like many big men in peak condition, the Scot moved with a sure-footed, almost silent grace, nodding his large, but fine-looking head in answer to the appreciative applause of the crowd.

The Laird was motioning for silence. 'Friends, there is one who has come to take up the challenge,' he announced. Then, with a dramatic pause, 'One from over the border.'

A buzz went around the crowd. Even though he had not yet been singled out, Bond could sense the hostility. He felt in his right hand trouser pocket to be certain that what he needed was there. Then he quickly slipped out of his anorak, handing it to Lavender.

'Look after this please, Dilly,' he said, grinning.

'James, take care. Last night . . . I wish we . . .' she whispered. Her sentence trailed off as the Laird called his name:

'From over the border. A Mr James Bond.'

Bond sprang on to the mats, holding up his hands

against the now angry mutterings of the crowd. 'Not altogether from over the border,' he cried out. 'I'll grant my mother did not come from here, but neither was she a Sassenach; and my father had good blood in his veins – a true Highlander – and I take up the challenge, Caber.'

'Well done!' The Laird thrust his head forward in his birdish manner. 'Well done, James Bond.' Then, quietly to Bond, 'I didn't know you had Scottish blood. How splendid.'

Bond, well-built and tall as he was, felt like a pygmy next to Caber, who merely smiled at him with the confidence of one who knows he has never been bested. There was only one way to deal with the situation, and Bond knew it – keep away from those hands for as long as possible; stop Caber from getting a deadly lock on him: then move at just the right moment.

The two men squared up, and the Laird asked each one if he was ready. Bond nodded and Caber said, 'Aye, Laird, it'll no tak' long.'

'Then . . . Wrestle,' Murik shouted, ducking out of the way.

Caber came straight at Bond, who sidestepped, attempting a trip with his ankle as he did so; but the huge Caber was very quick. Before he knew what was happening, Bond felt the man's hands grasp his forearms and he was lifted into the air and unceremoniously thrown, hitting the mats square on his back, the wind knocked from his body.

Caber made a dive for him, but this time Bond fractionally beat him to it – rolling clear so that Caber was forced to handspring back to his feet. He rounded on Bond, coming in fast again. Bond weaved, but it was no good; Caber performed a quick cross-ankle pick-up, sending Bond sprawling again.

This time there was no rolling free, for Caber had one arm and a good deal of weight on Bond's right shoulder. At the same time, the giant of a man drew back his right arm. Bond saw the motion and in a split second realised that

Caber was playing for keeps. The Scot's fist was balled, ready to strike hard into Bond's face. It was time to use science in all its forms.

Bond's left arm was free, and he just managed to roll his head to one side as Caber's blow came hurtling towards him. The fist grazed his ear and thudded hard, and painfully, into the matting beside his head.

Caber was slightly off-balance, but still holding down Bond's right shoulder. Time to use the left arm; and use it on the area of greatest weakness in all men – even a wrestler as strong as Caber. An instructor had once pointed out to Bond that you do not have to hit hard on what he called 'the golden target' to be effective. The little nutbrown instructor's voice was ringing in Bond's ears as he brought the left hand up, fingers pointed in a sharp jab at Caber's groin. As he heard the big man grunt with pain, Bond remembered that the move used to be called the 'Ganges Groin Gouge'. It worked, particularly when followed up by another, slightly stronger attack at the same target.

Caber grunted again, and Bond felt his shoulder freed as the Scot fell forward, rolling as he did so. Bond backed away. Caber was rising quickly, the pain of those two blows showing in his eyes. It was the moment for Bond to be most alert. He had hurt Caber who, like a wounded animal, was now enraged. That he had been willing to maim and mutilate at the start of the bout was clear to Bond. Now the big man would kill if he had to.

Bond let his right hand drop to the level of his trouser pocket, and, as Caber came in for the attack, Bond launched himself forward in a leg dive, the movement covering his right hand, which slid quickly in and out of the pocket.

He hit Caber's legs, though it was like diving into a wall. The big man hardly wavered, but Bond now had Q'ute's special Dunhill firmly clasped in his hand. He twisted, trying to bring Caber down, but the man just laughed and kicked hard, throwing Bond aside, stretching his arms out and diving for Bond again.

This time Bond's right hand came up as though to ward off the certain pinioning by the giant. His right hand moved across the face of his target, and, as Caber's tree-trunk arms caught his shoulders, so Bond readied the Dunhill.

Q Branch's version of the Dunhill lighter was cunning and efficient. It contained no flint or electronic mechanism to spark a light. Neither was it filled with inflammable liquid, though its contents could be expelled, in four specially measured bursts, by activating the flip-top.

The Dunhill was loaded, under pressure, with a liquid containing a high base of the anaesthetic Halothane. One burst of Halothane near the mouth or nose should have the desired effect, for the drug — first produced in the early 1950s — is quick-acting, highly potent, and yet produces no nausea or irritation of the mucous membranes. In Q'ute's own words, 'They won't know what hit 'em — before, during or after.'

Bond's hand was in exactly the right place to deliver the primary burst, Caber's mouth and nose being less than two inches from the hidden Dunhill as he flicked the flip-top. As he moved his fingers, so Bond prepared to roll clear. He had seen the lighter demonstrated and did not particularly want to get a whiff of the Halothane himself.

Caber simply kept on coming, like an aircraft landing heavily with its undercarriage down but not locked. Bond was just able to glimpse the look of surprise, then the glazing of the big Scot's eyes as he collapsed — Bond rolling clear just in time. As he rolled he grabbed at Caber's now inert arm. To the crowd, the whole thing would look like a clever, or lucky, jab to the face, and Bond had to leave some kind of mark. Twisting Caber's arm he turned the man over, though it was like trying to move a ton of lead. Once Caber was on his back, Bond dived at the shoulders, and delivered two swift blows, using the cutting edge of his hand to the jaw. Caber did not move. Even his head remained rigid.

As he sprang back and away Bond returned Q'ute's

useful little toy to his pocket. There were three more shots in that if he needed them.

A hush had come over the crowd. Then Murik, looking shaken, was by his side, and two men were leaning over the prostrate Caber. One of them – Malcolm this time – looked up at the Laird. 'Yon's oot cold, Laird. Oot cold.'

Murik swallowed hard, glancing uncertainly at Bond, who smiled pleasantly. 'Shouldn't you announce, or proclaim, or whatever you have to do?' he whispered. 'I think I'm your new Champion.'

There was a pause lasting only a few seconds. Then the Laird of Murcaldy gave a watery smirk, took a deep breath, and announced, 'Ladies. Gentlemen. Friends. People of Murcaldy. You've seen the result of this match. We have a new Champion – I have a new Champion – and you'll treat him with the respect and honour always afforded to the Champions of Murcaldy. I give you, Champion of Murcaldy, Champion of the Laird of Murcaldy – Mr James Bond.'

There was an uncertain silence, then the cheers began, and Bond was lifted shoulder-high to be carried around the Great Lawn with drums beating and the pipes skirling the strains of 'Highland Laddie'.

David and Goliath, Bond thought, knowing that it would be a good idea to keep out of Caber's way once the former Champion had regained consciousness. He had successfully played David to Caber's Goliath, and Q'ute had provided him with the ultimate in the slingshot syndrome.

Through the crowd he saw Lavender Peacock looking at him with warm admiration in her eyes. Well, if he worked on Murik with speed, Bond might even have all the information he needed, to get away before the next morning. Then, once M was alerted, there could even be time to get to know Dilly Peacock really well.

12

A CONTRACT, MR BOND

THOUGH ANTON MURIK had presented the major trophies for the Murcaldy Games, people seemed reluctant to leave. On the Great Lawn, groups still performed reels and strathspeys, while those who had not been good enough to enter the major competitions were now availing themselves of the equipment, and space, to practise or emulate their superiors in the arts.

The marquees and tents remained thronged; there would be many a sore head or upset stomach in the glen by the following morning. It was now just past six in the evening, and after an enthusiastic speech amidst much applause and cheers, the Laird had set off in the direction of the castle, motioning Bond to follow him.

Lavender was left with Mary-Jane Mashkin, who, Bond noted, was never short of young and well-built male company—a fact that seemed not to upset the Laird. The previous night's experiences still puzzled Bond, who had begun to wonder how genuine the two women were. It could be a case of playing the hard and soft roles, as in a classic interrogation. Yet of the two, he would rather have Lavender on his side.

Murik led Bond through the hall, past the main staircase, pushing open a set of swing doors that led to a corridor, blocked at the far end by the great dividing line between old-style servants and their masters — the green baize door.

The Laird stopped half-way down the corridor, bringing out the ever-present keys — this time from his sporran — to unlock a solid oak door strengthened with steel grilles.

Bond followed him down a wide flight of stone stairs. Tiny guide lights gleamed, throwing vague shadows in the darkness. Half-way down, Murik turned towards him. With his mane of white hair, against the face in darkness, the visage took on the appearance of a negative. When he spoke the Laird's voice echoed eerily. 'You've already seen my inner sanctum. We're going to the most interesting part of the castle this time. The oldest remaining relic of my heritage. Now you are my Champion, Mr Bond, you should know of it.'

The air smelled dank, and the stone stairs seemed endless, descending deeper and deeper underground until they came out into a flagged open space. Murik reached out to a switch hidden in the wall and the place was suddenly flooded with light. Huge arches supported the vaulted ceiling, which Bond thought must be as old as the original castle. There were two more doors, one on each side of the flagged space, while ahead of them another narrower passage continued. Murik nodded, 'That way leads to the old dungeons.' His jowl moved in a twitching smile. 'They are occasionally useful. To our right, a room which I do not like using. The old torture chamber.' He pushed open the door and Bond followed him in.

At one end of the room Bond identified a rack, bolts and chains set into the walls, a flogging frame, brazier, and all the old and sinister instruments – from whips and branding irons to pincers and gouges. Murik pointed out other devices: 'You see, Mr Bond, all the old Scottish pleasures – the thumbikins and pilniewinks, and, of course, the boots. Very nasty things, the boots. Having your feet gradually crushed with wedges is not the way to ward off fallen arches.'

'Nor deal with your corns.' Bond shuddered in spite of the light-heartedness. In his time, he had suffered much physical torture, and its instruments were not unknown to him. Yet when he looked towards the far end of the room his blood ran cold. The walls there were tiled in white, and in

the centre was an operating table. Cabinets along the far
wall were of modern design, and Bond guessed they would
contain more terrifying instruments than the brutal
weapons of pain – hypodermics and drugs to send the mind
reeling to the very edge of madness, and possibly even the
means of inflicting agony through electrodes attached to
the most sensitive areas of a man or woman. A man, well-
trained, might withstand the exquisite pain that could be
inflicted by the crude implements of torture; but few would
keep truth or secrets for long in the more sophisticated part
of this, Murik Castle's chamber of horrors.

'Very occasionally this room is put to use, Mr Bond.
Have care. All who serve me are given a guided tour. It
usually does the trick, as a salutary warning. You defeated
the good Caber, so you automatically serve me. Let your
glimpse of this place act as a warning. I demand complete
loyalty.'

Murik led the way out and across the flagged area to the
door facing that of the torture chamber. He turned, smiling
before he opened the door. 'My operations' room.'

The contrast was staggering. They were in a long,
low, vaulted chamber. Its grey walls were covered with
weapons: ranging, at the end nearest the door, from artistic
and obviously valuable broadswords, rapiers, dirks and
knives, through magnificently engraved crossbows decorated with inset stones, to wheel-lock, snaphance and flint-
lock pistols and muskets; and finally, on the far wall, there
were modern rifles, carbines, pistols and automatic
weapons.

'The most valuable part of your collection?' Bond recalled that Murik had already told him the best pieces were
elsewhere in the castle.

Murik smiled, and Bond could not resist one gibe. 'No
thermonuclear devices to bring it right up to date?'

The Laird's face darkened, then cleared into a seraphic
smile. 'We have no need. The world provides them. They
are all around us, sitting there ready and waiting to wreak

disaster at the right moment.'

Murik reached up, touching a large broadsword, 'A *claidheamh mor*,' he said. 'A two-handed sword that once belonged to an ancestor of mine.' Bond nodded. He was certainly impressed, but his gaze had moved beyond this unique collection of weapons to the far end of the vault which, indeed, looked like some kind of operations' room, with its long console desk, computer monitors, radio equipment and a large transparent map of the world covered in chinagraph markings.

Murik motioned him to the console table, gesturing to one of the comfortable leather swivel chairs behind it. He took the other chair himself and gave a throaty laugh. 'From here, Mr Bond, I control the destiny of the world.'

Bond, uncertain whether Murik was joking or not, laughed with him. There was an uneasy silence for a moment, giving Bond the opportunity to glance up at the map. Quickly he took in the fact that Indian Point Unit Three and San Onofre Unit One were both plainly marked on the American map. As he turned his gaze back to Anton Murik he knew that another couple of glances would probably give him the names of the targets in Europe. At the moment, however, it took all his will-power to drag his eyes back to the Laird. Don't seem too eager, he told himself, willing relaxation—even disinterest—into his brain.

'You know who I am?' Anton Murik was asking, and Bond replied that he was Dr Anton Murik, Laird of Murcaldy.

Murik laughed. There was far more to him than that. 'I am probably the greatest nuclear physicist who has ever lived,' he said in an alarmingly matter-of-fact way.

Nothing like modesty, Bond thought. Aloud he tried to say 'Really?' with a convincing gasp.

'Let me tell you . . .' Murik launched into his own version of his brilliant career. Most of what he said corresponded with what Bond already knew, deviating only when the Laird started to talk about his final disagreements

with the International Commission. In Murik's version, he
had resigned out of protest. 'Those who fight for the aboli-
tion of nuclear power stations in their present form are
right,' he said in a voice that had slowly been rising in
agitation. 'Note, Mr Bond, I say in *their present form*. They
are unsafe. Governments are keeping the truth concerning
their potential dangers from the general public. Government agencies have tried, again and again, to muzzle
people like me. Now they deserve a lesson. They say that
the only way out of the energy crisis is to use nuclear power.
They are right: but that power must be made safe. How is
electricity made, Mr Bond?'

'By turning a generator.'

'Quite; and the generator is operated usually by a turbine, in turn operated how, Mr Bond?'

'Water, in hydro-electric plants; boiling water producing
steam in other types of plant.'

'Good; and the steam is produced through boiling the
water, using coal, oil, gas – or the core of a nuclear reactor.'
He gave another little laugh. 'An expensive way to boil
water, don't you think? Using nuclear power?'

'I hadn't thought of it like that. It's always struck me as
being one of the few sure ways to produce energy and power
without using dwindling supplies of oil and fossil fuels.'

Murik nodded, 'In many ways I agree. I do not go along
with Professor Lovins when he says that using nuclear
power to boil water is like using a chainsaw to cut butter –
though he does have something on his side: wasted heat.
No, the problem, Mr Bond, is one of safety and control.
Nuclear reactors, as they now stand throughout the world,
put our planet and its people at risk . . .'

'You mean the problem of radioactive waste?'

'No. I'm talking about unavoidable accident. There
have already been incidents galore. If you're an intelligent
man you must know that: 1952, Chalk River, Ontario;
1955, Idaho Falls; 1957, Windscale, England; '58, Chalk
River, Canada; '61, Idaho Falls; 1970, Illinois; '71, Minne-

sota; '75, Alabama; '76, Vermont. Need I go on? Or should I mention the Kyshtym catastrophe in the U.S.S.R. when an atomic waste dump exploded in the Urals? Spillage, partial fuel meltdown. One day, with the kind of reactors we have at the moment, there will be catastrophe. Yet governments remain silent. The Carter Administration almost admitted it . . .' He rummaged among some papers. 'There. 1977 – "Between now and the year 2000 there *will* be a serious core meltdown of a nuclear reactor; but with proper siting such accidents can be contained". Contained? Proper siting? Do you realise what a core meltdown means, Mr Bond?'

'Is that something to do with what they call the China Syndrome? I saw a movie with Jane Fonda . . .' Bond continued to play innocent.

Anton Murik nodded. 'A nuclear reactor produces its enormous heat from a core – a controlled chain reaction, and as long as it's controlled all is well. However, if there is a failure in the cooling system – a ruptured pipe, a shattered vessel, the coolant lost – that's it. The core is just left to generate more and more heat; create more and more radioactivity . . .'

'Until it goes off like a bomb?' Despite Anton Murik's fanaticism, Bond found himself absorbed in what the man was saying.

Murik shook his head. 'No, not quite like the big bang, but the results are fairly spectacular. One of the great American-born poets wrote, "This is the way the world ends; not with a bang but a whimper." The whimper would be a kind of tremor, a rumble, with the earth moving, and one hell of a lot of radioactive particles being released. The core itself would become so hot that nothing could stop it, right through the earth – rock, earth, metal – nothing could stand in its way. Right through to China, Mr Bond; the Pekin Express – and that could happen in any one of the nuclear reactors operating in the world today. The trouble is that *I* could make it safe for them.' He gave a long slow smile, then a shrug. 'But, of course, as usual, the money men won't play. My system is foolproof, but they won't allow me to build it, or show them how.' He paused again, looking hard at Bond, 'Can you blame me, Mr Bond? I'm going to demonstrate how unsafe the present systems are and at the same time show them just how safe they could be.'

Bond shook his head. 'No, I wouldn't blame you for doing that if your system *is* as safe as you say.'

For a second he thought the Laird of Murcaldy was going to lash out at him.

'What do you mean?' Murik screamed. 'What do *you* know, Bond? *If* my system is safe? *If* my system is as safe as *I* say? I'm telling you, I have the only positively one hundred per cent safe nuclear reactor system; and because of grasping economists, because of contracts and profits, because of self-seeking politicians, they've tried to make a laughing stock of me.' He seemed to relax, drawing back into his chair.

During the long speeches about nuclear reactors, Bond had managed to steal two more glances at the large map. The American targets were ringed in red chinagraph. Now he had managed to identify the English and French locations. Heysham One and Saint-Laurent-des-Eaux Two. What was this man going to do? Was his brilliance so unhinged that he was prepared to expose governments or organisations he hated by sending suicide terrorists into nuclear reactor sites to manufacture disaster that might affect the entire world? Would his madness carry him that far? Meltdown – of course.

Murik was speaking again. 'I have prepared a master plan that will do both of the things I require.' He gestured towards the map, giving Bond the opportunity to take another look, his eyes moving unerringly to Germany. There it was, marked in red like the others.

Bond experienced a sinking deep in his stomach when he realised that there were two targets marked in the German area, one in the Federal Republic, the other in the East—in the DDR. So, even the Eastern Bloc had not been left out of Anton Murik's plans. In the East it was Nord Two-Two. The site in West Germany could be identified as Esenshamm. Now Bond had them all locked in his brain. The job would be to lead Murik on to reveal the bulk of his Operation Meltdown; though, even without further information, Bond considered the mission complete. If he could get out that night, M.I.5 would be able to track down and isolate Murik and with luck collar Franco through the American security agencies. Meltdown could be blown, and with it the instigator, Warlock: Anton Murik.

'My little plan will alert the world to the horrific danger that exists through the nuclear plants already built and working.' Murik gave another of his chuckles, rising to a full-throated laugh, 'It will also provide me with the necessary capital to build my own safe plant, and demonstrate to those cretins and profit-seekers that it is possible to use nuclear energy without putting the human race at risk.'

'How?' Bond asked, convinced that a straightforward question would produce a reflex answer. But Anton Murik, in spite of the hysterical outbursts was not easily trapped.

'It's a complicated business. But you will play your part, Mr Bond. Ours was a happy meeting; a pleasant coincidence.'

'What sort of part?' Bond dropped his voice, sounding wary.

'There is one essential piece of the operation: to ensure no legal action will be taken against me. It is something that has to be done so that nobody ever knows I have had a part in what will happen. Your job is to kill one man. A contract, Mr Bond. I am giving you a contract – that's the right terminology, I believe?'

'You think I'll just go out and kill someone?'

'I see no reason for you to be squeamish. From what I gather, you are not a man who values human life very highly. Also, the job pays well. According to my information you need around £20,000 quite soon. I'm offering £50,000, which I'm certain is more than your usual basic fee. It should also serve to keep you silent.'

'I don't know what you mean,' Bond said flatly. Inside, there was a mild sensation of elation. Anton Murik had been fed the entire cover story. 'I mean, you know nothing about me . . .'

'No?' Murik's eyes clouded, the old dangerous lava flow hot in their depths. 'I think you will find I know far more than is comfortable for you.'

'How . . . ?'

'There are ways, Mr Bond. *Major* Bond. Who won the Sword of Honour for your year at Sandhurst?'

'Fellow called Danvers . . .' Bond tried to make it sound spontaneous.

'And you used to call him Desperate Dan, yes?'

Bond allowed his face to take on a puzzled expression, 'Yes, but . . . ?'

'And you went into the Guards, like your father before you, like the late Colonel Archie Bond? Correct?'

Bond nodded silently.

'You see, James Bond, I have my informants. I know about your career. I also know about your heroism. I have details of the great courage you displayed while assigned to the SAS . . .'

'That's confidential information,' Bond blurted out, 'highly classified.'

Murik nodded, unconcerned. 'Like the name of all officers seconded to the Special Air Service – yes. But *I* know. Just as I am up to date with your failures: how they allowed you to resign rather than face a court martial after that unfortunate business with the Mess funds; how you have lived by your wits and skill ever since. I have details of the small jobs you have performed in Third World countries, and I also have a record of the unpleasant gambling gentlemen who would like to get their hands on either you or the £20,000 you owe them.'

Bond allowed his shoulders to slump forward, as though he had been defeated by some clever policeman. 'Okay,' he said softly, 'but how do you know all this about me?'

'By wits and weapons, James Bond: that's how you've lived since the Army let you go,' Murik went on, ignoring the question. 'Apart from mercenary engagements, I can make an informed guess concerning the contract killings you've performed.'

M had certainly placed the information well. Bond wondered exactly how Murik's informants had been manipulated as channels for Bond's mythical past. He sat up, his face impassive, as though Murik's knowledge of his supposed profession as mercenary and contract artist was something with which he could deal. 'Okay,' he said again. 'I won't deny any of it. Nor am I going to deny that I'm good at my job. It's not a profession of which a man can be proud, but at least I do it very well. How's Caber?' There was a tinge of malice in his voice. Bond had to show Murik he was unafraid.

The Laird of Murcaldy was not smiling. 'Bewildered,' he said coldly. 'Nobody's ever really beaten Caber until today. Yes, you are good, Mr Bond. If you were not, I wouldn't be offering you a sum of £50,000 for a contract killing now.'

'Who's the lucky client?' Bond assumed a straightforward, professional manner.

'A man called Franco Oliveiro Quesocriado.'

'I don't think I've had the pleasure.'

'No. Probably not. But at least you'll have heard of him. Hijackings, bombings, hostage-taking: his name is often in the papers – his first name, that is. He is said by the media to be the most wanted international terrorist on the books.'

'Ah.' Bond opened his mouth, allowing a flicker of recognition to cross his face. '*That* Franco. You're putting out a contract on him?'

Murik nodded.

'How do I find him?'

'By staying close to me. There will be no problems. I

shall point you in the right direction. All you have to do is remove him – but not until you're told. You will also do it in a prescribed way. The moment will come, in the operation I am about to set in motion, for Franco to disappear. Vanish. Cease to exist, leaving no trace.'

'For that kind of money I might even throw in his birth certificate.'

Murik shook his head. In a chilling voice he said, 'That has already been taken care of. *You* will be his death certificate.' Both men were silent for a moment. Bond looked down and absently fingered a knob on the console in front of him. Then he looked Murik straight in the eye.

'And the money? How shall I receive it?' he enquired firmly.

'You will be free to collect £50,000 in bank notes of any currency of your choosing a week from today at my bank in Zurich. I assure you it is the most respectable bank in Europe. I shall arrange for you to call them from here tomorrow – on the public telephone system, of course. I have no private connection. I shall leave you alone to ascertain the number from the Swiss telephone directory and verify the arrangement personally. But I can allow you only one call to Switzerland.'

'Sounds fair enough,' Bond said, wildly thinking that here was a heaven-sent opportunity for getting word out to M. But he knew full well the call would be monitored and intercepted the moment he tried any sort of bluff. It was on Bond's lips to ask what would happen should he fail and Franco escape, but he remained silent.

Murik stood up and began to walk calmly down the long room. 'I think we should get ready for dinner now, Mr Bond. Then I would suggest a good rest. It is likely to be an active and taxing week.' There was no suggestion that Bond might like to consider the proposal, no polite enquiry even as to whether he would accept. Murik had already assumed the terms were agreed and the contract sealed.

Bond started to follow Murik towards the door and as he

did so, caught sight of one of the weapons on display in the
Laird's collection. On a small shelf among grenades and
other devices stood a cutaway German S-Mine, from the
Second World War – a metal cylinder with its long protruding rod housing the trigger. Bond knew the type well,
and the display version showed clearly how deadly the
mine could be. You buried the thing until only the tip of the
slender trigger showed above the ground. An unlucky foot
touching the trigger activated the mine, which then leaped
about seven feet into the air before exploding to scatter
fragments of its steel casing, together with ball-bearings
loaded into the sides of the device.

The cutaway S-Mine had been so arranged as to show
the ball bearings in position, and also separately. A small
pile of these steel balls, each about a centimetre in dia-
meter, lay beside the weapon. They looked just the right
size for Bond's purpose. Loudly he asked – 'You're tied up
with this Franco fellow? In this scheme of yours?'

Before Murik had time to stop and reply, Bond had
quietly reached out his hand and scooped three of the ball
bearings from the display, slipping them into his pocket,
out of sight, as Murik turned.

'I am not going into the finer points, Mr Bond.' Murik
stood by the exit as Bond caught up with him. 'There are
some things you should know, I suppose.' Murik's voice
was low, with a rasp like the cutting edge of a buzz saw.
'Yes, friend Franco has contacts among all the major terrorist organisations in the world. He has provided me with
six suicide squads to infiltrate half-a-dozen major nuclear
power stations. They are fanatics: willing to die for their
respective causes if need be. For them, if my plan works, it
will mean vast sums of money set at the disposal of their
several societies and organisations. Terrorists always need
money, Mr Bond, and if the plan does not work, it is of no
consequence – to the suicide squads, at least.' He gave
another of his unpleasant chuckles, before continuing.

'All these men are willing to sit in nuclear control rooms

and, if necessary, produce what you have called the China Syndrome. If they have to do that, a very large part of the world will be contaminated, and millions will die from radioactive fallout. I personally do not think it will happen – but that is up to me. I have provided Franco with the means to get these squads into the reactor control rooms. I have, through Franco, trained them so they can carry out destructive actions at my command. At the end of the day there will be a huge ransom. Franco is to get half of the final ransom money, which he will split with the groups according to his prior arrangements. It is up to Franco to come to me in order to collect his share. He has even tried to tell me that the terrorist groups are pressing for assurances that the money will reach them. Lies, of course. It is Franco himself who needs the assurances. He will get none.'

They were now back in the main flagged hall. Murik quietly closed the door to the armoury.

'You will understand, Mr Bond, that I do not intend Franco to collect anything. For one thing, he is the only living person who would be able to tie me into this operation – identify me – when the security forces of several countries begin to question the terrorist squads. For the other' – he shrugged lightly – 'I need all the money myself in order to build my own reactor, to prove that I am right. It is all for the benefit of mankind, you understand.'

Bond fought down the desire to point out the terrible risk that Murik would be taking. The facts of Operation Meltdown were like a kaleidoscope in his mind; but of one thing he was certain: hired and fanatical terrorists are unstable in conditions of stress. However strongly Anton Murik felt about the ultimate threat, the situation might well be out of his control once the terrorist squads were in place.

More than ever, Bond realised that he must make a bid for freedom. They made their way slowly, side by side, to the foot of the stone stairway.

'There is one thing,' Bond said calmly, hands clasped behind his back.

'Go on,' Murik encouraged him. The two men might
have been discussing new staffing arrangements at a respectable City company.

'If you want Franco removed,' Bond continued politely,
'to – ah – protect your little secret and to save on expenses,
why should I suppose you'll not have Caber and his men
similarly dispose of me as soon as I've done the job? And
why not anyway simply put something in Franco's night-
cap and get Caber to dump him in the loch?'

Murik stopped in mid-stride and turned to beam at
Bond.

'Very good, Mr Bond. You show yourself to be the man
of wits I'd hoped for. You are right to question my trust-
worthiness. It would be all too easy for me to arrange
matters as you prognosticate. Except, of course, your last
suggestion. I would not wish Franco's remains to be discovered on my doorstep.'

Murik said this in a tone of mild parental shock. They
resumed strolling back to the stairs.

'As to your own wellbeing,' Murik continued, 'it is by no
means assured by my proposal. One false move would
certainly bring about Caber's longed-for revenge. He is a
savage man, Mr Bond, but I can control him. All the same,
I should point out that neither could you be sure, had you
declined my offer, that I would not be able to make your
future life – or death – very unpleasant. The choice remains yours. Even now you can walk out of here freely,
without a penny, and spend every minute of the days to
come wondering where and when I might catch up with
you. No one would believe the cock-and-bull story you
might think of imparting to the police, or anyone else. So
you have only my word for good faith. But remember,
much greater risks lie on my side of the contract.'

'You mean,' Bond interjected, 'that you are gambling on
my not taking up with Franco at the last minute, instead of
killing him, so as to aid him in collecting a much larger sum
even than the generous fee you have suggested for me?'

'Precisely.' Murik flicked the switch and the vault was once again plunged in gloom. They mounted the stairs in silence.

13

NIGHTRIDE

THE NAMES of the six nuclear power stations were in the forefront of Bond's mind for the rest of the evening, running like a looped tape in his head. His knowledge of nuclear power, and the location of reactors throughout the world, was sketchy; though, like his colleagues, he had done a short course on the security of such power plants.

Indian Point Unit Three was somewhere near New York City – he knew that because of a remark made during a seminar. A serious accident at any of the three Indian Point plants could cause grave problems in New York itself. It was the same with San Onofre One, situated a hundred miles or so from Los Angeles. There had been criticism of the siting of that plant so near a possible off-shoot of the San Andreas fault, he recalled.

Heysham One was in Lancashire, near the coast, and only recently operational. Saint-Laurent-des-Eaux Two, in France, he knew was in the Orleans area. As for the East and West German reactors – Nord Two-Two, and Esenshamm – Bond had no clues.

At least he had the names, and the knowledge that they were subject to terrorist squad takeover on Thursday. Small squads in the control rooms, the Laird had said. Get out, Bond's experience told him. Get the information to M and leave the rest to the experts. Sir Richard Duggan's boys from M.I.5 almost certainly had Murik Castle under surveillance, and it would not take long for troops to move in. If they were on the ball, Franco would already be in the F.B.I.'s sights in the United States. It should not take much to pull him; and if part of Meltdown was already under way, strict security at the target points would mop up the suicide squads.

Bond did not have time to start thinking of the delicate intricacies of Murik's plan. Already there was enough on his mind, and it was essential for him to appear completely relaxed in front of Murik, Mary-Jane Mashkin and Lavender Peacock.

The old adage about the best form of defence being attack might not be either tactically or strategically sound on a battlefield, but here, round the Laird of Murcaldy's dinner table, Bond knew it was his only salvation. He drew the talk around to his favourite subject of golf, and took over the conversation, launching into a long and amusing account of a game he had recently played. It was, in fact, a highly embellished description of a round with Bill Tanner, and Bond felt it was perfectly within the interests of the Service to slander M's Chief-of-Staff outrageously.

Even Murik appeared to be amused by the long tale, and Bond was so caught up in the telling that he had to pull himself from the half-fantasy when the ladies withdrew, coming down to earth as he faced Anton Murik alone over the table.

Little passed between the two men except an explicit warning from the Laird, who obviously felt he had already told Bond too much about his plans. As they finally rose, he placed a hand on Bond's arm and said, 'Stay alert,' the note of command clear in his voice. 'We shall probably be leaving here in a day or two, and I shall want you on hand all the time before you go out and earn your money. You understand?'

Bond thought of the old English word *wǣrloga* – one that breaks faith – and knew that, if Murik was going to break faith with desperate men like Franco's terrorists, there would be little likelihood, had Bond really been a contract mercenary, of any money coming his way. Franco's death would undoubtedly be followed quickly by Bond's own demise, whatever Murik said about his good intentions.

As he said goodnight to Murik and the ladies, Bond took heart from Lavender's quick, conspiratorial look, guessing that she would come to his room as soon as the castle was quiet.

Back in the East Guest Room, Bond heard the tell-tale thud as the electronic lock went on after the door was closed. Murik was not a man to take chances: great care would be required once Lavender arrived.

He now moved with speed, packing only the essential hardware and clothes into the larger case, then laying out other necessary items on the bed: the fake Dunhill, the pen alarm — which he would use to put M on alert once he was clear of the immediate vicinity of Murik Castle — and a small flat object that looked like a television remote control. This last he placed next to the car keys. When the moment came, speed would be essential. He wished now that there had been the opportunity to smuggle the Browning into the castle. He would have felt a small edge of confidence in being armed, for in the clear light of logic he should trust no person in this place, not even Lavender Peacock. But, as far as M was concerned, 007's job was complete — the basic information was to hand and ready to be reported. Maybe the Saab would have to run some kind of gauntlet, but if his luck held and Lavender really was the girl he thought, it would only be a matter of hours before M would have a special unit — maybe the SAS — smashing their way into the castle.

Last of all, Bond laid out a pair of dark slacks and a black roll-neck sweater, together with the dullest-coloured pair of moccasins he possessed. Then, after placing the three steel ball-bearings, filched from Murik's control room, near the door, he showered, changed into the dark clothing, stretched out on the Sleepcentre, and lit a cigarette. Near his right hand lay the last piece of equipment, a wide strip of thick plastic, one of many odds and ends, screwdrivers, wires and such, provided by Q'ute.

Time passed slowly, and Bond occupied himself by

working on the remaining pieces of the Meltdown puzzle —
should he not get through, it would be best to have some
operational diagram in his head.

Six nuclear power stations were to be taken over by small
suicide squads. Murik had stressed that the squads were
small, and would occupy the control rooms. This probably
meant that Anton Murik himself, with his many contacts in
the hierarchy of worldwide nuclear power, had been able to
supply identification and passes for the terrorist groups.

From what little Bond knew of nuclear power stations,
the control rooms were self-sufficient and could be sealed
off from the outside world. With desperate and determined
men inside, the situation would be tense and fraught with
danger.

If Meltdown did happen, and even if troops and police
were brought on to the six sites, it would take time to break
into those vault-like rooms. Besides the authorities would
be loath to precipitate matters, particularly if they knew the
terrorists were prepared to die — and take a lot of people
with them — by cutting off the cooling systems to the nuclear cores.

Logically, Anton Murik would be making demands at
some very early point. From what the little man had said,
the demands obviously concerned money or valuable convertible items alone. It would be a lot of money; and, if
Murik was as shrewd as he seemed, the time limit had to
be minimal. Whatever the governments of countries like
Britain, the United States, France and Germany had said
about never giving in to terrorist blackmail, Meltdown
would present them with the gravest dilemma any country
had yet faced.

With hostages, aircraft, embassies and the like, governments could afford to gamble and sit it out — establish a
dialogue and find a way to stall matters. Yet if this situation
arose, the governments would be left with no option. The
hostages would consist of large tracts of land; cities; seas;
rivers; and millions of people — all caught in a deadly pollu-

tion that would be devastating, and could even alter the whole course of the world for decades to come.

It was, Bond decided, the ultimate in blackmail – worse even than the threat of a thermonuclear device hidden in the heart of some great city. For this very real threat meant – technically at least – that six nuclear cores would not only wreck six plants, throwing their radioactive filth over large areas, but also bore their way, gathering heat, through the earth itself – possibly producing radioactive expulsion at other locations on the way, and certainly at the final point of exit.

Anton Murik was thorough. He would have worked out every move, down to the smallest detail, from the takeover by the terrorist squads, and the making of his demands, right down to the collection of the ransom, and the point where Bond would rid him of Franco – and he would rid himself of Bond.

Yet there was still one factor for which Murik had not accounted: the circumstances Bond had considered earlier – the trigger-happy, death-wish uncertainty of any terrorist group under pressure. This thought – above anything else – strengthened Bond's commitment to get out and back to M as quickly as possible.

It was almost one in the morning before he heard the click of the electronic lock. Bond sprang like a cat from the bed, the strip of plastic in one hand, the other scooping up the trio of ball bearings. Gently he pulled back on the door, allowing Lavender to enter the room. Raising a hand, he signalled silence, then slipped one ball-bearing into each of the circular bolt housings, softly tapping all three, so that the bearings rolled gently to the far ends of the housings. If Bond's thinking was accurate the metal bearings would make contact at the bottom of the bolt housings. By rights the 'on' lights would be activated in the castle switchboard room. If luck was with them the flicker as Lavender unlocked the door would have gone unnoticed.

Bond then inserted the thick plastic strip over the bolt

heads, to prevent them locking back into place. Only then did he partially close the door.

Lavender was still in the dress she had worn at dinner. In one hand she carried what looked like a pocket calculator, and, gingerly in the other, one of the duelling pistols, which Bond recognised as coming from the valuable set in the hall.

'Sorry I'm late,' she whispered. 'They've only just gone to bed. A lot's been happening. Caber came up to the house with some of the men. The Laird's been giving them instructions, Lord knows what about, but Caber's in a fury. I heard them talking in the hall. It's a good thing you're going, James. Caber is threatening to kill you; but I heard Anton say, "Not yet, Caber, your turn will come." Have you any idea what's going on?'

'A fair amount, Dilly: enough to call in help. Yes, it *is* serious, I'd be foolish not to tell you that much. While I'm away, I want you to keep to yourself as much as possible. If things get bad, try and hide somewhere – and would you please not point that thing in my direction?' He took the duelling pistol from her.

She told him it was safe: the hammer was down. 'I just thought you should have some kind of protection – some weapon; and I know how to load these. Anton showed me years ago. There's a ball in it, and powder, and a percussion cap.'

'Just hope it doesn't blow up in my hand if I have to use it.' Bond looked with some misgivings at the piece.

Lavender said it was fine. 'The Laird tests them regularly – about once a year. He told me once that he shouldn't, but he seems to enjoy it. That one's Monro's pistol, by the way. The man who won.'

Bond nodded, trying to hurry her along by asking about the main doors, and the best way out. She told him there was a red button high up on the top right-hand side of the main door. 'You'll find a small switch just beneath it in the down position. Move it up, and the alarm system'll be disconnected. Then just press the button, and the main door locks will come off. They'll know in the switchboard room straight away, so you won't have much time. I've checked, and your car's still in the same place outside.'

'And that?' Bond pointed to the flat black object.

'The main gates,' she told him. They apparently had a permanent guard on the gates, which were also equipped with electronic locks. 'Both Anton and Mary-Jane carry these in their cars.' She demonstrated that the flat box had two controls, marked Open and Close. The rest was obvious. If you started to press the Open button at around fifty yards from the gates they would unlock and swing back of their own accord. 'That's about all the help I can give you.'

'It's more than enough, Dilly, darling. Now I'm going to let you have about three minutes to get well clear, and back to your room, before I start. If everything goes to plan, I'll have help here, and there'll be some unmasking to do. I fear your guardian could end up in the slammer for a long time.'

'Just take care, James. Dear James.' She put her arms around his neck and he kissed her. This time there was no doubt about her intentions as she pushed close to him and their mouths locked. It was no way, Bond considered, to start out on a wild dash to safety. 'Take care,' she whispered again, and he opened the door – holding the plastic strip in place – wide enough for her to get out.

Bond slipped the remote control for the gates into a hip pocket, then slid the hard barrel of the duelling pistol into his waist band, making sure the hammer was right down, and thinking of the dangers he would be running if it wasn't. Next he picked up his car keys and the flat box of his own. This was also a remote operator – one of the many extras provided by Communication Control Systems for the Saab. With this, he could turn on the ignition and have the motor running almost before he was out of the main castle doors; that was unless somebody had wired a bomb to the ignition – the true security reason for having a remote starter anyway.

Taking several deep breaths, Bond clutched the car keys, remote ignition control, and the suitcase in his left hand, leaving the right free. Opening the door, he allowed the thick plastic to fall and pulled the door closed behind him. The bolts shot home, and he waited anxiously to see if the mechanism would jam against the ball bearings. It didn't.

For a few seconds Bond stood in the darkness of the corridor, letting his eyes adjust. Then, slowly, he moved towards the gallery.

A low wattage safety lamp burned at the top of the stairs. Bond stopped, peering down into the hall and along the gallery. The old building creaked twice. Quietly he made his way down the staircase, keeping to the side of the steps, where the wood is always more solidly based and unlikely to make any noise.

Once he got to the hall there was the normal desire to move too fast, an overwhelming need to get it all over. But long discipline made Bond cross to the door at a slow, tiptoe pace. He could see the small panel with the red button and switch quite plainly. Reaching up he flicked off the alarm and pressed the button. There were three heavy bolts on the main door, and the whole trio clunked back in unison, like a pistol shot. In the night silence of the house it was enough noise to waken the dead, he thought; and, at that very moment, with the door swinging back and the fresh air carrying the unique scent of the gardens and Glen Murcaldy into Bond's nostrils, all the lights went on and a voice told him to put his hands up.

It was Donal. Bond recognised the voice, and judged the butler to be somewhere just to the left of the stair bottom. Trusting his own experience and intuition, Bond's hand grasped the duelling pistol, cocking the hammer as he drew it from his waistband. He whirled around as the end of the barrel came clear.

It was a risky shot, and the pistol made far more noise than he had bargained for, the metal jerking in his hand like a trapped snake and a cloud of white smoke rising from the explosion. But Bond's senses had been accurate. Donal was just where his ears had placed him. A pistol of some kind clattered over the floor as the butler wheeled in a complete circle, clutching his shattered shoulder where the ball had struck and whimpering in a high-pitched squeal, like a terrified animal.

Of this Bond had only a brief and blurred picture, for he was already out of the main door, pressing his own remote ignition control and dropping the duelling pistol so that he could grasp the keys to the Saab. He had the impression of lights coming on and the shadows of running figures rising from the lawns near the great gravel sweep and heading towards the Saab as its motor sprang to life.

Almost dragging the case behind him, Bond sprinted to the car. The motor was ticking over gently as he thrust the key into the door lock. The key turned in the lock and came away as he pulled at the door. Throwing the case into the rear, he slid behind the wheel, slamming the door and flicking down the lock.

The click of the lock came almost at the same moment as one of the shadowy figures closed on the car. It was time to test C.C.S.'s special fitments. Working quickly, Bond unlocked the two hidden compartments, threw the Browning on to the ledge above the instrument panel and grasped the spare set of Nitefinder goggles.

There were at least five men around the car now; even before he had the goggles in place, Bond could see two of them carried what looked like machine pistols, pointing towards him. He thought Caber was there in the background, but he was not going to hang around to find out. One of the men was shouting for him to get out of the car. It was then that Bond hit the tear gas button.

One of the safety devices – a standard fitment in the C.C.S. 'Supercar', as they call it – consists of tear gas ducts placed near all four wheels. At the press of a button, the gas is expelled enveloping the car, and anyone attempting to assault it.

Bond heard the thud and hiss as the canisters opened up, then saw the effects as the five men began to reel away and the angry white cloud rose around the windows. There was a portable oxygen unit, with masks, within reach, in case the gas penetrated the car or the air ran out; but Bond was more concerned with getting the Nitefinder set around his head, slipping the remote control for the main gates on to his lap and putting some distance between himself and the castle. He snapped on the seat belt, slammed the machine into gear, took off the hand brake. Holding down the foot brake, he slowly pressed the accelerator, building up power. Then, suddenly taking his foot off the brake, Bond let the car shoot forward, skidding wildly on the gravel. Straightening as he gained control, he drove at breakneck speed away from the castle. Through the rearview mirror he could see the men coughing and reeling about, shielding their eyes, bumping into each other, and one huge figure — it could only be Caber — lunging into their midst, as though reaching out for a weapon.

He did not see the flashes; only felt the heavy bumps as a burst of automatic fire hit the rear of the Saab. Best not to be concerned about that: there was enough armour plating and bullet-proof glass around him to stop most kinds of weapon. Maybe an anti-tank gun would have some effect, but certainly not automatic fire.

Bond changed up, still with his foot hard on the accelerator. Then touching the brake, he took the turn in the drive too fast, and sent up a great spray of gravel as he slid outwards, before regaining control. There were two more heavy thuds. One of the tyres, he thought. No problem there: Dunlop Denovos — puncture and split-proof.

He could see the gates in the distance, and one hand went to the locking device on the gun port built in just below the dash. A turn and slide, and the port was open. Bond removed the old and unauthorised heavy Ruger Super Blackhawk ·44 Magnum, pushing it into a spot where he could easily grab the butt.

He changed to third, the gear stick moving with comforting, firm precision. The gates were coming up fast, and Bond's hand now went to the remote control given him by Lavender. It flashed through his mind that this might not work and he would have to run at the gates full-tilt, relying on the stressed steel ram bumpers fitted to front and rear. After the experience with Donal and the waiting men in front of the castle, Bond had begun to doubt Lavender and her instructions. So far, the events had all the marks of a set-up; so it was with some relief that he saw the gates start to move as he pressed the control button.

Then, from the right, he caught sight of a figure running towards the gates, one arm raised. A small yellow flash, followed by a thud; then another. The gatekeeper was firing at him. Bond went for the Blackhawk and, still keeping his eyes on the opening gates, thrust the muzzle through the gun port, twisting the weapon to the right to allow himself the most extreme field of fire.

The gates, still opening, came up with alarming speed as Bond let off three shots in quick succession, the noise and smell of powder filling the car and battering at his eardrums. The figure of the gatekeeper was now out of sight, but the slowly opening gates were on him. He felt both sides of the Saab scrape against the metal. There was one long ripping sound and he was free, changing up again, and hurtling along the metalled road away from the castle.

The speedometer showed well in excess of 85 m.p.h.; there was no moon, but the view was clear as day through the Nitefinders. In a moment the Saab would be off the metalled road and on to the wide track leading to the village. Time, Bond thought, to give M some warning. He reached for the pen alarm.

At first he imagined it had merely slipped inside his pocket, so often had he checked it. More than thirty seconds passed before he realised that the alarm was missing – dropped outside the castle, or rolling around somewhere inside the Saab. As the stark fact penetrated Bond's mind, he glimpsed the lights of another car, far back towards the castle. Mary-Jane's B.M.W., he would guess, crammed with Caber and the boys, carrying machine pistols and automatics.

Bond had to make up his mind in a matter of seconds. The village would have been alerted by this time. He reasoned that the most dangerous path lay straight ahead. The answer would be to take the Saab around, going back on his own heading, following the track which ran parallel to the castle—the way he had come to reconnoitre the previous night. Without lights, the Saab would be difficult to follow and he reckoned that, even on the rough track, it would not take long to make the road to Shieldaig. At some point there would be a telephone. A call to the Regent's Park building would bring all hell down upon Murik Castle in a very short time.

The car was bucketing badly along the uneven road, but Bond held his speed. In the mirror, the twin beams of the chase car did not seem to have grown any larger.

Keep the speed up, he thought. Hold her straight, and try for a feint at the village, which was now visible, and appeared uncannily close—the bulk of the kirk and other houses sharp against the sky, standing out like fists of rock. Would they be waiting? Bond tried to picture the junction near the kirk, with its little wooden signpost. Watch for the signpost and drag the car around.

Without warning a light came on, then another: twin spots from near the kirk. The reception committee; the spots wavered, then homed in on the Saab, like spotlights following the demon king in a pantomime. Bond started to pump the brakes, changing down, slowing, but still travelling at speed. Slow just enough to let them think you're going to run straight through. Make them think the spots are affecting vision. That was the godsend about the Nitefinder.

Bond took in a gulp of air as he saw the first flicker of

automatic fire from near the kirk, coming from between the spots. Then the slow, coloured balls curved towards him – tracer, lazy, but deadly. Once again he shoved the Black-hawk through the gun port, stood on the brakes and wren-ched at the wheel, slewing the car to one side and blasting off two more rounds as he did so. Then one more shot. That was the Blackhawk empty. He reached for the Browning, clawing it from the shelf as he saw, with some elation, that one of the spots had gone out.

Now, his subconscious seemed to yell. Now – drive straight at them. The Saab kicked and jarred on the rough heather and gorse as Bond spun the wheel to right and left in a violent Z pattern.

The remaining spot lost him, then caught the Saab again as a second burst of tracer began its arc towards him. Bond squeezed the Browning's trigger in two bursts of two, loos-ing four shots through the gun port as it came into line with the spot. For a second the firing ceased, and he realised he was driving flat-out towards the village, ears bursting with the noise and the car filled with the acrid reek of cordite. Get it as near as you can, then skid-turn on to the other road. In his mind he saw the pattern as a hairpin with himself travelling fast along the right hand pin. He had to negotiate the bend on to the left pin, and there was only one way to do that while still leaving the reception party wondering if he was going straight on – presumably into a second road block in the village itself. At speed it was a dangerous confidence trick. One sudden or misjudged action and he could easily run right out of road, or spin the car over on to its back.

He saw the little wooden signpost almost too late. There were figures of people running, as though afraid he would smash into them. Wrenching the wheel and doing an intri-cate dance between brake and accelerator, Bond went into the violent skid turn. The world seemed to dip and move out of control as the Saab started to slew round, the tyres whining, as though screaming because they had lost their grip on the rough surface of track, or heather. For a second, as the car spun sideways on, Bond knew that all four wheels had left the ground, and he had no flying controls. Then he felt a judder as the wheels took hold of the earth. He spun the wheel to the right, put on full power, in a racing change down, and began to slide, broadside on, towards the sign-post.

The car must have torn the post straight out of the ground. There was a teeth-jarring bump as the nearside door hit the sturdy sign. For a second Bond knew he was at a standstill; then he had his foot down again, heaving the wheel to the left. The Saab plunged like a horse, shuddering, shaking its tail violently, then smoothly picked up speed again. Briefly, in the midst of the noise, Bond thought he heard another engine running in time with his own.

He sighed with relief. He was now moving fast up the track which he had followed with such caution the night before. At least the dirt track was minimally smoother than the one he had just negotiated. There was no sign of the following lights, which he had assumed to be the B.M.W. He changed up, feeling confidence grow with every second. He needed as much speed as possible to cover the ground parallel to the glen and Murik Castle. He would not be happy until he was completely clear of the castle area, away somewhere to his left, on the far side of the rise.

For reassurance he felt down, touching the butt of the Browning, at the same time glancing towards the panel — something he rarely did; but with the lights off and instruments dimmed right down, the head-up display was not as clear as normal.

He looked up again and immediately knew he was in trouble. A shape showed through the Nitefinder goggles, above and just ahead. Automatically, he changed down and pumped the brake. Then the shape moved, splaying a great beam of light across his path and he heard the engine noise he thought he had imagined back at the turn near the kirk. The helicopter. He had not counted on the helicopter. But there it was, backing away slowly like some animal gently retreating, uncertain of its prey.

Well, if he hit the damned thing it was too bad. Bond did not slow down. Again he reached for the Browning, pushed the barrel through the gun port, pointed upwards and fired twice. The helicopter was dangerously low, yet remained directly in front, still backing away. Then, without warning, it lifted and retreated fast. From directly in front of the Saab came a massive flash and boom – like a huge version of the SAS 'flash-bang' stun grenade. The Saab shook, and Bond felt the inertia reel harness clamp hold of him. Without it he would have been thrown across the car. He slammed a foot on to the brake as he felt, with the intuition of experience, that another grenade would follow the first. Certainly the helicopter was coming forward, and low, again. Bond prepared to haul the wheel over and put power on the moment he saw the chopper alter attitude.

It came just as he expected – the same manoeuvre, a dipping of the nose, a fast slide up and back. Bond swung the wheel to the right, changed into second, and allowed his foot gently to increase pressure on the accelerator.

The Saab changed course, going off the track to the right as the second large 'flash-bang' exploded. His mind was just starting to grapple with the strategy he would need to use against the chopper when the Saab began to lift its nose.

With the horrific clarity of a dream over which one has no power, Bond realised what had happened. He had been fool enough to do exactly as the helicopter had wanted. The little metal insect had probably been watching his progress – on radar, or by other means – almost from his moment of escape. The sudden appearance of the machine, dropping its large 'flash-bangs' in his path, was a lure. They had wanted him to go to the right, and at speed. Had not Mary-Jane Mashkin told him about the digging? A new drainage system? Had he not seen the evidence of it on his visit to this spot?

All this flashed through Bond's head as he applied the car's brakes too late. The nose of the Saab reared up, and he was aware of the Mashkin woman telling him the size and depth of the pit. The wheels clawed at empty air, then the Saab began to drop forward, tipping to one side, bouncing and bumping in a horrible crunching somersault.

In the final moments Bond was buffeted around in his harness, and something, possibly the Blackhawk, caught him on the side of the head. He felt the numbness, but neither fear nor pain as the red mist came in, with ink in its wake, carrying him floating off into its black impenetrable sea.

Out on the track, the lights of the B.M.W. could be seen in the distance as the helicopter slowly settled on the heather. 'Got him,' said Anton Murik with a smile.

The pilot removed the Nitefinder goggles taken from Bond the previous night. 'They work well, these,' he said. 'Clear as sunlight up to over five hundred feet.'

14

HIGH FREQUENCY

THERE WAS A blinding white light. James Bond thought he could hear the noise and for a moment imagined that he was still in the Saab, rolling into the ditch.

'The bloody ditch,' Bond muttered.

'I told you it was dug for drainage, James. Fifteen feet deep and over twelve wide. They had to get you out with oxy-acetylene cutters.'

Bond screwed up his eyes and looked at the woman now coming into focus. It was Mary-Jane Mashkin, standing above him.

'Nothing much wrong with you, James. Just a little bruising.'

He tried to get up, but the harness held him tightly. Bond smelled the dampness, and turning his head, he saw where he was: in Murik's white-tiled torture chamber.

They had him strapped down on the operating table, and Mary-Jane Mashkin stood beside him wearing a white coat. She smiled comfortably. Behind her, Bond made out the figures of two men; a couple of the Laird's heavies, their faces sculpted out of clay, and no expression in their eyes.

'Well,' Bond tried to sound bright. 'I don't feel too bad. If you say I'm okay, why don't you let me get up?'

Anton Murik's voice came soft, and close, in his ear. 'I think you have some explaining to do, Mr Bond. Don't you?'

Bond closed his eyes. 'It's getting so a man can't even go out for a night drive without people shooting at him.'

'Very witty.' Murik sounded anything but amused. 'You killed two of my men, Mr Bond. Making off in secret, with the knowledge you have about my current project, is not the way to keep me as a friend and protector. All previous contracts made with you are cancelled. More to the point, I would like to know your real profession; for whom you work; what your present aim in life happens to be. I may add that I know what your immediate future will be: death; because I am going to bring that about unless you tell us the absolute truth.'

Bond's head was almost clear now. He concentrated on what was happening, feeling some bruising on his body, and a dull ache up the right side of his head. Memory flooded back: the night ride, the helicopter and the trap. He also knew what was going to happen, realising he would require all possible reserves of physical· and mental strength.

Start concentrating now, Bond thought. Aloud, he said, 'You know who I am. Bond, James, 259057, Major, retired.'

'So,' Murik purred, 'you accept work from me, and then try to blast yourself out of Murik Castle and the glen. It does not add up, Major Bond. If you *are* Major Bond – I have people working on that, but I think we'll probably get to the truth faster than they will.'

'Got windy,' Bond said, trying to sound tired and casual. In fact he was fully aware now, his mind getting sharper every minute, though he knew the stress of that drive would already have played havoc with him. The fatigue had to be just under the surface.

'Windy?' Murik sneered.

'Fear is not an unknown failing in men.' Concentrate, Bond thought; get your head into the right condition now. 'I got frightened. Just thought I would slip away until it was all over.'

Murik said he really thought they should have the truth. 'There is so little time left.' Bond saw him nod towards Mary-Jane, who stepped forward, closer to the table.

'I'm a trained psychiatrist,' Mary-Jane Mashkin

drawled. 'And I have one or two other specialities.'

Like being a nuclear physicist, Bond thought. Anton Murik's partner in nuclear crime. 'Proper little Jill-of-all-trades,' he muttered.

'Don't be frivolous, Bond. She can make it very unpleasant for you.' Murik leered at him. 'And you should know that we've been through your luggage. As a mercenary and retired army man, you carry very sophisticated devices with you. Interesting.' He again nodded towards Mary-Jane Mashkin, who rolled up Bond's sleeve. He tried to move against the restraining straps, but it was no good. His mind began to panic, casting around for the right point of mental focus, trying to remember the rules for what one did in a situation like this. A thousand bats winged their way around his brain in confusion.

Bond felt the swab being dabbed on his arm, just below the bicep: damp, cool, the hint of its smell reaching his nostrils. The panic died, Bond conquering the immediate fear of what would come. Focus. Focus. Bond; James. 259057, Major, retired. Straight. Now what should he keep in the forefront of his consciousness? Nuclear power: Murik's own subject. Bond had only an elementary knowledge, but he concentrated on the reading M had made him do before going on this mission. Blot out M. See the book. Just the book with its drawings, diagrams and text. Bond, James. 259057, Major, retired. If they were to use the conventional truth drugs on him, Bond had to remain alert. There were desperate mental counter-measures to interrogation by drugs, and 007 had been through the whole unpleasant course at what they called the Sadist School near Camberley.

'A little Mozart, I think,' Murik's voice called, away from the table. Mary-Jane Mashkin moved, and Bond winced slightly as he felt the hypodermic needle slide into his arm. What would they use? In their situation what would he use? Soap – the Service name for Sodium Thiopental? No, they would risk a more toxic substance.

The book: just keep the pages turning. Lazy. The pages. Probably a nice mix — Scopolamine with morphine: twilight sleep, like having a baby.

Bond felt his whole body slowly become independent of his mind. The book. See the pages. Far away an orchestra played. Violins, strings and woodwinds, a pleasant sound with a military rhythm to it; then a piano — all far away.

Walking in the park on a summer Sunday, with the band playing. Lavender was there. Holding hands. Children laughing; the ducks and water fowl. People. Yet he felt alone, even in the crowd, with Lavender — with Dilly — as they floated over the grass near the Mall to the sound of music.

Bond heaved his mind back. Bond, James. What was the next bit? The band played on, and he could smell the expensive fragrance of Lavender's scent as she held his hand tightly. No. No. Bond, James. 259057. Major, retired. The book. Nuclear power plants derive their energy from the splitting — or fission — of the uranium isotope U-235.

The music had changed, more gently, like Dilly's touch on his hand. Drag your mind back, James. Back. Don't let go. Then Lavender was asking the questions. 'James, what do you really do for a living?'

'Bond, James. 259057. Major, retired.' He knew that he should not have trusted her.

'Oh, not that rubbish, James, darling. What do you *really* get up to?'

Fight, James. Fight it. Even from outside his body. The echo in his own ears was odd, the speech blurred as he said, 'In a nuclear plant, steam is produced by the heat coming from the controlled chain reaction occurring inside the uranium fuel rods within the reactor core . . .' then he was laughing; and the band played on.

'You're talking scribble, James. Did your nanny say that when you were little? Talking scribble? You've got something to do with nuclear power, haven't you? Are you from the Atomic Research? The International Commission? Or the International Atomic Energy Agency in Vienna?'

Think, James, there's something very wrong here. Pull yourself up, you're dreaming and it's getting worse. Feel your body; get into your own mind. Be determined. Beat it. 'Nuclear power is a very expensive way to boil water.' That was what the book said; and there was a diagram next. Fight, James. Do everything they taught you at Camberley.

'Come on, who are you really?' asked Lavender.

'My name . . .' It wasn't Lavender. The other one was asking the questions. Yet he could smell Lavender's scent; but it was the American woman. What was her name? Mary-Jane? That was it, Mary-Jane Mashkin. Maybe Dilly was straight after all.

In a drowning pall of dark smoke, Bond shouted loudly, 'Bond, James. 259057. Major, retired. That what you want to know, Mary-Jane? 'Cause that's the truth.' He fought hard and stopped there, knowing to go on talking in this floating cloud of uncertainty, would lead him into babbling on like a brook. Brook. Babble. Book.

Another voice cut through, loudly. 'He's resisting. Increase the dosage.'

'You'll kill him. Try rewards.'

'Yes.'

Bond's body seemed to tilt forward. He was sliding down an invisible slope, gathering speed. Then something was pressed against his ears. Headphones. Music poured in on him. Beautiful liquid sounds that slowed up his descent, soothing him. Lord, he was tired. Sleep? Why not? The voice again – 'James Bond?'

'Yes.'

'What are your duties?'

'I am . . .' No, James, fight, you silly bugger. 'I am 259057 . . . Major, retired . . .'

The soothing music was still there in his head, and the voice snapped back, 'I want the truth, not that rubbish. When you don't speak the truth, this will happen – '

Bond probably screamed aloud. The noise filled his

head. The terrifying blinding noise, the screech and wail. NO . . . No . . . No . . . As suddenly as it started, the horrific, bursting blaze of sound stopped. It had been counter-productive, for Bond felt the nerve ends of his body again, and was quite clear for a few seconds about what was happening. If he gave them evasive answers they would pour the sound into his head again. The sound – high frequency white noise: waves of sound; waves on a non-uniform pattern. They brought pain, distress, and worse.

The soft music had returned, then the voice again. Murik. Anton Murik, Laird of Murcaldy. Bond had re-gained enough sense to know that.

'You were sent on a mission, weren't you, Bond?'

'I came here. You invited me.' His body started to slip away, the mind floating.

'You made sure I invited you. Who sent you here?'

Slipping. Watch it, James. Air brakes; slow up; slow up. The Saab's wheels clawing at the air and the crashing somersault . . . Then the agony, the screech of noise filling his head, bursting the brain, red in his eyes and the pain sweeping between his ears: great needles of noise against the screams – which he could not hear – and the faces of evil glaring out from the terrible high-pitched cacophony. His brain would burst; the soundwaves rising higher and higher. Then silence, with only the echoes of pain leaving his head the size of a giant balloon: throbbing.

'Who sent you here, and what were your instructions?' Sharp. Orders, like the crack of a whip.

No, James. Control. Concentrate. Fight. The book. The page. Bond knew what he was saying, but could not hear it. 'A nuclear plant's reactor core is suspended inside a steel vessel with thick walls like a giant pod . . .'

The white noise came in – a flood that swept away his cranium; whining, clawing, scratching, screaming into his very soul. This time it seemed to go on in an endless series of red-hot piercing attacks, not falling or letting up, but rising, enveloping him, filling the brain with agony, bursting at his eardrums, inflating him with its evil.

When it finally stopped, Bond was still screaming, on the very edge of madness, teetering on the precipice of sanity.

'Who sent you, Bond? What were you supposed to do?'

'The twelve-foot-long fuel rods are inside the core . . .'

The madness covered him again, then stopped.

Whatever drug they had used was now ineffective; for the ache in his great, oversized, head had taken over, and all Bond knew was the terrible aftermath of the noise.

'Tell me!' commanded Anton Murik.

'Sod you, Murik,' Bond shouted.

'No.' He heard Mary-Jane shout, so loudly, close to his ear, that he winced – as though the whole of his hearing and the centre of his brain had been branded by the white noise. 'You'll get nothing now.'

'Then we'll take him along for the ride. Dispose of him after the girl.'

Bond found it hard to understand what Murik was saying. The words were there, clear enough, but his concentration was so bad that he seemed incapable of sorting out the meaning. Each word had to be weighed and understood, then the whole put together.

'Get Caber,' he heard. Then:

'Quite extraordinary,' from the woman. 'His mental discipline is amazing. You'd normally expect a man to crack and blurt out everything. He's either for real – an adventurer of some kind who got frightened – or a very clever, tough professional.'

'I want him kept safe; and well away from the girl. Does she suspect anything?'

Mary-Jane Mashkin was answering, 'I don't think so. Went a little white when I told her Mr Bond had met with an accident. I think the silly bitch imagines she's in love with him.'

'Love! What's love?' spat Murik. 'Get him out.'

'I'd like tae do it fur permanent.' It was Caber's voice, and they were Caber's tree-like arms that picked Bond from the table. Bond could smell the man close to him. Then the weakness came, suddenly, and he felt the world zoom away from him, as though down the wrong end of a telescope. After that the darkness.

The next time he opened his eyes, Bond seemed to be alone. He lay on a bed that was vaguely familiar, but as soon as he shut his lids, all consciousness withdrew itself from him again.

Some kind of noise woke him the next time, and it was impossible to know for how long he had slept. He heard his own voice, a croak, asking to be left alone, and, louder, 'Just let me rest for a minute and I'll be okay,' before he drifted off again. This time into a real dream – not the nightmare from the torture chamber – with music: the band playing light opera overtures and Lavender close to him among the trees of St James's Park, with a cloudless London sky above them. Then an inbound jet stormed its way overhead, lowering its gear on a final approach to Heathrow; and he woke, clear-headed, with the pain gone.

He was in the East Guest Room, but it had been changed greatly. Everything movable had been taken out – tables, chairs, standard lamps, even the fitments in the Sleep-centre, on which he was lying, had gone. Bond's final wakening, he realised, had come because of another noise – the clunk of the electronic locks coming off. Caber's bulk filled the doorway. 'The Laird's seen fit tae feed ye.' He moved back, allowing his henchman, Hamish, to enter, carrying a tray of cold meats and salads, together with a vacuum flask of what turned out to be coffee.

'Very good of him,' Bond smiled. 'Recovered, have we, Caber?'

'It'll be a gey long time afore ye recover, Bond.'

'Might I ask a couple of questions?'

'Ye may ask; whether I answer'll be up tae me.'

'Is it morning or evening?'

'Ye daftie, it's evening.'

'And what day?'

'Tuesday. Now tak your food. Ye'll no' be bothered agin this night,' Caber gave him a look of unconcealed hatred. 'But we'll all be off early on the morn's morn.' The door closed, and the locks thudded into place again.

Bond looked at the food, suddenly realising he was very hungry. He began to tear into the meal. Tuesday, he thought; and they were leaving in the morning – Wednesday. That meant something. Yes, on Wednesday Franco had a date with someone who was to die. Cat-walk . . . palace . . . Majorca . . . high-powered air rifle with a gelatine-covered projectile. Murik's words in the torture chamber came floating back into his head. 'Dispose of him after the girl.' Could Murik have meant after Lavender, of whom Bond was not entirely sure? The pieces of the Meltdown puzzle floated around in his head for most of the night. He dozed and woke, then dozed again, until dawn, when the door locks came off and Caber threw in a pile of clothes, telling him to get dressed. There would be breakfast in half an hour and he should be ready to leave by eight.

High up in the building overlooking Regent's Park, M sat at his desk, looking grave and concerned. Bill Tanner was in the room, and 'The Opposition' had come calling again in the shape of Sir Richard Duggan.

'When was this?' M had just asked.

'Last night – or early this morning, really. About one thirty according to our people.' Duggan reported some kind of firefight, a car chase and a couple of explosions – a very large form of 'flash-bangs', near Murik Castle. 'They say your man's car was taken back to the castle this afternoon, and that it looked like a write-off.'

M asked if they were still keeping the place under watch.

'Difficult.' Duggan looked concerned. 'The Laird's got a lot of his staff out – beaters, people like that. They're making it look like some routine job, but they're obviously combing the area.'

'And Franco?'

'F.B.I. lost him. Yesterday in New York. Gone to ground.'

M allowed himself a few moments' thought, then got up and went to the window, looking down on the evening scene as dusk closed in around them. 007 had been in tight corners before; worse than this. If it were really desperate there would have been some word.

'Your man hasn't made contact; that's what I'm worried about. He was supposed to be in touch with my people. I hope you're not letting him operate on our patch, M.'

'You're absolutely certain he didn't follow Franco?'

'Pretty sure.'

'Well, that can only mean he's being detained against his will.' M allowed for a little harsh logic. 007 knew the score. He would make some kind of contact as soon as it was humanly possible.

'Do you think Special Branch should go in with a warrant?' Duggan was probing.

M whirled around. 'On what grounds? That an officer of my Service is missing? That he was sent to take a look at what was going on between the Laird of Murcaldy and an international terrorist? That your boys and girls have been watching his place? That's no way. If Anton Murik is involved in something shady, then it'll come to light soon enough. I would suggest that you try to keep your own teams on watch. I'll deal with the F.B.I. – tell 'em to redouble their efforts, and keep a lookout for my man as well. I may even talk to the C.I.A. Bond has a special relationship with one of their men. No,' M said with a note of finality, 'no, Duggan, let things lie. I have a lot of confidence in the man I've sent in and I can assure you that if he does start to operate, it will either be to warn your surveillance team or take action out of the country.'

When Duggan had gone, M turned to his Chief-of-Staff. 'Didn't like the sound of the car being smashed up.'

'007's smashed up cars before, sir. All we can do is wait.

I'm sure he'll come up with something.'

'Well, he's taking his time about it,' M snorted. 'Just hope he's not loafing around enjoying himself, that's all.'

15

GONE AWAY

As HE WAS sitting towards the rear of the aircraft, it was impossible for Bond even to attempt to follow a flight path. Most of the time they had been above layers of cloud; though he was fairly certain that he had caught a glimpse of Paris through a wide gap among the cumulus about an hour after takeoff.

Now, hunched between two of Murik's muscular young men, he watched the wing tilt and saw that it seemed to be resting on sea. Craning forward, Bond tried to get a better view from the executive jet's small window: the horizon tipping over, and the sight of a coastline far away. A flat plain, circled by mountains; pleasure beaches, and a string of white holiday buildings; then, inland, knots of houses, threading roads, a sprawl of marshy-looking land and, for a second only, a larger, old town. Memories flicked through the card index of his mind. He knew that view. He had been here before. Where? They were losing altitude, turning against the mountains, inland. The jagged peaks seemed to wobble too close for comfort. Then the note of the engines changed as the pilot increased their rate of descent.

Lavender sat at a window, forward, hemmed in by one of Murik's private army. The Laird had brought four of his men on board, plus Caber acting as their leader. At this moment Caber's bulk seemed to fill the aisle as he bent forward, taking some instructions from Murik, who had spent the entire flight in a comfortable office area with Mary-Jane, situated just behind the flight deck door. Bond had watched them, and there seemed to have been much poring over maps and making of notes. As for Lavender, he had been allowed no contact, though she had looked at him with eyes that seemed to cry out for help; or beg forgiveness. Bond could not make up his mind which.

The journey had started on the dot of eight o'clock, when Caber and his men arrived at the East Guest Room. They were reasonably civil as they led Bond down into the main building, through the servants' quarters to the rear door, where Caber gave instructions for him to be handcuffed – shackled between two men. Outside what was obviously the tradesman's entrance a small man loitered near a van, which looked as if it had been in service since the 1930s. Faded gold lettering along the sides proclaimed the van belonged to Eric MacKenzie, Baker and Confectioner, Murcaldy.

So. Anton Murik was taking no chances. The baker's van; a classic ploy, for the baker would, presumably, call daily at the castle. Any watchers would regard the visit as normal. Routine was the biggest enemy of surveillance. Simple and effective; the ideal way to remove Bond without drawing any attention.

He was dragged quickly to the rear of the van, which was empty, smelling of freshly baked bread, the floor covered with a fine patina of flour.

Caber was the last of Bond's guards to climb in, pulling the doors behind him and locking the catch from the inside. The giant of a man gave a quick order for Bond to stay silent, and the van started up. So the journey began uncomfortably, with Bond squatting on the floor, the flour dust forming patches on his clothes.

It was not difficult to detect that they were making a straightforward journey from the castle to the village, for the direction was plain, and the changes in road surface could be felt in the bumping of the van. Finally it started to slow down, then made a painful right-hand turn as though negotiating a difficult entrance. Eric MacKenzie, if it was he, had problems with the gearbox, and the turn was orchestrated by many grinds and judders. Then the van crawled to a stop and the doors were opened.

Caber jumped down, ordering everybody out with a sharp flick of his massive head. The van was parked in a small yard, behind wooden gates. The tell-tale smell of bread pervaded the atmosphere outside, just as it had done in the van. Bond thought you did not have to be a genius, or Sherlock Holmes, to know they were in MacKenzie's yard, somewhere in the middle of Murcaldy village.

Parked beside them, facing the wooden gates, was a dark blue Commer security truck with the words Security International stencilled in white on both sides. The Commer looked solid and most secure, with its grilled windows around the driver's cab, the thick doors, reinforced bumpers and heavy panels along the most vulnerable points.

Bond was now bundled into the back of the security truck, Caber and his men moving very quickly, so that he only just caught sight of a driver already in the cab, with a man next to him, riding shotgun.

This time Caber did not get in. The doors closed with a heavy thud, and one of the men to whom Bond was handcuffed operated the bolts on the inside.

There were uncomfortable wooden benches battened to either side of the interior, and Bond was forced on to one of these, still flanked by the personal guards. These well-built, stone-faced young men did not seem inclined to talk, indicating they were under orders to remain silent. Bond admitted to himself that Murik really was good on his security, even ruling out the possibility of their prisoner starting to build up some kind of relationship with the guards. When he tried to speak, the young heavy on his left simply slammed an elbow into his ribs, telling him to shut up. There would be no talking.

The journey in the security van lasted for almost six hours. There were no windows in either the sides or the front – connecting with the driver's cab – and it was impossible to see through the small grilled apertures in the rear doors.

All Bond could do was try to calculate speed and mileage. All sense of direction was lost within the first hour, though he had some idea they were moving even farther north. When they finally stopped, Bond calculated they had come almost two hundred miles – a slow, uncomfortable journey.

It was now nearly three in the afternoon, and when the doors of the truck were unbolted and opened, Bond was surprised to see Caber already waiting for them. A sharp breeze cut into the truck, and Bond felt they were probably on an area of open ground. Again it was impossible to tell, for the rear of the truck had been backed up near to a small concrete building, only a pace or so from a pair of open doors. The view to left and right was screened by the truck's doors, now fully extended. Nobody spoke much, and almost all the orders were given by grunts and sign language – as though Bond was either deaf or mentally deficient.

Inside the concrete building they led him along a narrow passage with, he noted, a slight downward slope. Then into a windowless room where, at last, the handcuffs were removed and the freedom of a wash room was allowed; though this too had no windows, only air vents fitted high, near the ceiling. Food was brought – sandwiches and coffee – and one of the guards remained with him, still impassive, but with his jacket drawn back from time to time so the butt of a snub-nosed Smith & Wesson ·38 was visible. It looked to Bond like one of his own old favourites, the Centennial Airweight.

From the moment of departure from the castle, Bond's mind hardly left the subject of a possible breakaway. This, however, was no time to try anything – locked away in what seemed to be a very solidly built bunker, in an unknown location, kept close with armed men and the giant Caber. He thought about Caber for a moment, realising that, if they had been through all his effects, the huge Scot would know the secret of Bond's success in the wrestling match. Caber was going to be a problem; but at least things were moving, and Bond had been heartened by one item of his clothing they had returned to him – his thick leather belt, the secrets of which he had checked, to find they had not been discovered.

In his luggage there were three belts of different design and colour, each containing identical items of invaluable assistance. Q Branch had constructed the belts in a manner which made their contents practically undetectable – even under the most advanced Detectorscope, such as the sophisticated J-200 used extensively by Bond's own service. With everything else – watch, wallet and the rest – removed, he at least had the fall-back.

Bond sat looking at his guard, giving him the occasional smile, but receiving no reaction. At last he asked the young Scot if he could be allowed a cigarette. The man merely nodded, keeping his eyes on Bond as he withdrew a packet of cigarettes and tossed one towards 007's feet. Bond picked it up and asked for a light. The man threw over some book matches, telling him to light up, then drop the book on to the floor and kick it back. There would be no blazing-matches-in-the-face routine.

At around four o'clock there were noises from above – a helicopter very low over the building, chopping down for a landing. Then, a few minutes later, Caber entered with the other guards. 'Ye'll be joining the Laird now,' he was ordering Bond, not telling him. 'It's only a wee walk, so ye'll not be needing the irons. But I warn ye: any funny business, and ye'll be scattered to the four winds.' Caber sounded as if he meant every word, and would be more than happy to do the scattering personally.

Bond was marched up the passage, between his original guards, and through the door. The security truck had gone, and they were standing on the edge of a small airfield. It was clear now that they had come out of the basement of what must be a control tower.

A couple of Piper Cubs and an Aztec stood near by.

Away to the left Bond saw the helicopter, which he presumed was from Murik Castle. In front of them, at the end
of a metalled runway, a sleek executive jet shivered as if in
anticipation of flight, its motors running on idle. It looked
like a very expensive toy — a Grumman Gulfstream, Bond
thought — in its glossy cream livery with gold lettering,
which read Aldan Aerospace, Inc. Bond recalled the company's name in the dossier on Anton Murik which M had
shown him.

Caber nodded them towards the jet and, as they walked
the few yards — at a smart pace — Bond turned his head.
The neat board on the side of the control tower read: Aldan
Aerospace, Inc. Flying Club: PRIVATE.

Anton Murik and Mary-Jane Mashkin were already
seated, as was Lavender with her minder, when they
climbed into the roomy little jet. The pair did not even turn
around to look at their captive, who was placed with a
guard on either side, as before. A young steward passed
down the aisle, fussily checking seat belts, and it was at this
point that Lavender turned to lock eyes with Bond. During
the flight she repeated the action several times, on two
occasions adding a wan smile.

They had hardly settled down when the door was slammed shut and the aircraft moved, pointing its nose up the
runway. Seconds later the twin Rolls-Royce Spey jets
growled, then opened their throats, and the aircraft began
to roll, rocketing off the runway like a single seat fighter,
climbing rapidly into a thin straggle of cloud.

Now they were reaching the end of the journey, with the
sun low on the horizon. The mountains were above them,
seeming to lower over the bucking aircraft. Bond still
peered out, trying to place their location. Then, suddenly,
he recognised the long, flat breast of the mountain to their
left. The Canigou. No wonder he recognised it, knowing the
area as well as he did. Roussillon — that plain circled with
mountains, and bordering on the sea, hunched against
Spain. They were in France, the Pyrénées Orientales, and

the old town he had spotted was the ancient, one-time seat
of the Kings of Majorca, Perpignan. He should have spotted the towers that remained of the old wall and the vast
fortress which had once been the palace set among the
clustered terracotta roofs and narrow streets.

Roussillon? Roussillon Fashions. The blurred and spor-
adic conversation, overheard after the bug had been dislodged from Murik's desk, came back to Bond. It was down
there at the ancient palace, dating from medieval times,
when the area had been an independent kingdom, ruled
over by the Kings of Majorca, that Franco was to admin-
ister death: through a high-powered air rifle on Wednesday
night – tonight – the day before Operation Meltdown. The
target? Bond knew with fair certainty who the target would
be. The situation was altered beyond recognition. Whatever the risk, he must take the first chance, without hesitation. More than at any time during the whole business,
Bond had to get free.

Of course. They were on the final approach to Perpignan
airport, near the village of Rivesaltes, and only three or four
miles from the town itself. Bond had even been here in
winter, for the skiing, as well as spending many happy
summer days in the area.

The engines flamed out and the little jet bustled along
the main runway, slowing and turning to taxi away from
the airport buildings, out towards the perimeter of the
airfield.

The aircraft turned on its own axis and finally came to a
halt, the guard next to Bond placing a firm restraining
hand on his arm. The top brass were obviously going to
disembark first.

As Murik came level with Bond, he gave a little swooping
movement and his bulldog face split into a grin. 'I hope you
enjoyed the flight, Mr Bond. We thought it better to have
you with us, where we can keep an eye on you during this
most important phase. You will be well looked after, and
I'll see that you get a ringside seat tomorrow.'

Bond did not smile. 'A hearty breakfast for the condemned man?' he asked.

'Something like that, Mr Bond. But what a way to go!'

Mary-Jane, following hard on Murik's heels, gave a twisted little smirk. 'Should've taken up my offer when the going was good, James.' She laughed, not unpleasantly.

Murik gave a chirpy smile. 'We shall see you anon, then,' and he was off, doing his little bird hop down to the door.

For the first time Bond was one hundred per cent certain about Lavender. He looked up, giving her a broad, encouraging grin as she passed down the aircraft, her brawny escort's hand clamped hard on to her arm. A flicker of nervousness showed in her eyes, then the warmth returned, as though Bond was willing courage and strength into the girl.

They were parked alongside a huge hangar, with adjacent office buildings, topped by a neon sign that read Aldan Aerospace (France), Inc. Bond wondered what had prompted Murik to choose this Catalan area – the Roussillon – as his headquarters for this part of Europe. Roussillon Fashions, for sure, but there had to be some other reason. Bond wondered how much of it concerned Meltdown.

The guards acted like sheepdogs, closing in around Bond, trying to make the walk from the aircraft look as natural as possible. The hangar and offices were no more than a few yards from the perimeter fence of the airport, where a gaggle of ancient Britannias rested, herded together like stuffed geese, each with the legend European Air Services running above the long row of oval windows. The fence was low, and broken in a couple of places. Beyond, a railway track with overhead wiring ran straight past; behind that, a major road – the Route Nationale – slashed with cars, moving fast. Going to, or coming from Perpignan, Bond thought; for in this area all roads led to that town.

At full stretch he could be away and through that fence in a matter of thirty seconds. Thirty seconds: he actually considered it as they neared the offices. The muscular Scots around him would be prompt in their reaction. Yet Bond was almost hypnotised by the idea of escaping this way through the fence, should the opportunity present itself.

It was to happen sooner than he expected. They were within a few paces of the office doors when, from around the corner, in a flurry of conversation and laughter, there appeared a small group of men – four in the dark blue uniforms of a commercial air line. They were close enough for Bond to make out the letters E.A.S. entwined in gold on their caps. European Air Services. A fragment of English floated from the conversation, then a quick response in French, for the aircrew were accompanied by two young French customs officers – the whole group strolling lazily towards the Britannias.

Murik and Mary-Jane were almost at the office door, accompanied by one of the guards; behind them, Lavender was being led firmly by her minder, and Caber walked alone between her and Bond, still flanked by his two men.

It would be one of his biggest gambles. The odds flashed through his mind: putting everything you owned on the turn of a card; on one number at the roulette table; on the nose of a horse. This time it *would* be everything he owned: life itself. If Murik's men could be so shocked into holding fire or chase, even for a few seconds, he might just do it. In this fraction of time, Bond weighed the chances. Would Murik wish to call attention to himself and his party? Would they risk other people being hurt, killed even? It was a matter of audacity and nerve.

Later, Bond thought the appearance of the train probably made up his mind; the sound of a horn in the distance, and the sight of a long railway train snaking its way along the tracks, about a mile off.

He slowed, dropping back a couple of paces, causing one of the guards to nudge him on. Angrily, Bond shoved the man. 'You can stop that,' he said very loudly. 'I'm not interested in your bloody meeting.' Then, looking towards the group of aircrew and customs men, he raised his voice and shouted 'Good grief', already taking one step away from the nearest guard, who moved a hand to grab him. Bond was quick. The bet was laid. *Le maximum: faites vos jeux.*

Bond had stepped away, and was moving in great long strides, his hand up, towards the group of uniformed men. 'Johnny,' he shouted. 'Johnny Manderson: what the hell are you doing here?'

The uniformed men paused, turning towards him. One smiled broadly; the others looked puzzled.

'Get back here.' Caber tried to keep his voice low as he started forward; and Bond heard Murik hiss, 'Get him. For God's sake. Take care.' But, by this time, Bond had reached the group, his hand stretched out to one of the aircrew, who in turn put out his hand in a reflex action of cordiality, while beginning to say something about a mistake.

'It's good to see you, Johnny.' Bond pumped his hand wildly, still talking loudly. Then he pulled the man towards him, spinning around to put him, as a shield, between Murik's people and himself. Caber and two of the guards were advancing warily, hands inside their jackets and, doubtless, on the butts of their weapons. Behind them the others were moving slowly into the building, Murik glancing up, his face a mask.

Bond dropped his voice. 'Terribly sorry,' he said, grinning. 'A little problem about non-payment of dues. I should watch out for those blokes. Hoods, the lot of them. Must dash.'

Using the group of uniformed men for cover, he was off, going flat out in a low crouch, weaving towards one of the jagged gaps in the fence. There were shouts from behind him, but no shots. Only the sound of pounding feet, and an argument of sorts, between Caber's men and the aircrew and customs officers. Bond dived through the gap, sliding down the small embankment on to the railway track – the train now bearing down on him, its roar shaking the gravel, the sound covering everything else. If there was going to be shooting, it would happen in the next few seconds, before the train reached them.

The big engine was coming from his right – from the direction of Perpignan, he thought. There was no time for further reflection. It was now or never, in front of the train looming above him. Bond chanced it, leaping in two long strides across the track, and doubling his body into a ball, rolling as he reached the far side; the engine almost brushing his back as it passed with a great *parp* of its horn.

The horn sounded nothing like that unmistakable *too-too-too-too-toot* of the hunting field; but, for a second, Bond was transported, hearing the noise of hooves heavy on grass, the baying of hounds and the huntsman's horn, 'Gone away'. He had never cared much for foxhunting, and now – casting himself in the role of the fox – he liked it even less. How the hell did you go to earth in a foreign country with Murik's hounds at your heels?

In an instant Bond was on his feet running down the far bank towards the Route Nationale, his thumb already up in the hitch-hiker's position. But luck was still with him. As he reached the edge of the road he saw a small, battered pickup truck pulled into the side. Two men were being dropped off, and there were four others in the back, shouting farewells to their comrades. They looked like farmworkers going home after a long backbreaking day in the vineyards.

'Going into Perpignan?' Bond shouted in French.

The driver, a cigarette stuck unlit in the corner of his mouth, nodded from the window.

'A lift?' Bond asked.

The driver shrugged, and one of the men in the back called for him to jump up. Within seconds they were edging into the traffic, Bond crouched down with the other men – thanking providence for his own facility with the

French language. He sneaked a peep towards the airport side of the railway tracks. There was no sign of Caber or the others.

No, Bond thought, they would be running for cars – Murik would be well organised here – his men would already be taking short cuts into Perpignan to head Bond off.

Cars already had their headlights on, as the dusk gathered quickly around them. Bond asked the time, and one of the workmen told him it was after nine, holding out his wrist with pride, to show off a brand new digital watch, explaining it was a gift from his son. 'On my saint's day,' he said. The digits showed four minutes past nine, and Bond realised that they were in a different time zone, an hour later than British time. 'We'll have to move if we're going to see the fun,' the man said.

Fun? Bond shrugged, explaining he had just come in on a flight, 'with freight'. He was very late, and had to meet a man in Perpignan.

'All men are in Perpignan tonight. If you can find them,' laughed one of the workers.

Bond scowled, asking why. 'Something special?'

'Special?' the man laughed. It was Perpignan's night of nights.

'Fête,' one explained.

'*Vieux Saint Jean,*' said another.

A third gave a bellow, lifting his arms histrionically, '*La Flamme arrive en Perpignan.*'

They all laughed. Bond suddenly remembered that he had been here before for the fête. Every town in the Mediterranean had its own rituals, its battle of flowers, processions, carnivals – usually religious. In Perpignan it was the great feast of St John; when the whole town was crammed to the gills, and there was dancing in the streets, singing, fireworks, spectacle. The festivities started when bonfires were lit by a flame, brought, with Olympian cere-mony, by runners from a high point in the Canigou mountain itself. He could not have arrived in this ancient place at a better time. There would be crowd cover until the early hours; and with luck, enough breathing space to find a way of making contact with London and M.

- 16 -
FÊTE AND FATE

THEY DROPPED HIM off on the corner of the Place de la
Résistance, which was already full of people standing
shoulder to shoulder, pushing along the pavements. There
were plenty of police in evidence, directing traffic, closing
off streets, and – presumably – keeping an eye open for
troublemakers.

Bond stepped back into the crowd. It was some years
since he had been here, and first he had to get his bearings.
In the middle of the crush of people, Bond realised, with a
sudden stab of fear, that his legs were shaking. Directly in
front of him there were three great bonfires ready to be lit.
To the left he saw a bridge spanning the well-kept canal,
banked here by green lawns and flowers, which runs, above
and below ground, through the town: a tributary of the
river Têt.

A platform had been built over the bridge and was even
now crowded with musicians. A master of ceremonies
spoke into an uncertain microphone, telling the crowds
about the next *sardana* they would be playing, keeping
things going until the flame arrived to ignite both bonfires
and excitement. The musicians burst into that music,
known to anyone who has passed even briefly through
either the French or Spanish Catalan lands: the steady bray
of pipe, drum and brass in 6/8 time to which the *sardana* is
danced. The groups of dancers, some in traditional costume, others in business suits or jeans and shirts, formed
their circles, clasping hands held high, and launched into
the light, intricate, foot movements: a dance of peace and
joy; a symbol of Catalonia.

On the far side of the bridge, other circles had taken up the dance in front of the towering red Castillet – the old city gateway, still intact, glowing russet in the light from the street lamps; its circular tower and battlements topped by what looked like a minaret.

The crowds began to thicken, and the music thumped on with its hypnotic beat and lilting melodies, the circles of dancers growing wider, or reforming into smaller groups – young and old, impeccable in their timing, and dancing as though in a trance. It was as if these people were reaching back through the years, linking hands with their past.

Bond thought that if there were to be any future for them – or at least a chance of one – he had better move fast. Telephone London. Which was the best way? Call from a telephone box on the direct dialling international system? For that he would need money. It would have to be quick, for telephone booths – particularly on the Continent – are highly unsafe, and Bond had no desire to be trapped in a glass coffin, or one of those smaller, triangular affairs which would preclude keeping an eye on his rear.

The first move was to lose himself in the swelling throng, which rose and fell like a sea. Above all else, he had to be watchful, for Murik's men could be already among the crowds, their eyes peeled for him; and if they saw him Bond knew what he could expect. Most likely they would use dirks, sliding the instruments of death through his ribs, covered by the crowd, in the middle of the celebrations. There was no point in going to the police – not on a night like this, without identification. They would simply lock him up and perhaps tomorrow, when it was too late, telephone the British Consul.

Bond took a deep breath and began to move through the crowd. It would be best to keep to the fringes, then disappear into a side street.

He had just started to move when a large black Mercedes swept into the Place, only to be halted by a gendarme, who signalled that it should turn back. The road was about to be closed. The driver spoke to the policeman in French, then turned to the occupants of the car. Bond's heart missed a beat. Next to the driver sat Caber, while the three other big Scotsmen were crammed into the rear.

Caber got out, two of the men joining him, while the gendarme made noises suggesting they get the car out of the way as soon as possible.

Bond tried to shrink back into the crowd as he watched Caber giving orders. The men dispersed – Caber and two of them crossing the Place, the last diving into the crowd a little to Bond's right. The hounds were there, trying to spot him or sniff him into the open. Bond watched the big lad shouldering himself away. Then he moved, taking his time, along the fringe of the crowd, going slowly out of necessity, and because of the density of the shouting, laughing, chattering people.

Bond kept looking back and then scanning the way ahead and across the road. The band had stopped and the master of ceremonies was saying that the Flame, carried from near the summit of the Canigou by teams of young people, was now only a few minutes from its destination. A few minutes, James Bond knew, could mean anything up to half an hour.

The band started up again and the dancers responded. Bond kept to the edge of the crowd, slowly making his way across the now sealed-off road, towards the towering Castillet. He was looking for a street he recalled from previous visits: an ancient square almost entirely covered by tables from the cafés. They should be doing a roaring trade tonight.

He reached the Castillet and saw another bonfire ready and waiting to be lit. A great circle of dancers around it was going through the intricate patterns, slightly out of time to the music, which was distorted on the night air. On the far side of the circle he spotted one of Caber's men turning constantly and searching faces in the throng.

Bond held back, waiting until he was certain the man

was looking away from him; then he dodged nimbly through the crowd, sidestepping and pushing, until he found a clear path through the archway of the Castillet itself. He had just passed the café on the far side, and was about to cross the road, when he had to leap into a shop doorway. There, walking slowly, scanning both sides of the street, head tilted, as though trying to catch his quarry's scent, was the giant Caber. Bond shrank back into the doorway, holding his breath, willing the Scot not to see him.

After what seemed an age, the giant walked on, still constantly scanning faces with his eyes. Bond edged out of the doorway and continued up the street. He could already see the intersection for which he was searching, marked by the bronze statue of a nude woman who looked unseeing down the wide road to his right. Crossing over through the thinning crowd, Bond arrived at his goal – Perpignan's Loge de Mer, once the great financial centre of the town: its Rialto. Indeed, many people felt the street contained many an echo of the glories of Venice – particularly the old Bourse with its grey stone walls, high arched windows and intricate carving. Right on the corner of this building the original weathervane – a beautifully executed galleon – still swung gently, but the Bourse itself, like the buildings opposite, had been given over to a different kind of financial transaction, for it was now a café. Here it was hard cash for hard liquor, coffee, soft drinks or beer. The old marble pavement was a litter of tables and chairs and people taking refreshment before joining in the festivities.

Bond walked straight into the corner Bar Tabac and asked for the *toilette*. The bartender, busy filling orders and being harassed by waiters, nodded to the back of the bar where Bond found the door marked with the small male symbol. It was empty, and he went into the first *cabinet*, locking the door behind him and starting work almost before the bolt slid home.

Quickly his hands moved to his belt clasp – a solid, wide

U-shaped buckle with a single thick brass spike, normal enough until you twisted hard. The spike moved on a metal screw thread. Six turns released it, revealing a small steel knife blade, razor sharp, within the sheath of the spike. Bond removed the blade, handling it with care, and inserted the cutting edge into an almost invisible hairline crack in the wide U-buckle. With hard downwards pressure the buckle came apart, opening on a pair of tiny hinges set at the points where it joined the leather. This was also a casing — for a tiny handle, complete with a thread into which the blade could be screwed. Equipped with this small but finely honed weapon, Bond pulled the belt from his waistband and began to measure the length. Each section of the double-stitched leather contained a small amount of emergency foreign currency in notes. German in the first two inches, Italian in the next, Dutch in the third— the whole belt containing most currencies he might need in Europe. The fourth section was what Bond needed: French francs.

The small toughened steel blade went through the stitching like a hot knife laid against butter, opening up the two-inch section to reveal a couple of thousand francs in various denominations. Not a fortune—just under two hundred pounds sterling, the way the market was running — but ample for Bond's needs.

He dismantled the knife, fitted it away again, and re-assembled the buckle, thrusting the money into his pocket. In the bar he bought a packet of Disque Bleu and a book of matches, for change; then sauntered out into the Place, back along the way he had already come. His target was the post office, where he knew there would be telephone booths. A fast alert to M, then on with the other business as quickly as possible.

Music still thumped out from the other side of the Castillet. He continued to mingle with the crowd, keeping to the right of the circling *sardana* dancers. He crouched slightly, for Murik's man was still in place, his head and eyes roving, pausing from time to time, to take in every face in the ever-changing pattern. Bond prepared to push himself into the middle of a group heading in his direction. Then, suddenly, the music stopped. The crowd stilled in anticipation, and the amplifier system crackled into life, the voice of the French announcer coming clear and loud from the horn-like speakers, bunched in little trios on the sides of buildings and in trees.

'My friend' – the announcer could not disguise the great emotion which already cut in waves through the gathered crowds – 'the Flame, carried by the brave young people of Perpignan, has arrived. The Flame has arrived in Perpignan.'

A great cheer rose from the crowds. Bond looked in the direction of the watcher by the Castillet, who was now searching wildly for signs, not of Bond, but of this great Flame. The fever pitch of excitement had got to everyone.

The loudspeakers rumbled again, and with that odd mixture of farce and sense of occasion which besets local feasts – from the Mediterranean to English country villages – the opening bars of Richard Strauss's *Also sprach Zarathustra* climbed into the air, shattering and brilliant, associated as it was with the great events of the conquest of space.

As the opening bars died away, so another cheer went up. A group of young girls in short white skirts came running, the crowds parting at their approach. About eight of them, each with an unlit brand held aloft, flanked the girl who carried a great blazing torch. Taking up their positions, the girls waited until the torch was set to a spot in the middle of the bonfire. The tinder took hold, and flames began to shoot from the fire, rising on the mild breeze. The girls lowered their own torches, to take flame from the fire before jogging away in the direction of the Castillet entrance.

The crowd started to move, backing off to get a better view. Bond moved with them. It was only a matter of turning to his left and he would be at the post office within minutes.

The bonfires in the Place went up, other groups of girls having jogged down the far side of the canal to do their work. Another roar from the crowd, and the band started up again. Before he knew what was happening, Bond was seized by both hands, a girl clinging to each, giggling and laughing at him. In a second, Bond was locked into part of the large circle of *sardana* dancers which was forming spontaneously. Desperately, and with much help from the girls, he tried to follow the steps so as not to draw attention to himself, now an easy target for Caber and his men.

Then, just as suddenly as it started, the *sardana* stopped, all eyes turning towards the Castillet, where the girls, with their blazing brands, occupied the spaces on the battlements, holding the torches high. A rocket sped into the air, showering the sky with clusters of brilliant fire. There followed three more muted explosions, and a great flood of light appeared to rise from the battlements on which the girls stood, their brands flickering, making a breathtaking spectacle. The effect was as though the whole of the Castillet was on fire, gouts of crimson smoke rising from the turrets, battlements, even the minaret; and from this, more rockets pierced the darkness of the night, exploding with shattering sound and shooting stars.

Bond at last freed himself from the two girls, looked around carefully, and set off again, pushing and shoving through the wall of people whose eyes could not leave the dazzling spectacle of starshells, rockets and Roman candles.

The entire area around the Castillet was tightly packed with shining faces – old men and women, who probably could remember this fête when it was not done on such a grand scale; children getting their first view of something magical; tourists trying to capture the experience for their home movies; and locals who entered into the spirit of the fête.

Bond saw all these faces — even teenagers aglow and delighted, not blasé, as they might have been in Paris, London or New York. He saw none of the enemy faces and finally pushed through the crowds, walking fast towards the less-populated streets and in the direction he remembered the post office to be.

The noise, music and fireworks were behind him now, and the streets darker. Within a few minutes he recognised the landmark of the Place Arago with its palm trees, shops and attractive bars. On his last visit Bond had often sat at the large café occupying the centre. The post office was only a minute away, in a street straight ahead to the left of the canal.

The street was narrow — buildings to his left and trees bordering the canal to the right. At last Bond saw the line of open telephone booths, each dimly lit and empty — a row of grey electronic sentries beside the post office steps. He drove his hand into his pocket, counting out the one franc pieces from his change. Six in all. Just enough to make the call, if the duty officer allowed him to speak without interruption.

Swiftly he dialled the 19–44–1 London prefix, then the number of the Regent's Park building. He had already inserted one of the franc pieces into the slot from which it would be swallowed when contact was made. In the far distance he was aware of the whoosh and crackle of the fireworks, while the music was still audible through the noise. His left ear was filled with clicks and whirrs from the automatic dialling system. Almost holding his breath, Bond heard the sequence complete itself, then the ringing tone and the receiver being lifted.

'Duty watchman. Transworld Exports,' came the voice, very clear, on the line.

'007 for M . . .' Bond began, then stopped as he felt the hard steel against his ribs, and a voice say quietly, 'Oot fast, or I'll put a bullet into ye.'

It was the watcher who had been standing near the

Castillet. Bond sighed.

'Fast,' the voice repeated. 'Put down yon telephone.' The man was standing very close, pushed up behind Bond.

Primary rule: never approach a man too close with a pistol. Always keep at least the length of his leg away. Bond felt a twinge of regret for the man as he first turned slowly, his right hand lowering the telephone receiver, then fast, swinging around to the left, away from the pistol barrel, as he brought the handset of the telephone smashing into the Scot's face. Murik's man actually had time to get one shot away before he went down. The bullet tore through Bond's jacket before ricochetting its way through the telephone booths.

Bond's right foot connected hard with his attacker's face as the man fell. There was a groan, then silence from the figure spreadeagled on the pavement outside the open booth. The blood was quite visible on his face. A telephone, Bond reflected, should be classified as a dangerous weapon. He had probably broken the fellow's nose.

The handset was wrecked. Bond swore as he rammed it back on to the rests. He bent over the unconscious figure to pick up the weapon. Cheeky devil, he thought. The gun was Bond's own Browning, obviously retrieved from the Saab.

In the distance, among the noises of the fête, there came the sound of a klaxon. It could well be a fire engine, but someone might have heard the shot or seen the scuffle. There had to be another place from which to get a message to M. The last people Bond wished to argue with tonight were the *flics*. He pushed the Browning into his waistband, turning the butt hard so that the barrel pointed to the side and not downwards, and then set off at a brisk walk, crossing the road and returning in the direction from which he had come.

At the Place Arago he stopped for traffic, looking across the road at an elegant poster prominently displayed on the wall of the large café. It took several seconds for the poster to register: ROUSSILLON HAUTE COUTURE. GRAND SHOW OF

THE NEW ROUSSILLON COLLECTION ON THE NIGHT OF THE
FESTIVAL OF OLD ST JOHN. PALACE OF THE KINGS OF MAJORCA.
ELEVEN P.M. There followed a list of impressive prices of
admission which made even Bond wince. Eleven – eleven
o'clock tonight. He gazed wildly around him. A clock over a
jeweller's shop showed it was five minutes past eleven
already.

Franco . . . the cat-walk . . . air rifle . . . death with a
gelatine capsule . . . Now. M would have to wait. Bond
took a deep breath and started to run, trying to recall from
his previous visits the quickest way to the ancient Palace,
and the easiest clandestine way into it. If he was right, the
girl would die very soon. If he was right; and if he did not
get there in time to prevent it.

DEATH IN MANY FASHIONS

THE PALAIS DES ROIS DE MAJORQUE stands on the higher ground at the southern part of Perpignan, and is approached through narrow sloping streets. The original Palace was built on a vast knoll, in the eleventh century, and was later walled in with the citadel—which rises to a height of almost three hundred feet and is wide enough at the top to accommodate a two-lane highway. On the inside, the walls dip to what was once the moat, making the whole a near-impregnable fortress.

Bond had visited the Palace several times before, and knew that the approach is made from the Street of the Archers, up flights of zig-zagging steps, which take the normal sightseer underground, to the main entrance, and then into the large cobbled courtyard. Above the entrance is the King's Gallery, while to the left are apartments closed to the casual visitor. On the right stands the great and impressive Throne Hall, while opposite the entrance runs a cloister with a gallery above it. Behind the cloister stands the lower Queen's Chapel, and above that, off the gallery, the magnificent Royal Chapel, with its series of lancet, equilateral and drop arches.

Above the two chapels the keep climbs upwards to a small bell-tower. This is the extent of the Palace usually on view to the public. Bond knew, however, that there was a further courtyard behind the cloister, gallery, chapels and keep. This area was still used: the yard itself as a depot for military vehicles and the surrounding buildings as billets for some of the local garrison; the bulk of whom lived below the citadel, in the Caserne Maréchal Joffre.

On his last visit to the area – some three years before – on a skiing holiday in the nearby mountains, Bond had fallen in with a French army captain from the garrison. One night, after a particularly lively après ski session, the gallant captain had suggested drinks in his quarters, which lay within the second courtyard of the Palace. They had driven to Perpignan, and the Frenchman had shown Bond how easy it was to penetrate the barracks by entering through a narrow alley off the Rue Waldeck-Rousseau, and from there follow the transport road which climbed steeply to the top of the citadel. It was not possible to enter the rear courtyard through the main transport gates, but you could squeeze through a tiny gap in the long terrace of living quarters forming the rear side of the courtyard. It was on that night Bond also learned of the archway through the rear courtyard, which leads straight into the main Palace area.

So it was to the barracks, the Caserne Maréchal Joffre, that he was now running as if the plague was at his heels. He knew there was little chance of gaining admittance to the main courtyard by following the normal route. Concerts were held there, and he had few doubts that this was where the Roussillon fashion show was being staged – under bright illuminations, and with the audience seated in the cobbled yard – or occupying the windows in the old royal apartments, the King's Gallery, and the gallery in front of the Royal Chapel.

It took nearly fifteen minutes for Bond to find the alley that led into the barracks, then another five before he could start the gruelling climb up the dusty, wide transport track. Bond forced himself on – heart pumping, lungs strained and thigh muscles aching from the effort required to move swiftly up the steep gradient.

Above, he could see the burst of light from the main courtyard; while music and applause floated sporadically down on the still air. The fashion show was in full swing.

At last he reached the rear of the buildings that formed the very far end of the second courtyard. It took a few minutes to find the gap and, as he searched Bond was conscious of the height at which he now stood above the town. Far away fireworks still lit up the night in great starbursts of colour, shooting comets of blue, gold and red against the clear sky. Squeezing through the gap, he hoped that the bulk of the garrison would be away, down in the town celebrating with the locals on this feast of feasts.

At last Bond stood inside the dimly lit courtyard. Already his eyes were adjusted to the darkness, and he easily took in the simple layout. The large gateway was to his left, with a row of six heavy military trucks standing in line to its right. Facing the gates in single file and closed up, front to rear, were four armoured Creusot-Loire VAB, *transports de troupes*, as though in a readiness position. Few lights came from the barrack blocks which made up three sides of the yard. But Bond had few doubts that the *transport de troupe* crews would be in duty rooms near by.

Keeping to the shadow of the walls, he moved quickly around two sides of the square, to bring himself close to the final dividing wall which backed on to the main palace. He found the archway, with its passage and, stepping into it, he was able to see up the wide tunnel, the darkness giving way to a picture of colour and activity.

If his memory was correct, a small doorway lay to the right of the tunnel. This would take him up a short flight of steps and out on to the gallery in front of the Royal Chapel. He was amazed at the lack of security so far, and could only suppose that Murik had his men posted around the main courtyard or still in the town searching for him. Suddenly, from the shadows, stepped a gendarme, holding up a white-gloved hand and murmuring, '*Monsieur, c'est privé. Avez-vous un billet?*'

'*Ah, le billet; oui.*' Bond's hand went to his pocket, then swung upwards, catching the policeman neatly on the side of the jaw. The man reeled against the wall, a look of surprise in his already glazing eyes, before collapsing in a small heap.

It took a further minute for Bond to remove the officer's pistol, throwing it into the darkness of the tunnel, then to find, and use, the handcuffs, and, finally, gag the man with his own tie. As he left, Bond patted the gendarme's head. '*Bon soir*,' he whispered, '*Dormez bien*.'

Within seconds he found the doorway and the short flight of steps leading to the gallery. It was not until he reached the elegantly arched passage that the full realisation of his mission's urgency penetrated Bond's consciousness. So far, he had pushed himself on, thinking only of speed and access. Now the lethal nature of matters hit him hard. He was there to save a life and deal with the shadowy Franco — terrorist organiser and unscrupulous killer.

The gallery was lined with people who had obviously paid well for the privilege of viewing the fashion show from this vantage point — even though it allowed standing room only. People stood at the high arched windows of the Throne Hall to his left and at those of the former royal apartments on the right of the courtyard. Across the yard, the King's Gallery was also crowded; and below, in the great yard itself, the show was in full swing. The main entrance, below the King's Gallery, led to a scaffold of carpeted steps, arranged to accommodate a small orchestra. A similarly carpeted cat-walk stretched out from directly below where Bond stood, probably starting at the edge of the cloister in front of the Queen's chapel. It ran the length of the courtyard, to end only a short distance from the orchestra, and was flanked by tiered scaffolding rising in wide steps on either side, to give the best paying customers a good close view — each step being arranged with those small gilt chairs so beloved by the organisers of major fashion shows the world over.

Murik's organisation had certainly drawn a full house, all well-heeled and immaculately dressed. Bond caught sight of Murik himself on the first step to the left of the cat-walk, sitting, resplendent in a white dinner jacket and maroon bow tie. Next to him was Mary-Jane Mashkin, swathed in white silk, a necklace sparkling at her throat.

The setting for the Roussillon show was undoubtedly magnificent: brilliantly lit by huge arc lights, and the ancient arches and cobbles glowed soft and warm in tones of grey and red, sandstone and terracotta. The place was almost tangibly steeped in the history of eight hundred years.

The fashion show which Bond was now watching had an ambience that did not match others Bond had attended. It was a minute or so before he realised that the difference lay in the music. Looking closer, he saw that the musicians comprised a consort, a kind of chamber ensemble, using copies of early, probably fifteenth- or sixteenth-century instruments. James Bond knew little about old instruments, having been a devotee of popular music during his schooldays; yet, as he looked, the shapes and sounds began to take on names, slipping into his mind from long-forgotten lessons. He recognised instruments such as the lute, the viol, the cittern, an early flute, pipes and the tambour. The noise they produced was pleasing enough: simple, dance-like, romantic, with strong texture and melody.

Bond did not have to look further than the cat-walk to understand the choice of music for this show. There were six models: three gorgeous black girls and a trio of equally delicious white ones, following each other on to and off the cat-walk with amazing speed and precision. As he looked down, Bond saw Lavender just prancing off as another girl reached the far end of the cat-walk, and yet another was stepping on, to take Lavender's place. The music was provided to match the dress designs. This year's Roussillon collection had undoubtedly been created to reflect medieval costume and patterns.

The materials were silks, brocades, chiffons and cords:

the designs ranging from long-waisted dresses, with wide drooping sleeves; to elaborate costumes incorporating trains and surcoats. There was also a monastic look, with heavy circular collars, wimples and cowls; and off-beat little suits, made up of tunic and tight hose, with long decorated pallia which fell to the ground from the neck, or trailed behind the wearer. The colours were dazzling, the varied cuts and shapes enchanting, as they flared, rustled and floated around the models. Bond reflected that these clothes were, like so many collections of *haute couture*, the stuff that dreams were made of, rather than the clothing of everyday life.

Lavender reappeared, whirling to a slow dance, clad in a loose gold creation of multi-layered chiffon, with a short embroidered surcoat dropping ecclesiastically in front and behind. Bond had to use a surge of will-power to drag himself from his reverie: before the sights and sounds below took control and plunged him into a kind of hypnotic trance. It must be well after eleven thirty by now. Somewhere, above or below him, Franco was waiting with a pellet of death, which he intended to use before the fashion show had ended.

Bond's eyes moved carefully over the crowds, up to the roofs, and any other possible vantage point for a marksman. There seemed to be no place for a man to hide. Unless . . . the answer came to him, and he glanced upwards, towards the gallery ceiling. Directly behind him lay the Royal Chapel. Above that, the keep rose, topped with the small bell-tower. Above the keep, he knew, there was a loft that had once served as the ringing chamber and store room. The ringing chamber had at least three unglazed windows, or openings. All these looked straight down into the courtyard.

The door to the keep was set into the wall, to the right of the Royal Chapel door, not more than a dozen paces from where he stood. Behind that, a tight stone staircase coiled upwards to various landings in the keep; and finally to the ringing chamber itself.

Bond whirled around, striding towards the Norman arched door, with its long iron hinge-plates and great ring latch. He tried the ring and it moved smoothly, soundless and well oiled. Gently he pulled the door open and stepped through. He was aware of a smell in the darkness – not mustiness, but the scent of oil mixed with an after-shave lotion, possibly Yves Saint Laurent. The stone spiral of stairs was narrow and slippery from hundreds of years' usage. Bond started to climb as quietly and quickly as he dared in the darkness. His thigh muscles felt weak now, after the exertions of the last half hour or so; but he plodded on silently, cheered by occasional shafts of light at the wider turns in the spiral and on the landings.

Three times he stopped to control his breathing. The last thing he could afford was to reveal his presence by any noise. Even through the thick walls, the sounds from the courtyard floated upwards. If the ringing chamber was indeed Franco's hideout, the killer would have to be invested with an extra sense to detect him, unless Bond made some unnecessary sound.

As he neared the top of the climb, Bond felt the sweat trickling from his hairline and down the insides of his arms. Slowly he took out the Browning and slipped off the safety catch.

Holding his breath, Bond reached the topmost steps, his head just below the aged wooden-planked floor of the chamber. There were five more steps to negotiate to bring his feet level with the floor. Putting all his weight on the right foot, Bond slowly lifted his body so that his eyes came just above floor level.

Franco was at right angles to him, lying in the classic prone position of a marksman. The killer's concentration seemed to be centred completely on the scene below, his eyes close to a sniperscope fitted on top of the powerful Anschütz ·22 air rifle. The butt was tucked against his cheek and pressed hard into his shoulder. Franco's finger was on the trigger, ready to fire. Bond could not afford to miss if he fired the Browning. And anyway the rifle could still go off on a reflex action. If Bond jumped the man, he might only precipitate the marksman's deadly shot.

There was no time for further appraisal of the situation. Bond lept up the remaining steps, calling out softly but sharply, 'Franco! Don't shoot!'

The marksman's head swivelled round as Bond heard the dull plop from the air rifle, a sound inaudible to anyone but Franco and Bond, high in the keep. In the same second, on an impulse, Bond flung himself on to the prone figure of Franco, landing with a bone-shattering crash across the marksman's shoulders. In a flash, lying spread-eagled across the terrorist's shoulders, James Bond took in the scene below, looking from Franco's viewpoint down through the rough square opening.

Lavender Peacock was alone in the centre of the cat-walk, pirouetting in magnificent scarlet which drooped in long folds, like a crimson waterfall, around her body. Her arms were outstretched, her feet moving to a haunting jig played by the consort. Slightly to her left and behind her, Anton Murik sat partly turned in his chair, frozen for a moment, looking towards Mary-Jane Mashkin who had half-risen, one hand at her throat, the other like a claw to her chest. Almost exactly in line with Lavender, she was doubling forward, and, in what seemed like slow motion, she tee-tered, hovered, and then pitched headlong among the chairs.

Underneath Bond, Franco was cursing and struggling to free himself from 007's grip on the back of his neck, '*Mierda*! I hit the wrong one. You'll . . .' His voice evaporated in a hiss of air as he let his muscles relax, then arched his back and jerked his legs to dislodge his assailant. Bond was taken by surprise and thrown off, his shoulder thudding against the wall on the far side of the chamber. Franco was on his feet in a second, his hand dropping to his hip and coming away with a small revolver. Bond, winded from the throw, levered himself from the wall and kicked wildly at the terrorist's hand, loosening his hold on the gun. It was enough to send Franco weaving and ducking down the narrow spiral stairs.

The staircase would be a deathtrap for either of them, and no place for a shooting match. Taking air in through his mouth, Bond regained his lost balance and started after the terrorist, glancing quickly down into the courtyard as he went. The music had stopped, and a small huddle of people were gathered around where he had seen Mary-Jane fall. He could see Lavender, who had come off the cat-walk, and one of Murik's guard, who stood very close to her. Caber was also there, with Murik apparently shouting orders to him. From the main entrance, two white-clad figures came running with a stretcher.

Bond waited at the top of the stairs until he was certain Franco had passed the first landing. Then he began the difficult descent, the Browning held in front of him, ready to fire back, even if one of Franco's bullets caught him in the confined space.

But Franco was being just as careful. He had a head start. Bond could hear him, cautiously going down, pausing at each landing, then quickly negotiating the next spiral.

At last Bond heard the door close below, and took the last section of stairs in a dangerous rush, grabbing at the door, pushing the Browning out of sight and stepping out into the gallery, where a great many people were craning over, or leaving to get down into the courtyard. Franco was just ahead, making for the small flight of steps that would bring him into the archway through which Bond had made his entrance into the Palace. Taking little notice of people around him, Bond went after his quarry. By the time he reached the archway, there was no one to be seen, except the huddled figure of the gendarme, still out cold.

At the far side of the archway, the noise came only from behind. Nothing in front, from the rear courtyard: just silence and the shapes of the heavy trucks lined up along the wall near the gate to his far right.

Franco was there though. Bond could almost smell him, lurking in the shadows, or behind the line of *transports de troupes*, maybe taking aim at this very moment. The thought quickly sent Bond into the shadow of the wall to his right. Now he must out-think Franco. This man was clever, a survivor, a terrorist who, in his career, had passed through whole dragnets. Did he know of the narrow gap between the buildings on the far side, through which Bond had come? Or did he have another way? Would he wait among the shadows or by the vehicles, sweating it out, knowing that only Murik and his present assailant were aware of his presence?

Slowly, Bond began to crab his way along the wall, edging to the right, deciding that Franco would most likely have made for the cover of the vehicles. Eventually the man would have to run a long way, for his contract had gone awry in the most deadly manner. A gelatine capsule, Bond thought. That had been the missile, which reached a low velocity as it hit, and had some thin coating which burst on impact, leaving little or no mark but injecting something – probably untraceable – into the victim's bloodstream. It would have to be very fast-acting, for Mary-Jane had collapsed within seconds.

It had been meant for Lavender. Bond had no doubt about that. Now Franco would know that the full might of Murik's private forces would be out to hunt him down, just as they were already in full cry after Bond.

He was getting close to the first truck. If Franco was hidden there he would certainly keep his nerve, holding back a natural desire to be rid of his pursuer by chancing a shot which could only call attention to his position.

But Bond had misread the hunted man. Maybe Franco had been rattled by what had occurred in the ringing chamber. The shot came directly from beside the rearmost *transport de troupes*, a single round, passing like an angry hornet, almost clipping Bond's ear.

Dropping to the ground, Bond rolled towards the trucks parked against the wall, bunching himself up to present only the smallest target and coming to a stop beside the great, heavy rear offside wheel of the first truck. He had the Browning up, held in the two-handed grip, pointing towards the flash from the shot.

Once more Bond set himself the task of out-thinking his enemy. Franco would have moved after firing, just as Bond rolled towards the truck, which was only a few yards from the rear armoured *transport de troupes*.

What would he – Bond – do in that situation? The trucks were at right angles to the little line of armoured troop carriers facing the gate. Bond thought he would have moved down to the second *transport*, protected by its armour, and then skipped across the gap between the line of *transports de troupes* and the truck behind which Bond was sheltering. If he was right Franco should at this moment be coming around this very truck and trying to take Bond from the rear.

Moving on tiptoe, crouched low, Bond silently crossed the few yards' gap between his truck and the rear *transport de troupes*. Whirling around, he dropped on to one knee and waited for Franco's figure to emerge from the cover which he had just relinquished.

This time, his thinking was right. Bond heard nothing but saw the shape of the hunted man, pressed hard against the bonnet of the big truck, as he carefully felt his way around it, hoping to come upon his opponent from behind.

Bond remained like a statue, the Browning an extension of his arms, held in a vice with both hands, and pointing directly towards the shadow that was Franco.

Still Franco's reputation held up. Bond was staking his life on his own stillness, yet the terrorist detected something. With a sudden move, the man dived to the ground, firing twice as he did so, the bullets screeching off the armour plating of the *transport de troupes*.

Bond held his ground. Franco's shots had gone wide, and the target remained in line with the Browning's barrel. Bond fired with steady care: two pairs of shots in quick succession, a count of three between the pairs.

There was no cry or moan. Franco simply reared up like an animal, the head and trunk of his body arching into a bow from the ground then bending right back as the force of all four shots slewed him in a complete circle, then pushed him back along the ground as though wrenched by an invisible wire: arms, legs and what was left of his head flailing and flopping as a child's doll will bounce when dragged along the floor.

Bond could smell the death — in his head rather than nostrils. Then he became aware of lights coming on, running feet, shouts and activity. He moved, faster and even more silently than before, sprinting towards the minute gap between the far buildings, and so down the sandy track to the Caserne Maréchal Joffre. When he reached the Caserne, Bond slowed down. He was breathing hard. Never run away from an incident, they taught you — just as you should never run after lighting an explosive fuse. Always walk with purpose, as though it was your right to be where you were.

He saw nobody on the way back to the private entrance shown him by the French captain; stepping with a smile into the Rue Waldeck Rousseau. He was home and dry: the street was empty.

Bond had walked four paces when the piercing whistle came from near by. For a second he thought it was a police whistle. Then he recognised the human sound: the whistle of a man who has been brought up in the country, the kind of noise one makes to call in hounds, or dogs, or other beasts. Now it brought in the Mercedes, bearing down on him, lights blazing. A pair of steel-like bands took him from the rear, pinioning his arms to his sides and pressing so that pain shot down to his hands and fingers. The Browning dropped to the pavement.

'I suppose ye got Franco, then. But it'll do ye nae bluddy guid for yersel, Bond,' Caber whispered in his ear. 'The Laird's mor'n a mite upset – and wi' good reason. Ocht man, he's longing tae set his eyes on ye. Just longing for it. I doubt he has some grand plans for ye.'

The car came alongside and Caber propelled Bond into the back seat as soon as the door was opened.

- 18 -

A WATCHED PLOT

M SAT GREY-FACED, listening to the tape for the sixth time. 'It's him all right.' He looked up and Bill Tanner nodded in agreement. M turned to the Duty Officer. 'And the number?' he asked.

The telephone equipment at the Regent's Park building was the most sophisticated in the country. Not only were all incoming calls monitored and taped, but a selective print-out was immediately available. The print-out included both the words spoken and the number from which the call had been dialled.

The Duty Officer shifted in his chair. 'It's French. We're sure of that because of the code.' He was a young man, in his first year of duty following the four-year training period. He sighed. 'As to its origin ... well ...'

'Well?' M's eyes flashed angrily.

'You know what it's like, sir. They're co-operating, of course, but at this time of night ...'

'I know,' Bill Tanner cut in. 'It *is* tricky, sir. But I'll go off, with your permission, and try to ginger them up.'

'You do that, Tanner.' M's grey eyes showed no emotion. 'At least we're certain it was France?'

The Duty Officer nodded.

'Right.' M picked up his red telephone. 'Then it's time Duggan's people did something positive. Time for them to go into that damned castle – on suspicion of dirty work, or however they want to put it. It's safe enough now.'

'I shoulda finished yon man off long ago, Laird.' Caber spoke softly. Everyone around the Laird of Murcaldy had become quiet, almost reverent. A death in the family, Bond thought grimly. Would it have been like this if the real target had been hit?

Anton Murik looked shaken – if anything a shade shrunken in height – as he waved Caber away. 'I think not.' He looked hard at the huge Scot. 'You did as you were bidden: brought him back alive. A quick breaking of the neck or an accurate bullet's really too good for him now, Caber. When the time comes . . .' He gave a thin smile.

They were in a comfortable room, fitted simply with what Bond considered to be Scandinavian furniture – stripped pine desk, table and chairs. There was only one padded and comfortable swivel chair, which was Murik's own preserve.

This time they had taken no chances. In the car, Bond had been immediately handcuffed. Now he sat shackled by wrists and ankles. He knew they were inside the Aldan Aerospace offices at the airport, but there were no windows to this room, which Murik had described as 'Spartan, but suitable for our needs'. He added that they had at least one very secure room in the place, 'from which the great Houdini himself could not escape'.

The Laird dismissed Caber and sat, looking at Bond, for a long time. Then he passed a hand over his forehead wearily. 'You must forgive me, Mr Bond. I have been at the hospital, and with the police for some time. Everybody has been most kind.'

'The Franco business?' Bond asked.

'In a way.' Murik gave a bitter little laugh and repeated, 'In a way. You did it then, Bond. Finished off Franco.'

'There was no option. Even though you had cancelled my contract.'

'Yes.' The Laird gave a small sigh, almost of regret. 'Unhappily you have not only interfered a little early, but caused me great grief. Franco's death is, I gather, being treated simply as some gangland vendetta. They have yet to identify him.' He sighed again. 'The common flatworm,' he muttered. '*Leptoplana tremellaris*. It seems strange that my dear Mary-Jane has perished at the hands of the common flatworm. We've spent many years together, Mr Bond. Now you have been the cause of her death.'

Bond asked coolly if Murik would have mourned greatly had the death been that of his intended victim.

'Not in the least,' Murik flared. 'She is a useless little strumpet. Unnecessary. Mary-Jane was a brilliant scientist . . .' He lapsed into silence, as though the death of his mistress and its repercussions had only just made themselves felt. Then he repeated, 'The common flatworm.'

Bond pressed home on the man's emotional disadvantage, asking what he meant by the common flatworm.

'Killed her.' The Laird became matter-of-fact now. 'There's no getting away from it, Franco was a clever devil: an organiser of ingenuity and a killer of even greater skill. He explained it to me, Bond, after I had arranged things.'

Franco, it appeared, had access to scientific work on untraceable poisons. In great detail, as if talking to himself, Murik explained. 'For years we've known that a poison produced by the epidermal skin glands of the flatworm brings about cardiac arrest in animals. Very quick. A heart attack. It is only in the last year that an extract removed from the flatworm's skin has been made strong enough to bring about the same reaction in humans. A very small amount will bring on a perfectly natural heart attack in a matter of minutes, or seconds.'

Franco had arranged with his tame scientists to prepare a delivery system for the poison: a gelatine capsule of just the right thickness, fired over a specific distance, through a specific weapon, in this case the powerful Anschütz ·22 air rifle. The passage of the projectile, both through the barrel and, at its maximum velocity during its trajectory, would strip some of the gelatine away, leaving only a very thin layer. 'In fact it overshot the calculated distance.' For the first time Murik smiled. 'Yet still worked. A tiny sting — hardly felt by the recipient — but strong enough to just break the skin and inject the poison into the wound. Enough to produce a heart attack – and death.'

Bond asked if the authorities suspected anything. No, not a thing Murik told him. As far as everyone was concerned, Mary-Jane Mashkin had suffered cardiac arrest. 'I have the certificate.' He patted his pocket. 'We shall bury her when Meltdown is complete.' As he said it, the Laird's mood changed, as though he had become his old self again. 'She was a soldier, killed in action for my cause. It would be wrong to mourn. Now, there are more important things to be done. Really, Mr Bond, it is a pity we cannot work together. I have to admit some admiration for you. The play-acting after our arrival at Perpignan airport was worthy of a professional. But, then, it appears that you are a professional of some kind, aren't you?'

'If you say so.' Bond was tight-lipped. It must now be well after one in the morning. Already two attempts to beat Anton Murik had failed. Third time lucky – if there was to be a third time; for the sands were trickling out fast. Less than twelve hours to go before the sinister Laird's Meltdown project went into action, with Warlock leading the way.

Murik leaned forward with one of his little pecking movements. Strange, Bond thought, how the man could look so distinguished, with that mane of white hair, yet give the impression of being a bulldog and a bird at one and the same time.

'The man whose face you smashed up in the telephone booth, Mr Bond.' Murik smiled again. 'He heard the words you used. I can only presume that you are 007 – a code of some kind. Who is M?'

Bond shook his head. 'Haven't the foggiest.'

'Well, I have.' The Laird of Murcaldy leant further across the desk. 'In my time as a nuclear physicist, I too have signed the Official Secrets Act. I have been privy to what the novelists call the secret world. M, if I am correct, is the designation used for the person romantics like to call the head of the British Secret Service.'

'Really?' Bond raised his eyebrows. Put your mind into overdrive, he told himself; knowing that, at the very least, the London headquarters would be able to identify the general locality of his telephone call. If they had already done so, Murik and his crew would have been flushed out by now—a depressing thought. He consoled himself with the fact that M would eventually put his finger on Aldan Aerospace. Yet there was no use pretending. It was going to be a damned close run thing.

Murik was speaking again, and Bond had to pull his attention back to the little man's words. '. . . not much of a message to M, was it? I don't think we can expect too much trouble from that source.' He gave a little cough, clearing his throat. 'In any case, I am anxious to get Meltdown underway; there's no chance of stopping that chain of events now. Our late, unlamented Franco has seen to that. And my demands will go out the moment I receive information that certain nuclear power stations are in the hands of the departed Franco's fanatical, so-called terrorists.'

'Six nuclear reactions, I believe,' Bond said smoothly. He must do everything possible to ruffle the calm surface of Murik's confidence.

The bulldog face broke into a radiant smile. 'Yes. Six.' He sounded pleased, as though he had pulled off a clever trick.

Push him, thought Bond. 'Six: one in England, one here in France, one in the Federal Republic of Germany, one in East Germany and two in the United States.'

Murik spread his hands. 'Clever, James Bond. So you know the locations; just as I know you cannot have passed them on to anyone who matters.'

The wretched little man refused to be rattled. But Bond would not give up that easily. Quickly he recited the names of the nuclear plants: 'Heysham One; Saint-Laurent-des-Eaux Two; Nord Two-Two; Esenshamm; Indian Point Three, and San Onofre One.'

'Excellent. Yes, by the time we leave here, just before one o'clock local time, tomorrow afternoon – noon in England – Franco's hardboiled suicide squads will be preparing their individual assaults . . .'

'Which could go wrong.' Bond wanted to say something about Murik's statement that they were leaving, but held his tongue. Maybe the Laird would spill everything without being pressed. Leaving for where? And how would they leave?

'I very much doubt that,' Murik chuckled. 'Meltdown has been a long time in the making.'

'Good preparation or not, the security on those places just about precludes any serious terrorist activity.' The conversation had become bizarre. Like a pair of wargamers discussing moves. It had about it a distinct air of unreality.

'From within?' Murik asked with mock surprise. 'My dear Bond, you don't think something as important as this has been left to chance. Originally I provided poor Franco with a long list of possible targets. The ones we're going for were chosen because they were the easiest to infiltrate.' He slapped the pine desk with the flat of his hand. 'They were infiltrated about a year ago. We've had to be very patient. A year can seem a long time; but patience pays off. There are four of Franco's contacts working at each of the targets, four trusted people, there now, at each reactor. They all have skills, and they've proved their loyalty, worked hard, done their jobs. Over the year, each person has managed to reach a position where he or she is beyond reproach, his face is known to the security men; and each one has been most successful in smuggling in the equipment necessary for the task.'

'Weapons can sometimes backfire.' Bond tried hard not to crease his brow with the worry now nagging at him, opening an empty pit of horror within his mind.

'The weapons are only small things.' Murik's eyes again stirred into that unpleasant deep movement – the deadly molten lava, which seemed to betray a hint of madness. That he was wholly mad, in his genius, Bond did not doubt. Only a maniac would take the kind of risks this small monster was about to embark upon. 'The weapons are needed for one moment only. The men and women, all twenty-four of them, will be on duty in their various plants at the required moment. All have access to the control rooms. Weapons will be used as a last resort only – possibly as a threat. The takeover of the control rooms in all six plants should be quite bloodless. And the staff inside will be freed immediately.'

'How well do you know people like that?' Bond kept any hint of feeling out of his voice. Murik now began to look more like a slug than a bulldog, but one could not but have some awe for what was obviously such careful planning.

'I?' Murik looked up with surprise. 'I do not know them at all. Only Franco, and he acted on my instructions. Franco, as I've said, was a highly intelligent man. I taught him all the necessary things. In turn he instructed the teams. I do assure you, James Bond, that we even went through each phase with plans – plans of the plants concerned. Nothing has been left to chance. You see, the initial moves in the control rooms will be elementary precautions only. First, the remote switches will be cut: this means that no master control can scram the plants in question.'

'Scram?'

'It is a word we use. Scram means the sudden shutdown of a fission reactor. Remote control insertion of the control rods. In all but one of our target reactors there is a central master control covering several reactors. So each squad will first isolate its reactor so that it cannot be rendered safe from the master control.' His smile was as unpleasant, and nerve-twitching, as the lava look in his eyes. 'It would defeat our purpose if the squads did not have complete control over their destinies.'

Bond's muscles had gone as rigid as his tightened lips. Tension built steadily through his body. He had gone over the dozen or so possibilities which might defeat the terrorist assaults before they even had a chance to get off the ground. The facts concerning infiltration and the immediate isolation of the target reactors removed a whole range of opportunities.

'And the other thing?'

'Oh,' Murik pecked his head forward. 'The most obvious one, of course. As they separate themselves from the master control, they will also cut all communication lines to the outside world.'

'No contact at all?'

'They won't need contact. That can lead only to a dangerous lack of concentration. We cannot possibly allow any dialogue between the squads and the authorities. They have their orders; the times and details.' He gave his humourless smile once more. 'They have one, and only one, method of communication. That lies with me. It will be used most sparingly.

'Each group is equipped with a small but immensely high-powered transceiver, developed by one of my own companies. This company. It is the most important item that the teams have smuggled in; and each one is set to a particular frequency. Once they're in and completely isolated, each team will signal one code word, together with an identification. Only one person in the entire world will be able to receive those messages.' Smugly he tapped his chest. 'Myself. In turn, the groups will be the only people able to receive my message – another code word of course – to inform them to abort their mission. That instruction will be given only when my demands are met in full: and it has to be received by them within twenty-four hours of their messages that the various takeovers have been successful. If they do not receive my abort signal . . .' He gave a sad little gesture with his hands. 'If they do not receive it, they'll go ahead – on the dot – with the action. They will cut off the cooling systems to each of their reactors.'

Bond's face was set like stone, his eyes locking with those

of Anton Murik. 'And if they do that, millions of lives will be lost, large parts of the world will be rendered uninhabitable for a long time, there will be huge damage and pollution . . .'

Murik nodded like a Buddha. 'It is possible that the *whole* world will suffer despoilment, yes. Yes, Mr Bond, that is why the governments concerned – and, almost certainly, other governments too – will not allow it to happen. My demands will be met; of that I am one hundred per cent sure.'

'And how will the world know of your demands?'

'You will see, Bond; you will see. You'll have a ringside seat.' He chuckled. 'You'll be able to observe everything, from start to finish.'

'But . . .'

'And after it is all over.' He spread his hands in a gesture meant to convey an inevitability. 'Well, Franco had to go at some point. You have done that for me. You see, I could never have let Franco pass any of the ransom money on to his various terrorist organisations, because I need to keep it myself. It is essential that I retain every penny made from this operation, in order to bring safety to the world. This is truly a case of the end justifying the means.' Murik shifted uncomfortably in his chair, adopting a slightly sad tone as he went on, 'Of course, I do feel it a little dishonourable witholding *your* small fee. After all, you did achieve success of a sort, even if not in the way I would have wished. And I have, as I say, rather taken to you, my friend. But then you have from the beginning betrayed my trust in you. And, in the circumstances, I cannot allow you to remain in possession of the facts. However, if you have any next of kin, I am prepared to make a token . . .' Murik's voice tailed away.

'So you'll kill me?'

'Something like that. I had a nice idea originally, but since Mary-Jane's death, I think you deserve a longer agony. Surely you would like an exciting end, James Bond?'

'And Lavender?'

Murik hit the table hard, with a balled fist, 'She should already be dead, instead of my Mary-Jane. But don't worry, Bond, she'll be with you – right up to the very end.' A throaty chuckle. 'Or right down to the very end.'

'You bastard.' James Bond spoke quietly, in control of his emotions. 'You've already tried to murder your ward, and you'll do it again. Your own ward . . .'

'Who has been a thorn in my side for many years.' Murik also spoke with no trace of emotion. 'Just as you have turned out to be a thorn over the past few days. My work will continue with no possible disruption, once Miss Lavender Peacock has disappeared.'

'Why?' Bond stabbed in the dark. 'Why? Because she is the rightful heir to your title, estate and money?'

Anton Murik raised his eyebrows. It was a movement which made the pugnacious face even more repellent. 'Astute,' he said, sharply, uttering the word clearly, in two distinct syllables. 'Most astute. There's no harm, I suppose, in you knowing; for there is very little to prove it. Yes, she is the rightful heir. I came to my own position by devious means, you see . . .'

'You mean the business with your grandfather? And then the doubts about your own mother being the rightful wife to your late lamented father?'

For the first time in the whole conversation, Murik looked bewildered, then angry. 'How do you know this?' His voice began to rise.

Bond, feeling he was gaining a small ascendency, took his mind back to the moment M had explained the chequered and dubious history of the Muriks. 'The business in Sicily? It's common knowledge, Laird. The graves at – where was it? – Caltanissetta? Those of your father and your mother's maid? The facts about that are well enough documented. I should've thought you'd'vę known. After all, the Lord Lyon King of Arms has been carrying out a very lengthy investigation . . .'

Murik's face twitched, then his voice returned to normal.

Even the smile came back. 'Ah, maybe. But nothing can be proved.'

'Oh, I don't know. Your own mother was your father's maid, wasn't she, Anton?' It was the first time Bond had dared use the familiarity of his Christian name.

Murik nodded. 'But I was *his* son.'

Once more, Bond stabbed in the dark: 'But you had a brother — a half-brother anyway. By your father and his true wife. A brother born at the time of the bandit episode in Sicily, when *your* mother, the maid, was already pregnant. What did he do? Come back to haunt you?'

'He came back with a wife, child, and every possible legal document,' snapped Murik.

'And died, with his wife, in an air disaster.'

Murik chuckled. 'Oh, most certainly. He was what you might call intrepid: a man of many parts. Or at least he was when he died.' A further chuckle. 'The Sicilians have faults, but they love children. The bandits kept him, trained him, made him one of their own, and then told him the truth — after making sure he had been moderately well educated. Like myself, he was good at waiting. But not so good at judging character. Of course I told him I would relinquish Murcaldy and Murik Castle to him. He believed me. A mad flyer. Such a pity. They said it was a fractured fuel line or something; I forget the details.'

'But you made certain his wife was with him.'

'How could I stop her?'

'Why didn't the child — Lavender — go along?'

Murik's eyes took on a distant look, as though he could see back into the past. 'He wanted a new aeroplane. I encouraged him to buy it. After all, he was inheriting the money. He actually flew it into the glen: only a light thing. Wanted to give it a good test the next day, show it off to his wife and the child. I was not there, of course. I had to go to Edinburgh to see the lawyers about relinquishing my title: they had to peruse the documents. The child was taken ill; with a colic, as I remember it. They said it was terrible. You know, he avoided crashing into the castle by a matter of feet. Very brave. They both died instantly. At the time, everybody said the infant had a lucky escape.'

Bond nodded. 'You had to get back quickly, so the lawyers never saw the documents?'

Murik shook his head, in mock sadness. 'No, they did not see them. Nobody's seen them. They lie safe in the castle, where nobody will find them. But they'll not be needed. Not after tomorrow. So now you know. And if you've been doing a little work on behalf of the Lord Lyon King of Arms, he's out of luck. Just as you and Lavender have run out of luck — and time.' His hand reached for a button by the telephone. 'We all need a little rest. Tomorrow will be quite a day — or today, I should say, for it is very late, almost three in the morning. I'm afraid our facilities here are cramped. You'll have to share the one secure room with my ward; but you'll find she's not been harmed. As yet. There's always tomorrow.'

Just before Caber came in to lead him away, Bond asked the final question. 'You said we would be leaving here.'

'Yes?'

'And that I'd have a ringside seat.'

'Yes?'

'Where?'

Murik pecked forward. 'Of course, you don't know. I mentioned the powerful transceivers we'll be using; well, tomorrow my company here will be conducting tests with just such equipment — on another frequency, of course. Several influential people are interested. You see, not only are they incredibly powerful but, like my nuclear reactor design, they're ultra-safe. My clever associates here have developed high-frequency transceivers which have what we call a safety-screened beam; this means their signals *cannot* be monitored. Nobody, Mr Bond, can listen in, or even detect them. We have a large aircraft,' he gave another little chuckle, 'provided, incidentally, by the United States. It is our flying testbed, and not only can it carry all the equipment we need, but also stay aloft for a little more than twenty-four hours. Extra fuel tanks. All the time we need. That's where you'll get your ringside seat.'

Caber and one of the other men arrived, took orders from the Laird and led Bond away down a series of passages. They handled him roughly, but Caber undid the shackles once they reached what he referred to as 'the secure room'.

'Ye'll no be gettin' oot o' here,' Caber sneered. Bond could not fault Caber's confidence, for the place was simply a narrow cell with no windows and only a tiny ventilation grille set well back high in the wall. The door was of eight-inch steel, with no handles on the inside, and so hung that it became part of the wall when closed. It was like being pushed into a large safe – a use the room was almost certainly put to on occasions. There were two beds and one small light, which burned perpetually behind thick glass and a mesh cover, flush with the ceiling.

Lavender had been dozing on one of the beds, but woke with a start as soon as they shoved Bond into the cell. She leaped up, then, with a little squeal, grabbed at her blanket, embarrassed by the fact that she wore only her tiny lace underwear.

All modesty seemed to disappear when she realised it was Bond. 'James!' She dropped the blanket and was in his arms. 'Oh God, they caught you. I hoped that you, at least, had got away.'

'No such luck. Not in the car; and not now . . .'

She looked up at him. 'James, you do know I had nothing to do with how they caught you – with the car, I mean?'

He nodded, allowing her to go on.

'The first thing I knew about it was when the Laird told me you had been in a driving accident. I was forbidden to have any contact with you. They threatened, and Mary-Jane . . . Did you know she was dead? She's had a heart attack.'

This time Bond stopped her talking with a kiss that developed, just as it had done on the last occasion he had been with her, saying farewell on the night of his abortive escape in the Saab.

She began to move backwards. On the bed she looked up at him. 'Oh, James. I really thought you'd get away and bring some help. Terrible things are going on . . .'

'You can say that again.' Bond smiled down at her. 'Really terrible,' he mused. 'I don't know how long I can stand it.'

The worried look on her face turned to one of delight. 'It *is* terrible, isn't it? As far as I can see there's only one answer.' She began to remove what little she was wearing.

An hour or so later, they lay together on the bed, side by side, their faces turned towards each other. 'James,' she whispered. 'If we ever get out of this . . . ?'

He stopped her again, with a kiss. She was a tough young girl, under that soft frilly exterior, and Bond felt it only right that she should know the truth. 'Listen, Dilly,' he began, and then with tact – missing out only the tiny details – told her the real facts of Mary-Jane Mashkin's heart attack, and how it had been meant for her. He also briefly outlined Murik's plans for the morning.

She lay silent for a time. Speaking at last with a voice that was calm and almost resigned, she said, 'Then it looks as if we've had it. Darling James, thank you. You saved my life; but I wonder if it would have been better to go then. At the Palace. Suddenly, Anton's a reptile, and I should imagine he has something very very nasty planned for us.'

Bond put a finger to her lips. 'It hasn't happened yet.' He tried to make light of things, saying that there was still time for help to arrive, that even he could find some way out. 'Anyway, Dilly, I've never been thrown out of an aeroplane before. Could be exciting. Like being here with you: at least we'll be together.'

She bit her lip and nodded bravely, then pulled his head down to hers so that they were again united by passion. To Bond it felt as though they had both escaped from time and trouble and were floating with increasing joy towards a whirlpool of earthly delights.

Later, they fell asleep, entwined on the small bed.

It was almost six in the morning before Bill Tanner returned to M's office with the bad news that, because of it being the middle of the night, they had not yet received a positive trace on the number from which James Bond had dialled.

'They'll have it for you before nine o'clock,' he said wearily.

M looked washed out, his skin like parchment and deep creases of worry around discoloured eyes. 'Nobody seems to know the meaning of urgency any more,' he growled. Deep inside, M had a nasty feeling that they were close to something terrible; even catastrophic. Logic told him that Anton Murik's disappearance, Bond's telephone call, and the fact of the F.B.I. having no trace on Franco, were all linked. Maybe they now stood on the edge of a precipice, constructed during all those meetings between the international terrorist and the former nuclear physicist.

'Duggan's the same,' he snorted. 'Got shirty with me when I reversed my views about him going into Murik Castle. But the issue's been forced now. They had to get some magistrate out of bed to sign the search warrant. Anyway, they've all buzzed off like a swarm of daft bees – Duggan, his men, and a load of Special Branch to lead the way.' He gave a sigh. 'Even so, they won't be able to do anything much before nine either.'

Bill Tanner, worried as he was, tried to make light of it, 'Should've sent a gunboat in the first place, sir.'

M grunted. 'Send some coffee, that's more like it. Get some coffee up now, Chief-of-Staff. Black, hot, sweet and strong. I've got a feeling it's going to be a long hard day.'

19

ULTIMATUM

THEY CAME ARMED, and in strength. Caber and three of the hoods; Caber carrying an automatic pistol, two of the hoods with trays.

'It's a special breakfast the Laird's been pleased to order for ye. He said ye'd understand.' Caber motioned for the trays to be set down, and Bond vividly recalled his conversation with Murik just after their arrival at Perpignan the previous day: about the condemned man eating a hearty breakfast.

The hoods disappeared and Caber backed into the doorway. 'And ye'll no try coming for us wi' them knives and forks when we collect the trays. All of us have got the wee shooters. Naebody's gonna get away this time.'

One of the hoods brayed with laughter from behind him: 'There's only the one way they'll be gettin' oot, eh Caber?'

'Shut yer gob, cretin.' Caber stepped back, swinging the door. Before he could close it, Bond called, 'What about washing and things?'

'Och aye.' Caber pressed something outside the door before slamming it. The great panel of metal thumped home and at the same time a small section of the wall slid back to reveal a little alcove containing the bare necessities – a washbasin, towels and lavatory. Bond examined it, but the alcove was as solid as the rest of the cell. 'I can't shave,' he said, trying to sound bright, 'but at least we'll both be clean.'

The trays contained steaming plates of bacon, eggs, sausages, two large silver pots of coffee, plenty of toast, butter and marmalade—laid out under ornate covers on the Laird of Murcaldy's personal china. Even the glass butter dishes were engraved. 'Butter in a lordly dish,' said Bond, realising that the Biblical quote had sinister undertones – murder of some kind, he seemed to remember: an Old Testament character smiting someone with a tent peg after bringing in his butter. Caber came with guns, not tent pegs.

Lavender pushed her tray away. 'It's no good, James. I can't eat it. I couldn't swallow.'

Bond went over, catching her by the shoulders. 'Dilly, where's your faith, girl? We'll find a way out – *I'll* find a way out: cling on to that. Murik'll be only too happy if you're frightened and show your fear. You have to fight with strength. Come on.' He had no idea how they could possibly escape, or even stop the events which were now, he knew, rolling inevitably towards what could be a holocaust of tragic and catastrophic proportions. Yet all Bond's experience told him Murik would only be beaten by some show of character.

Lavender swallowed and took in a deep gulp of air. 'Okay,' she nodded.

'At least have some coffee,' Bond said, more kindly.

She gave a little shiver. 'Of course, James. I've come a long way with Anton as well. Let's try and get the bastard.'

Bond set an example, even though he too found it hard to eat. The bacon and eggs stuck in his throat, but he managed to wash it down by consuming cup after cup of coffee, taking in a lot of sugar. At least his body would be provided with something on which to feed; and extra energy was what he needed. Lavender did her best, nibbling on toast and sipping coffee. When they had finished, Bond stretched out on the bed, turning his face away while she completed her toilet and dressed.

He then got himself ready, stripping off and washing from tip to toe. Pity about not being able to shave. If they were to die, he would rather go looking his best. Negative thinking. Bond cursed himself. From now on, it was his duty to be positive and alert; aware of everything going on; ready to take advantage of the smallest chink that showed in Murik's plan or actions.

There was no way of telling the time, but Bond guessed they had been allowed to sleep late. It must now be after midday, French time. The deadline here was one in the afternoon — noon in England. They would not have to wait much longer.

Five minutes later Caber and the other men reappeared. The trays were swiftly removed, and the two prisoners were ordered from the cell at gunpoint. They were taken through silent passages, narrow corridors and finally up steps which led to a metal fire door — Caber striding ahead, opening the door and waving them through.

Bond heard Lavender gasp behind him. They stood in the hangar he had seen on their arrival — a vast structure into which you could have easily fitted a block of houses: huge and echoing, smelling of oil and rubber, its temperature cool from the fans high up among the girders. The most impressive sight, though, was the aircraft standing in the centre, its tail pointing towards the towering roller doors and a yellow tractor already hooked to the nose.

Bond recognised it at once. He also wondered at the sheer size of the aerial monster. It was the massive Lockheed-Georgia C-14 — the Starlifter: the great American strategic transport aircraft with a wing span of over forty-eight metres and a length of over forty-four metres, towering to a height of nearly forty feet.

Even the hangar seemed dwarfed by this magnificent brute, decked out in standard United States camouflage, but with the added blue, white, red and yellow insignia of the French Armée de l'Air. Towards the rear of the wide fuselage the words Aldan Aerospace had been added. Below, Bond could see the outline of the huge rear ramp which could be hydraulically lowered, even in flight, for loading or dropping men and materials — tanks, vehicles of all kinds: even helicopters.

Murik could get everything he needed into this beast — from technicians to all the electronic equipment he needed for his shielded radio beams. Starlifter was a good name for the aeroplane, Bond thought, saying the word aloud.

'Yes, Mr Bond, the Starlifter.' Murik stood at his elbow, dressed casually in jacket and slacks. 'A good name, I think. Specially modified, of course. You will be interested . . . It's time to go aboard.'

From the front of the hangar came the sound of the roller doors starting to move. Caber prodded Bond with his pistol, and they began to climb the steps up to the forward doorway, low in the fuselage behind the flight deck.

Murik led the way, and Bond caught sight of the crew through the flight deck window, going through the pre-takeoff check. Two of Murik's men remained at the foot of the steps, while another couple who had been standing near by followed behind Bond, Lavender and Caber.

Inside, the fuselage had obviously been altered to Murik's own specifications. The doorway took them into a brightly decorated canteen with a bar, small round tables and seating capacity for a dozen people. A deep pile carpet lay under their feet and Bond, looking forward, could see two men already at work in a galley.

'I'm afraid you'll not be eating here, with the rest of us,' said Murik, looking from Bond to Lavender. 'That is one pleasure I shall, reluctantly, have to forgo. What will happen in the next hours needs great concentration and timing, so we cannot have you roaming around the aircraft. However, I shall see you do not go hungry or thirsty.' He pointed towards the sliding hatchway leading to the rear of the fuselage. 'I should be grateful if you would take care when passing through the next section. It contains the intestines of my electronic labours, and is, perhaps, the most important part of the whole project.'

On the far side of this hatchway, the fuselage seemed to narrow and the carpet disappeared. The section ran back down the fuselage for about forty feet, its sides crammed from deck to the upper bulkheads with banks of electronic equipment housed in metal units and high cabinets. Towards the centre there was a recess on either side, with two men in clean white coveralls sitting in each, at complex control consoles. As Murik's party passed Bond asked loudly if they could get Beethoven's Fifth. He was rewarded with a jab from Caber, and a filthy look shot at him by Murik.

At the end of this electronic cave there was another sliding hatchway, which was, to Bond's experienced eye, bullet and fireproof. He judged they had covered just over half the length of the aircraft. Murik paused, his hand on the sliding latch. 'My personal preserve,' he announced, tugging the door to one side. They stepped into a circular area lit by shaded lights, giving off a restful greenish glow. 'The nerve centre of my operation.' Murik gave a smug look around him as the door closed with an automatic hiss. 'This is where I shall control Meltdown.'

Two small oval windows, one each side, had their blinds down to keep out any extraneous light. On either side of the door, facing forward, was a pair of wide curved desks, each backed by another complicated array of electronic wizardry.

Three body-moulded swivel seats were bolted to the deck in front of each of the desk consoles and behind them four seats were ranged, as though for spectators. Leading aft, towards the tail of the Starlifter, another hatchway was outlined in scarlet. In large letters on this door a legend had been stencilled: DO NOT ENTER IF RED LIGHT IS ON. Near this exit yet another, smaller passage was visible to the right. Murik gestured towards it. 'The usual offices, as the estate agents say,' he said smiling. 'We have everything on board for a pleasant day trip over the sea. Now, if you'll just take your seats . . .'

Bond felt Caber's arms gripping him, and at the same time he saw the two other men close in on Lavender.

'You will sit next to me,' said Murik, turning to Bond. 'On my left, I think.'

Caber manhandled Bond into one of the chairs in front of the console on the right of the door—facing forwards—fastening a normal seat belt around his stomach.

'We have made certain modifications to the safety harnesses for you and my ward.' Murik slid into the seat to Bond's right, and as he did so his jacket rode back slightly, revealing a holster behind his hip and the curved butt of a small deadly Colt Python: the four-inch model. Bond could have identified that weapon anywhere. Well, it was something – within reach anyway.

Seconds later, Bond's hopes of the weapon being within reach were dashed.

'Put yer arms behind yer back, Bond,' Caber hissed. He saw a short webbing strap in Caber's paw, then felt his hands being pressed together and the strap encircling his wrists tightly as the big Scot pulled it secure. Then, holding him firmly in the seat, Caber began to fit what Murik called the modified safety harness. Two further webbing belts, anchored to the underside of the seat, were now crossed over Bond's chest and shoulders and pulled hard. He felt them being adjusted and locked somewhere at the back and underneath the seat, holding him immobile.

Murik had clipped on a seat belt, and was already adjusting the console in front of them, his hands moving with professional precision as pin-lights and visual units started to glow. Rising like a snake's head from the centre of the desk was an adjustable microphone, a large 'Speak' button set into a protective box directly in front of it.

Bond studied the row of digital clocks, each marked with a time zone, covering all six locations of the targets. British time showed at ten minutes to noon.

He glanced over to the other console, where Lavender had been fastened in exactly the same way as himself between two of Murik's men, who were now concentrating on the equipment facing them. These, Bond realised, were not just heavies, but trained technicians. At that moment he felt the deck beneath his feet tremble. The yellow tractor was moving, giving the aircraft a push-back from the hangar.

Murik looked up. 'I promised you a ringside seat, Bond,' he said, grinning, 'and here it is. Everything.'

Bond turned to see Caber disappearing through the red-outlined hatchway to their rear. He asked where it led, and Murik gave a loud, mocking laugh. 'The exit,' he almost shouted. 'There's a ramp, you know. Everybody's seen pictures of vehicles being driven up that ramp, in the more conventional Starlifter, or parachute troops hurling themselves down it. I had thought of hurling you down it, Bond. Then a better idea came to mind.'

'You didn't say what . . . ?' Bond began, then the first of the four powerful Pratt & Whitney turbo-fans began to throb. The Starlifter was coming alive. The second started; then the third and fourth.

'No, I didn't say.' Murik glanced at the instruments in front of him. 'But all in good time.'

Caber returned and nodded to Murik, as though passing a message. 'Good,' said Murik in acknowledgment. Then, pointing to the seat on his right, he commented that Mary-Jane should have been sitting in it. 'She's here in spirit, though.' He did not smile. 'Sorry about the restraint, Bond, but I felt it necessary. My people were working on those harnesses all night, putting in the locks and releases, well out of anybody's reach under the seats.'

The engines surged, one after another, then synchron-ised and the aircraft swayed along the taxiway. A metallic click from somewhere in the roof near the main entrance signalled contact being made from the flight deck. 'Captain to all crew and passengers of Aldan Five-Six.' The voice was English, with a drawl. One is usually wrong about putting invisible figures to voices, but it immediately made Bond think of a rather slim, tall, louche-looking man with long hair, starting to thin and bald. 'Please fasten your seat belts and extinguish cigarettes. We shall be taking off shortly.'

'And it's going to be a bumpy ride,' muttered Bond.

The British-time digital clock clicked towards 11·54 as the engines settled, then rose into a blasting roar as their combined 84,000 pounds' static thrust pushed the crew and two captives back into their seats.

As the aircraft ceased bumping along the runway, tipping itself smoothly into its natural element, Murik leaned over, placing a pair of foam-padded headphones over Bond's head. 'You will hear everything; and I shall also be able to speak to you through these.' He raised his voice. 'A running commentary, like the Boat Race.' He glanced towards the time displays. British time showed two minutes before noon. 'The witching hour.' Murik's chuckle had begun to irritate Bond. 'Very soon you'll hear the terrorist squads making their reports.'

Less than five minutes before the Starlifter rose from the runway at Perpignan, events were taking their course the world over. M, having now received information regarding the location of Bond's call, had checked on all possible connections with Anton Murik. His investigation led naturally to Aldan Aerospace (France), Inc. and their headquarters at Perpignan airport.

There had been rapid telephone calls to Paris and through the various police and security networks, to Perpignan itself. It had, however, been slow work, and a van carrying members of the SDECE—the French Secret Service—together with a squad of armed police was only now tearing towards the airport.

They had received further encouraging news at the Regent's Park headquarters. A Mary-Jane Mashkin, close friend of Dr Anton Murik, had died of a heart attack in the middle of a fashion show in Perpignan; while the body of a man – originally thought to be the victim of a gangland shoot-out near the fashion show – had been identified as the much-wanted terrorist known as Franco.

'007's work, sir?' Bill Tanner was not really asking.

'Could be. Two of 'em out of it, anyway.'

'Then there's a very good chance . . .' Tanner began.

'Don't count your chickens, Chief-of-Staff. Never do that. We could still be too late, fiddling around half the night waiting for information. Time's not with us.'

On M's orders, several of his own officers were now on their way, by military aircraft from Northolt.

All too late. Just as M had predicted.

A little over sixty miles from Paris, not far from the city of Orleans, deep under the vast complex which makes up the nuclear power stations known as Saint-Laurent-des-Eaux One, Two and Three, certain people were quietly going through a well-rehearsed routine.

Two men tending the large turbine of Plant Two left their normal posts at just before twelve-fifty. A maintenance man, whose job was to keep the air conditioning system in good repair, excused himself from the duty room where he had been playing cards with three of his colleagues. The security man at the entrance leading down to the main control room some fifty feet below ground waited anxiously while the other three made their way along the pipe-lined, stark passages, picking up pieces of cached equipment as they went. At two minutes before one, French time, they met at the head of the emergency stairs near the elevator shaft and went down one flight to the gallery immediately outside the plant's control room, where they joined their companion, the security guard. It was one minute to one.

Inside the control room, the half a dozen men who watched the dials and controlled the flow of power, keeping an eye open for any unexpected fluctuation or change in the system, went about their work normally. One of them turned, shouting irritably at the security man as he opened the large main door. 'Claude, what are you doing? You know you're not allowed . . .' He stopped, seeing the automatic pistol pointing at him, and a second man with a folding stock Heckler & Koch sub-machine gun, its barrel sweeping the room.

The security man called Claude was the only one to speak: 'Hands on your heads. Stand away from all equipment. Now. Move, or you will be killed. We mean it.'

The tone of his voice convinced the six men. Flustered, they dropped clipboards and pens, clamped their hands to their heads and stepped clear of any piece of monitoring equipment. So hypnotised were they by the weapons that it is doubtful if they even saw the other two men slip past their comrades, and move quickly and unerringly to two points in the room. In a matter of seconds these two were giving the thumbs-up sign to their armed colleagues. They had cut off all links with the outside world by severing the communications cables and pulling the external control override switches. The reactor operating at Saint-Laurent-des-Eaux Two could be handled only from this room, which now had no contact with the outside world.

The man who had severed the communications link was completing the job by tearing the three telephone leads from their sockets as the gunmen ordered the six technicians to line up, facing the door.

A series of images flashed through the minds of these half dozen unfortunates – pictures of their wives and families crossing bleakly with incidents they had seen on television newsreels: hostages held in terrible conditions for long periods; hostages shot and killed as a warning to others; the drawn and haggard faces of men and women who had lived through ordeals like this. It was therefore with a sense of both great surprise and relief that they heard the gunmen tell them to leave quietly through the main door and get up the stairs.

'It would not be advisable for anyone to take panic action,' the gunman called Claude told them. 'Just report to the authorities and say that a message with certain demands will be coming through from outside within a few minutes. Any sudden move before that and we shut down the cooling system. We cause a China Syndrome. Tell them that, okay?'

The six men nodded, shakily leaving their place of work. The heavy door to the control room slammed behind them and the two gunmen clamped on the interior safety locks, watching through the reinforced glass which ran the length of the gallery as the released operators slowly filed away.

The other two men had been busy removing their most essential piece of equipment, the transceiver, from a canvas haversack. One of the men now ran out a cable and plugged it into a wall socket. The security guard, Claude, who was the squad leader, switched on the small, box-like, transceiver and watched as the red light glowed, then turned green. Pressing the transmit button he said loudly and distinctly, 'Number Three. War.'

Similar scenes to these were being enacted in five other nuclear power stations, in Europe and the United States.

James Bond heard the words clearly through the headphones:

'Number Three. War.'

'That's the French one,' Murik said, his voice interrupted by another quick message: 'Number One. War.'

'England.' Murik was ticking off the names of the plants on a clipboard lying in front of the console.

'Number Four. War.'

'Number Five. War.'

'Number Two. War.'

They came in quickly, tumbling into the earphones, as though someone was speaking within Bond's head. Then a long pause. Bond saw Murik's hand clench and unclench. He looked hard at the man who was embarked on an operation from which there could be no turning back. The wait had Murik worried, drumming his fingers on the edge of the console. Then after what seemed an eternity: 'Number Six. War.'

'All in.' Murik grabbed Bond's arm, nodding his head

excitedly.

'Now,' he said, his voice strange, almost out of control, 'now for *my* message. In a moment I shall activate the ultimatum. You see, everything is ordered, outside human control – except for the reaction of the governments concerned. Throughout Europe and the United States we have a series of hidden powerful micro-transmitters controlled by a signal from this aircraft. The transmitters will relay a translated message to every European country, and a number of Asian and Eastern countries too. The transmission is locked into the normal broadcasting frequencies of the countries concerned and will cut in on any programme already going out.' He adjusted a dial and watched a pair of needles centre themselves on a VU below it. 'You will hear the ultimatum in your own language, Mr Bond. You'll realise the seriousness of the situation, and how it is impossible for me to lose.'

Murik leaned forward, threw two switches and prepared to press a red button on the console. He added, 'By the way, you will not recognise my voice. But it *is* me, even though I sound like a woman. There is an ingenious device called in the trade, the Electronic Handkerchief. By using it, you can alter your own voice beyond recognition. I have chosen the voice of a rather seductive lady. Now, listen.'

Without warning, Bond heard the voice in his headphones; sharp and commanding at first, then calmer as it dictated a message. Slowly the full impact, and Murik's sheer ingenuity, came home to Bond, his eyes widened and he felt a sickening lurch in his stomach.

Almost an hour later M sat with members of the government, security services, and chiefs-of-staff who make up the secret crisis committee known as COBRA – in the Cabinet Office Briefing Room deep under Whitehall. They were listening again to a recording of that sudden, audacious and terrifying ultimatum. It was the seventh hearing for M, but the message still had its impact – an impact it had made on people all over Europe, the United States and many other parts of the world.

The only action M had taken was to call the French police back from Perpignan airport. But, by the time he had made contact, M discovered that they had been recalled anyway. They too had heard the message, on the radio in their van.

The voice relaying that message was a woman's. M thought of clandestine propaganda broadcasts during the Second World War, like those of Lord Haw-Haw and Tokyo Rose.

'Stop whatever you are doing. Stop now. Stop and listen. This is an emergency broadcast of extreme urgency to every man, woman and child. Stop. Stand still and listen,' the voice clipped out, sharp and commanding. Then it continued, calm and deliberate. 'This is a message of great urgency. It concerns everyone, but it is mainly directed at the governments of Britain, France, the Federal Republic of Germany, the German Democratic Republic and the United States. This message is being broadcast in all necessary languages throughout Europe and the United States, as well as to some countries not immediately affected. It will be the only message, the only set of instructions to the governments concerned.

'At exactly twelve noon British Summer Time, that is, G.M.T. plus one, today, six nuclear reactor power plants were seized by terrorist groups. These groups now occupy and hold the main control rooms of the following nuclear plants.' The voice went on to list the full names of the plants and their precise locations. The tone rising, it continued, 'I must make two things clear. The men who hold these nuclear power plants are dedicated to a point that some would call fanaticism. They will die if necessary. Second, all lines of communication have been cut between these groups and the outside world. They can make contact with one person only – myself. They are under orders to do the following: if an attempt is made to assault any one of the six power plants my men will immediately turn off the cooling system to the core of the nuclear reactor. This will cause immense heat to build up. Within a very short time there will be an explosion similar to a mild earthquake and a very large area surrounding the plant will be contaminated by radioactive material. The core of the reactor will proceed to burn its way through the earth. Eventually the core will find an exit point where further, possibly more devastating, radioactive material will be expelled. That is known, to those who have not heard of it, as the China Syndrome.

'These men are under instructions to carry out this same operation exactly twenty-four hours after I stop speaking unless certain demands are met. Let me repeat that the men who have taken over these nuclear plants will not hesitate to follow their orders to the death. If in twenty-four hours this becomes necessary the results will be catastrophic for the whole world. It will mean an end to all life in large areas; certainly an end to the growth of food, the keeping of livestock and fish, in even larger tracts of land. It is no exaggeration to say that it could well mean the end of the world as we know it. There will be no way to stop such a disaster if my demands are not met.

'These are my instructions: I require a ransom payable only in cut gem diamonds to a value of not less than fifty billion dollars, that is, five zero billion, B for Bertie, dollars to be paid in cut gem diamonds at their current rate — today's rate. These diamonds — easily obtained through the markets in London, Holland, Belgium and America — are to be placed, packed neatly in one large-sized yellow naval flotation bag. The bag is to be equipped with a normal naval or army recovery hoop. This consignment is to be dropped by aircraft at the following point.' The voice calmly went on to give the latitude and longitude, repeating it three times so that there could be no error.

'Before the diamonds are delivered, an area of fifty square miles around the dropping point is to be cleared of all shipping, and once its mission is completed the aircraft

employed is to fly well out of the zone. I shall not give the
order for the nuclear plants to be released until the diamonds have been dropped. Until I have picked them up in
safety and have been assured of the amount, and its lack of
contamination. I have experts to hand, and this operation
will take me approximately two hours from the moment of
dropping. Thus the governments concerned have in reality
around twenty-two hours to comply with my demands. If
the ransom is *not* dropped; if I do *not* pick it up, and get it
away in time, without any action being taken against me, no
word of command will go out, and those who control the six
nuclear power stations will carry out their threat.

'I stress that this is no hoax. This broadcast is my ultimatum. There will be absolutely no other contact. I repeat
that any attempt to communicate with those holding the
plants can only result in tragedy. You have exactly twenty-
two hours. Message ends.'

The Prime Minister, who had been brought back to
London from an engagement in Hampshire – the car being
driven at breakneck speed with a police escort – was chair-
ing the meeting.

'I have been in touch with the President of the United States and the heads of all other governments concerned.' The Prime Minister looked worried; but the
natural poise was still there. 'We are all agreed that, no
matter how difficult, this is one terrorist action in which we
have no choice. We are being asked for a very large sum of
money, but at this moment all the threatened countries are
gathering diamonds of good quality. We have experts
working on it in London, and diamonds are being flown by
the fastest possible methods to Paris, where a French military aircraft is standing by. A co-ordination unit is being set
up there to ensure that there are no hitches, and to check
the quality of the stones. As you know, the dropping zone is
in the Mediterranean and at the moment we are scheduling
a drop to be made at nine o'clock our time tomorrow. The
most difficult thing, apparently, is to clear the area of all

shipping. There are specialists working on this now. I am, personally, depressed by this action. It is the first time this country has given way to blackmail by terrorist groups, but our combined advisers seem to think there are no options open. Has anybody got any further points to contribute?'

M cleared his throat. 'Yes, on behalf of my Service, Prime Minister: we think we know who is behind this ingenious and horrific act. We also think we know where this person is: in an aircraft over the Med now. With permission of the Chiefs-of-Staff, I am going to ask for this aircraft to be shadowed by the Armée de l'Air, by fighter-borne radar, of course. I know we can take no action until the terrorists have left the nuclear power plants, but it is a lead, and we might just be able to retrieve the diamonds after the event.'

The Prime Minister nodded. 'I read your confidential report on my way here. You mention something about one of your agents?'

'I can't be sure' — M looked solemn — 'but there is a possibility that one of my people is on board the aircraft. However, I'm certain he would be the last person to ask for any special consideration.'

'That's not the point.' The Prime Minister looked down at the documents on the table. 'Do you think he might be able to do something about the situation?'

'If he can't halt this ungodly mess, Prime Minister, nobody can.'

20

WARLOCK

Bond SAT IN FRONT of the console, the facts fighting each other in his mind, as though trying to drag him into despair. He recognised the symptoms: as when, caught in the sea a man decides he can swim no farther; or feels the onset of fatigue in snow, making him lie down exhausted, to be encompassed by that strange euphoria that comes before death by freezing.

Murik had planned, using his great knowledge and privileged information. He had mustered his forces through the most elusive international terrorist in the world and set up a complicated, and admirable, tactical operation. There was little to stop him at this stage. For his own safety, Murik would have to get rid of both Bond and Lavender. Why Murik had not already killed them was almost beyond Bond's comprehension. After all, the Laird was ruthless enough to set an almost impossible deadline to his ultimatum. Bond could only presume they were still alive because Murik's vanity needed to feed on the applause of doomed witnesses.

Don't let yourself go, Bond told himself. Keep alert. Do anything; try to combat the inevitable. He began by trying to feel the flight pattern being followed by the Starlifter. It appeared to him that the aircraft, having reached its cruising height, was locking into a wide, oval holding pattern, each circuit covering around fifty miles or so. That made sense: maximum altitude, with the aircraft using the minimum fuel and the Aldan Aerospace technicians in the forward compartment going about their prescribed tests with the equipment.

He glanced towards Lavender and smiled. She returned the look with a twist of her lips, bravely struggling with the horrors that must have been going through her head.

Anton Murik rarely stopped talking. 'You see,' he said, 'we'll descend to the pick-up point some ninety minutes before the deadline runs out. By then we'll know, by our radar, when their aircraft has made its dropping run. I want to keep them on the edge of their seats until the last moment. If the flotation bag is there – as I'm certain it will be – it's a simple matter: my air crew has been well-trained in the art of picking up from the sea. All we need is a couple of low-level passes while we trail a cable with grappling hooks from the rear of the aircraft. Once we've hooked on, we just winch up the bag. A rise in the price of diamonds, eh?' He cackled at his weak joke.

'A rise'll be right,' Bond replied. 'You'll get a glut. Could mess up the market.'

'Oh, my dear Bond, why do you always underestimate me? I'm a patient man: waited too long for this. You don't think I'm going to send out a troop of Boy Scouts with the diamonds, and flood the market next week.' He gave an irritated little sigh. 'This has taken too long to set up. I don't mind waiting a little longer – a year or two. Softly, softly. The diamonds'll trickle on to various markets. I've enough money to start work on my own reactor now. I simply wish to recoup from this little hoard.' Looking straight at Bond he gave a broad smile. 'All for free. They'll fall over themselves to pay up.'

'And if they stand fast? If they *don't* come up with your precious fifty billion?' Bond realised this was unlikely.

Murik held his gaze coldly. 'Then the world will not be the world any more. Not as we know it.'

'You're really going to let the terrorist teams close down the cooling systems?'

Murik gave a dismissive wave of the hand. 'There'll be no need. The governments will pay up and look happy. They have no option.'

'But . . .' Bond was about to repeat his constant worry — that either one of the terrorist squads would lose control, or some idiot security force would try an assault. There was a further possibility: that the governments would give in to the ultimatum, yet would lack time to fulfil Warlock's requirements. But what was the use? There was no point in arguing or even trying to reason with Anton Murik.

If argument would do no good, Bond had to think of some other way. Strapped into his seat, with Lavender in the same situation, he knew chances of survival were slim: He must go on searching for further chinks in the armour. Bond might play on Murik's vanity for a time, yet in the end that could not affect the outcome. To do anything concrete he had to be free and mobile. After that, there was the problem of taking out Murik, Caber and the two heavies sitting with Lavender at the other console.

Bond gazed blankly at the vast array of electronic units before him, particularly those directly in front of Murik. Think logically, he told himself. What would he do if free and unhindered? The earphones had been plugged into a unit bright with pin-lights, VUs, a digital frequency display and half a dozen tuning dials. He had no doubt that this was the most important piece of equipment in Murik's impressive array; in particular the microphone with its transmit button. Press that button, speak, and you would be through to the squads holding the control rooms in the nuclear power plants. This was all too obvious. It was what Murik would do once he was away and safe with the diamonds, plucked from the sea. But what would he say? How would Murik defuse the situation?

Vanity. Use it. Play on the vanity. 'What happens to the terrorist squads?' Bond asked, casually.

Murik gave him a sly look. 'What d'you mean, what happens to them?'

'Well, nobody can fault you on anything, Anton.' Bond again chanced the familiarity. 'This is probably the most brilliantly organised terrorist strategy of the century. But,

when you've picked up the diamonds and got safe home –
presumably not Perpignan . . .'

Murik laughed. 'Unfortunately you won't be around to
see.'

Bond nodded, as though the point was academic. 'I
realise that. But I suppose you call off the dogs: radio, on
your shielded beam, and give them the word. They give up.
So what happens to them?'

Murik shrugged: the sly look again. 'Franco's department.' He lowered his voice. 'And Franco isn't with us any
more. Those people have dealt entirely with him. They
expect to die in action. A nuclear death from radiation. As
far as I can gather, if they're ordered to abort, they simply
come out with their hands up. Custody. Interrogation.
Trial. A trip to the bridewell.'

'They're willing to die for their various causes; so they're
equally willing to serve a term in jail?'

'And, if any of them breaks, he can only point the finger
at Franco, who is missing, believed killed in action.' He
paused, glancing up at the dials in front of him. 'I imagine
they won't be in jail for long. There will be hostages,
deaths, demands.'

Bond nodded slowly. 'And you have to call up all six
groups? Or does a blanket code cover it?'

For a second, Murik was caught off his guard. 'Same
code, but each group enumerated in case I want to leave
one active until the others get clear. That was the arrangement. But, naturally, none are going to get clear.'

'You don't think any of them'll be stupid enough to fight
their way out?'

Murik shook his head very slowly.

It was enough for Bond. He needed the defusing code
word; and, having already heard each of the groups come in
with their 'Number One . . . War; Number Four . . . War'
and the rest, it required only common sense to work out the
way in which the occupying groups could be made to stand
down. At least that was a logical step in the right direction.

He had a reasonable idea of what to do *if* he managed to get free. But how to accomplish that part of the trick?

If only he could release his arms. Every time Murik moved, Bond glimpsed the butt of the Python revolver under the jacket. If his arms were free and the right moment could be found . . . Go on thinking. Work it out. There had to be a way, and there was still time. If he managed anything it would have to be late in Murik's scheme of things. Sometime tomorrow. A message to the terrorist squads now would only alert their suspicions. From what he knew of terrorist operations, Bond was clear about the psychological factors. For the first hours, hijackers or hostage-takers were suspicious of anyone and everything. Better to wait.

As he began to wrestle with the most difficult problem of all, the earphones suddenly came to life. He recognised the pilot's voice: 'Captain to the Laird of Murcaldy, sir. Could you send someone up here for a moment?'

Murik gave a quizzical tilt of the head and beckoned Caber. 'Up to the flight deck with you. See what it's all about.'

Caber left with a nod. Murik glanced at his watch. 'Hope it's nothing too drastic. Time for some food, I think.'

Caber was gone for around ten minutes, returning with a puzzled look. He bent low and muttered in Murik's ear. The Laird's face underwent no change as his hand gently eased Caber away and he swivelled his chair towards the console opposite. 'The captain says they're picking up an intermittent trace on the flight deck radar scope, just on the periphery, to the north. They've tracked other aircraft – commercial stuff – but they appear to have two blips coming up every now and then, as though they were holding station with us. See what you can do.'

The men bent over viewers, through which they were probably looking at radar screens. 'What's your range?' Bond asked Murik coolly, knowing that if aircraft were shadowing the Starlifter, M had probably succeeded, late in the day, in getting the right answers to some difficult problems.

'On the flight deck? Around a hundred miles.' There was no smile on Murik's face now. 'In here a little more – nearer a hundred and fifty.'

'There it is,' one of Caber's men exclaimed. 'Two of them. In and out of this screen very quickly.'

Nobody spoke. Then, about five minutes later, the same man said they were there again. 'Could be shadow aircraft. Just keeping out of range. Coming in for an occasional look.'

'Well, it won't do them any good,' snapped Murik. 'They can't take action.'

'Not until you've collected your diamonds and given the stand-down order.' Give him the facts now, Bond thought. Murik would come to it soon enough.

'And then?' asked the Laird with a lopsided smirk.

Bond sighed. 'Blow you out of the sky. Force you down. Anything. Even shadow you to your lair.'

Murik looked at him gravely for a full minute, then burst out laughing, his white hair ruffling as he threw his head back. 'You think I've not taken precautions against that possibility? After all the planning, you think I've left *that* to chance?'

'A man of your capabilities? I shouldn't think so.' Bond's stomach churned. The bastard. No, of course a man like Anton Murik would not take risks. Of course he had already eliminated any possible gamble from the Melt-down operation.

'Let them have their fun.' Murik was still laughing. 'Just keep an eye on them until the time comes.' He spoke to the men at Lavender's console, then turned back to Bond. 'You think I would undertake this without having some radar-jamming gear on board? If they really are shadow aircraft, then we'll fuzz their pictures as soon as we turn in to pick up the loot.'

'And if they are? They'll already know where you're

going – for the diamonds, I mean.'

'I'll be away and out of it long before they'll dare come near. I'll hold off on the terrorist squads until, literally, the last moment.' He gnawed his lip, something Bond had not seen him do before. 'Anyway, they may have nothing to do with us. Routine. Coincidence. Could be.'

'Could be. But somehow I don't . . .' Bond left the sentence unfinished.

Far away to the north of the Starlifter, the two Armée de l'Air Super Mirage fighters from the Fourth Fighter Wing turned in unison. Below, the pilots could see another pair of Mirages coming up fast. The leader of the pair which had been keeping station clicked on his transmitter and spoke. 'Watchdog Five,' he said.

Through his headphones came a voice from the approaching aircraft. 'Watchdog Five, this is Watchdog Six on routine patrol. We take over now. Instructions you return to base and refuel. Over.'

'Watchdog Five,' the pilot of the first Super Mirage replied. 'Instructions understood. All quiet. Headings as before. Good luck.'

Watchdog Six acknowledged the message, the pilot turning his head in the shining cockpit to follow the first two Mirages as they peeled away. Then he called up his wingman and the two new aircraft swung into a long, looping pattern high over the sea. It was good exercise, he thought. But there must be more to it than a routine shadowing. It wouldn't be a Russian they were following; and he had not believed his squadron commandant, who had told them this was a snap defence exercise. For one thing they were armed to the gills – everything from cannon to rockets.

The pilot bent his head to look at his small radar screen. The blip came up at the expected place. The two aircraft turned away, to begin another long circuit. If the blip vanished, they had orders to close until they made contact again.

Away to the south at Perpignan Airport, SEPCAT Jaguars sat, off the main runways, as though waiting to leap into the air for a kill. In the airport's operations' room, senior Armée de l'Air officers were going over the flight plan filed by Aldan Aerospace for their Starlifter. So far it had not deviated. The aircraft had made a long climb out to sea, and then maintained a holding pattern while testing Aldan's specialised equipment. The holding pattern would continue, at almost 30,000 feet, for the best part of twenty-one hours. After that Aldan planned to descend almost to sea level before turning in to make their return approach to Perpignan at just before one o'clock the following afternoon.

In the building overlooking Regent's Park in London, M examined the latest reports radioed to him from France. Anton Murik's Starlifter was maintaining its filed flight plan. Yes, he thought, it probably will. Right up until the last moment, when he's got the ransom aboard. Unless—M hoped—unless James Bond was on board, and could do something about it.

It was a long and tiring evening: prelude to an even longer night of intense fatigue. Murik had drilled his staff to perfection, so that they followed a prescribed routine. Quite early on he told Bond that he did not expect the ransom aircraft to arrive anywhere near its DZ until around nine or ten the following morning. 'They can manage it by then—or so the computers tell me. That's why I set a minimum deadline. Twenty-four hours is just enough time.' He grinned—a clever pupil showing off. 'And it makes them jump: doesn't give them time to think hard.'

Rest and eating periods were staggered, and either Murik or Caber was always left with Bond, just as one of the other two men remained next to Lavender. Caber, in fact, was there most of the time.

As for Bond and Lavender, they were fed—mainly on coffee and sandwiches—where they sat, their wrists being freed only for eating, or when they were taken to the wash room by an armed man, who locked them into the simple closet and stood outside the door, letting them out at a knock from the inside. On returning, they were carefully strapped into their chairs again, always under the wicked eye of at least one pistol. On no occasion during the night would there have been any opportunity to reverse the situation, but Bond had far from given up hope. Already, in the wash room, he had begun to act.

On his last visit, Bond had quickly taken a large wad of tissue from the cardboard packet. This he had rolled into an elongated ball, around three inches in length, and a good three inches thick. On being released, and led back to his seat, Bond placed both hands behind his back, ready for his wrists to be strapped. At the same time he manipulated the wedge of tissue from the palm of his hand, up and between the wrists, which he held tightly together.

It was an old trick, favoured by escapologists. When the wrist strap went on, Bond started to work with his fingers, pulling the tissue down from between his wrists. It was a lengthy business, but when the entire ball of tissue was removed and once more in his palm, the strap was looser around his wrists. There was freedom of an inch or so for him to work the strap around with his fingers and pick away at the fastening. The entire job took over an hour, but at last Bond knew that if he placed his wrists tightly together, then elongated his fingers in an attitude of prayer, the strap would slide away leaving his hands and arms free.

Near dawn, he decided. Near dawn, when they were all tired, and at their lowest ebb. It would be then, if the opportunity came, that he would act, whatever the consequences.

At around five-thirty in the morning, just after Murik had been to the forward part of the aircraft for coffee, Caber asked if he could go to the canteen.

'As long as it's only for coffee, Caber,' Murik said, laughing, while his eyes scanned the equipment in front of him.

The big man saw nothing funny about the remark, gruffly saying that of course it would be coffee. He slid the door open and let it slam back into place as he disappeared.

Bond knew his movements would have to be both very fast and accurate. Murik seemed preoccupied with the apparatus in front of him, and Bond feigned sleep. The other two men were still at Lavender's console. One had his eyes closed but did not seem to be fully asleep, merely relaxed and resting. The other was intent on watching his screen through the viewer.

Gently James Bond flexed his hands, allowing the wrist strap to come free. He clenched his fists a few times to get the circulation going, making up his mind for the last time as to his plan of action.

Then he dropped the strap and moved. His right hand came up, arrowing towards the gun inside Murik's jacket, while the left swept round, with all the force he could muster, in a vicious chop at the Laird's unsuspecting throat. The blow from the heel of his left hand was slightly inaccurate, catching the side of his victim's neck instead of the windpipe. Nevertheless it had all Bond's strength behind it, and as it landed so the fingers of his right hand grabbed at the butt of the Colt Python, which came out of the holster easily as Murik crumpled on to the deck. Bond, still strapped in, swivelled his chair around with his feet, holding the Colt up firmly in a two-handed grip.

He fired almost before Murik's unconscious body hit the ground, yelling to Lavender, 'Stay quite still.' Of the two men at the console, the heavy technician at the radar screen moved first, snapping his head up and going for his own gun a split second before his partner. As Bond squeezed the trigger it crossed his mind that this was one of the most foolhardy exploits he had ever attempted. Each bullet had to find its mark. One through the metal of the fuselage and bang would go the pressurisation. The long hours on various firing ranges paid off in full. In all, he fired twice: two

burst of two—the 'Double Tap' as the SAS call it—the
·357 ammunition exploding like a cannon in the confines of
the cabin. Four bullets reached their individual targets. He
could not blame Lavender for screaming as the first of her
captors spun to one side, a bullet lodged in his shoulder.
The second caught him on the side of the head, hurling him
into eternity with a great spatter of blood leaping from the
wound. Yet while the blood was still airborne, Bond had
fired his second two shots. The man who had been resting
with his eyes closed caught both rounds in the neck, top-
pling backwards, the sound of his gargling fall emerging
from the after-echo of the shots.

Then there was silence except for a small whimper of
fright from Lavender. 'It's okay, Dilly. The only way. Sorry
it was so close.'

She looked in horror at the bodies, then took in a breath
and nodded. Her guards lay dead, and her clothes dripped
with their blood. She shivered and nodded again. 'It's
okay, James. Sorry. It was unexpected, that's all.
How . . . ?'

'No time now. Got to do something about those bloody
terrorist squads before anything else.' Transferring the
revolver to his left hand, 007 grasped the microphone on its
snake-like, jointed stand. Now he would see how far logic
went. Having heard the squads report in with their 'Number one . . . War; Number Two . . . War' there was, for
Bond, only one way to stop the nuclear operation from
proceeding. He pressed the transmit button and began to
speak, slowly and distinctly:

'Number One . . . Lock; Number Two . . . Lock; Number Three . . . Lock' right through all six of the squads —
completing the word Anton Murik had used as his personal
cryptonym for Meltdown — Warlock.

'Now we pray.' He looked towards Lavender, still strapped helplessly in her seat. Bond's hands went to the buckle
on his belt in order to reassemble the small knife concealed
in its various components — the knife he had used to strip off

the section of the money belt in Perpignan. He worked
calmly, though it was a frustrating business. As he glanced
towards Lavender, smiling and giving her a few words of
confidence, he saw the means to his quick escape were very
near the girl, if only she were free.

The technician who had been watching the radar screen
when Bond's bullets had swept him from existence lay
slumped in his seat, turned slightly towards Lavender. The
man's trouser leg had ridden up on the right side, revealing
a long woollen stocking into which was tucked a Highland
dirk, safe in its scabbard. Bond had fleetingly feared, when
amongst the festive crowds in Perpignan, that death would
come silently by means of a dirk like this. It was the obvious
weapon for these people to carry. Now, just when he needed
the weapon, it was out of reach. As he completed fitting his
own small knife together, he drew Lavender's attention to
the dirk.

'Just get on with that handy little gadget you've produced from Lord knows where, James.' Her face betrayed
her frantic state of mind. 'Caber's already been gone for
nearly fifteen minutes. If you're not free by the time . . .'

'Okay, Dilly. *Nix panicus*, as my old Latin master used to
say.' He was already attacking the webbing straps binding
him to the seat. The small blade was sharp, but its size did
not make for speed: one slip and he could slash himself
badly.

As he worked there were no sounds about them except
for his own breathing counterpointed with that of the unconscious Laird of Murcaldy. Bond wondered how badly
he had damaged Murik. If his aim had been really accurate
the man would now be dead from a shattered trachea.

The first cross-strap came clear, but he was still not free.
Bond sawed away at the second belt – an easier task, for
with the first strap gone, he had more room in which to
move. It still seemed an age before the tiny blade ripped its
way through the tough webbing. It only remained for Bond
to unclip the seat belt and he was completely out of the

harness, springing up and flexing his muscles to get the blood flowing again.

In a second he was with Lavender, on his knees, feeling under the anchored chair to find the release mechanism, which he unclipped, so that her restraining harness fell away. Another couple of seconds to undo the wrist strap and she too was free.

'Hadn't you better stand by with that gun?' She nodded towards the other console, where Bond had left the Python.

'Don't worry, Caber's not going to cause us much . . .' He stopped, seeing her eyes turn towards the sliding door, widening with a hint of fear.

Bond whirled around. Caber had returned and now stood in the doorway, one huge hand still holding the partition open, while his eyes darted around the control room, taking in the carnage. Both Caber and Bond were frozen for a second, looking at each other. Bond's eyes flicked towards Murik's console, and the Python; and, in that second, Caber also saw the weapon.

As Bond came up from his crouched position, so Caber let out a great roar – a mixture of fury and grief for his master – and launched himself at Bond. For the first time, Lavender expressed her pent-up fear in a long, terrified shriek.

21

AIRSTRIKE

THE PREVIOUS DAY M had set up his own operations' room, next to his suite of offices on the ninth floor of the head-quarters' building overlooking Regent's Park. He dozed fitfully, half dreaming of some odd childhood incident: running along a beach with water lapping at his feet. Then the familiar sound, which began in his dream as his long-dead mother ringing the bell for tea, broke into M's consciousness. It was the red telephone by the camp bed. M noted it was nearly five o'clock in the morning as he picked up the handset and answered with a throaty 'Yes?'

Bill Tanner was on the line, asking if M would come through to the main operations' room. 'They've surrendered.' The Chief-of-Staff made no attempt to disguise his excitement.

'Who've surrendered?' M snapped.

'The terrorists. The people holding the nuclear reactors. All of them: those here, in England, the French groups, the two in the United States and the Germans. Just walked out with their hands up. Said it was over.'

M frowned. 'Any explanation?'

'It only happened a short while ago.' Tanner's voice now resumed its normal, calm tone. 'Reports are still coming in, sir. Apparently they said they'd received the code message to abort the mission. Our people up at Heysham One say the terrorists seem to think their operation's been success-ful. I've spoken to one of the interrogators. He believes they've been given the call-off by mistake.'

M grinned to himself. 'I wonder,' he grunted. 'I wonder if it was an engineered mistake?'

'007?' the Chief-of-Staff asked.

'Who else? What about the Starlifter?' M was out of the camp bed now, trying to hang on to the 'phone and wrestle with his trousers at the same time.

'Still keeping station. The French are going in now. Two sections of fighters are on their way. They held off just long enough to get the okay from the technicians at the nuclear reactors, which all appear to be safe and operating normally, by the way.'

M paused. 'The French fighters? They're briefed to force the Starlifter down?' His grip on the receiver tightened.

Tanner's voice now became very calm: almost grave. 'They're briefed to buzz it into surrendering, then to lead it back to Perpignan.'

'And . . . ?'

'If that doesn't work, the orders are to blast it out of the sky.'

'I see.' M's voice dropped almost to a whisper.

'I know, sir.' The Chief-of-Staff was fully aware of what must have been going through M's mind. 'We just have to hope.'

Slowly, M cradled the receiver.

Bond did not stand a chance of getting to the revolver, which was still lying on the console. Murik's chief lieutenant was enraged, and dangerous as a wounded bull elephant. His roar had changed into the bloodcurdling cry of a fighting man who could only be stopped by a fusillade of bullets, as he seemed to take off through the air and catch Bond, half-way across the cabin. Bond felt his breath go from his lungs as the weight of the brute landed on him with full force. Caber was yelling obscenities and calling on the gods for vengeance. Now he had Bond straddled on the floor, his legs across Bond's thighs and the enormous hands at his victim's throat. Bond tried to cry out for Lavender's help as the red mist clouded his brain, but Caber's pressing fingers prevented him. Only a croak emerged. Then, with the same swiftness of Caber's attack, the whole situation changed.

The Starlifter's engines, which until now had been only a steady hum in the background, changed their note, rising and straining in a roar, while the deck under the struggling men lurched to one side. Bond was conscious of the aircraft's attitude altering dramatically as he rolled, still locked with Caber, across the cabin floor. He caught a glimpse of Lavender, all arms and legs, being flung forward, as a great buffeting of the airframe ensued. Then the Starlifter lurched again, wallowing like a great liner plunging in a heavy sea. This action, followed by yet another sudden and violent change of attitude, as though they were making a steep downward turn, threw Caber free.

Bond swallowed, his throat almost closed by the pressure of Caber's hands, then heard Lavender calling that there were aircraft attacking. 'Fighters,' she yelled. 'They're coming in very close.'

Bond's ears started to pop, and he swallowed painfully again, trying to get to his feet and stay upright on the unstable deck, which was now angled downwards, juddering and bucking as though on a rollercoaster ride. He finally managed to prop himself against the forward door and began to make for the revolver. Out of the corner of his eye he saw that Lavender appeared to have been thrown some distance, and was lying huddled near her console. There was no time to do anything for her now. Caber, on his hands and knees near Murik's console was bracing himself for another attack, an arm stretched out towards the revolver.

The giant leaped forward, landing unsteadily on the rolling floor, his mask of fury giving way to a smile of triumph. 'I'd rather do it another way,' he shouted. 'Not by the bullet. I ken a bullet's too guid for ye.' His hand almost hid the Python revolver, which pointed directly at Bond's chest, motioning his victim to the other side of the cabin, towards the large hatchway marked out in red, and bearing the legend DO NOT ENTER IF RED LIGHT IS ON.

'Ye'll get over there,' Caber growled, keeping his balance, even though the aircraft was undoubtedly in a nose-down attitude, descending rapidly.

There was no way to avoid the order without ending up with his chest torn away by the Python's bullets. Bond crabbed across the cabin towards the hatchway.

'Now' – Caber had managed to get close behind him, but not near enough for Bond to try a tackle – 'now ye'll slide that thing open, and hold it until ma own hand's on it.'

Bond did as he was bidden; felt the revolver barrel jab at his back and saw Caber's hand take over the weight of the sliding hatchway as, together, they stepped through into the high sparred and girdered rear of the Starlifter. The aircraft made another fast and unexpected turn, throwing them apart, so that Bond banged his right arm against a rising, curved spar.

'I'm still behind ye, Bond, with the wee shooter, so dinna do anything daft. There's a wee bit of a lever I have to pull over here.'

The rear loading bay was cold: a bleak airborne hangar of metal, smelling of oil and that odd plastic scent of air that you get inside aircraft. The buffeting was worse here, almost below the high tail of the Starlifter. Bond had to grip hard on the spar to keep his balance, for the big aeroplane seemed to be turning alternately left and right, still going down, with occasional terrifying bucketing and noise – which Bond now clearly recognised as other aircraft passing close and buzzing them.

'There we go,' Caber called, and Bond heard the solid sound of a large switch going down. It was followed by the whine of hydraulics and an increased reverberation. Bond twisted around, to see Caber leaning against a bulkhead just inside the hatchway, the revolver still accurately aimed, while his left hand was raised to an open metal box inside which a two-foot double knife-switch had just been pulled down and was locked into the 'on' position. There was another great wallowing as the huge plane dropped a couple of hundred feet, and both men clung hard to their precious holds. Caber laughed. 'The Laird had some daft idea of pushing ye out an' trailing ye along with the pick-up line when we went fur the ransom. I'm gawn tae make sure o' ye, Bond.'

There was a distinct decrease in temperature. Bond could feel air blowing around him. Looking back towards the tail end of the hold, he saw the rear sides of the fuselage moving away, long curved sections, slowly pivoting outwards, while an oblong section of the deck gently dropped away to the increased whine of the hydraulic system. The ramp was going down. Already he could see a section of sky.

'It'll tak aboot twa minutes,' Caber shouted. 'Then ye'll have a nice ski slope there. Ye'll be goin' doon that, Bond. Goin' doon it tae hell.'

Bond's mind raced. If he was to die, then Caber would have to kill him with the gun. It was not likely that he could even get within grappling distance of the man. They were a good twenty feet from each other, and the Starlifter, still with its nose down, was yawing and performing what he recognised as evasive action of the most extreme kind. Perhaps it was his imagination, but Bond thought he could hear the metal plates singing and stretching with near human cries of pain as the aircraft was flung about the sky.

There is a dread, deep within most people, of falling to their death from a great height. James Bond was no exception. He clung on to his spar, transfixed by the quickly widening gap between metal and sky. Sudden death had never bothered him – in many ways he had lived with it for so long that it ceased to bring nightmares. One minute you would be alive, the next in irreversible darkness. But this would be different. He felt the clammy hand of death on his neck, and the cold sweat of genuine fear closed over him.

With a heavy rumble and thump, the ramp locked down, sloping away and leaving a huge open hole the size of a

house in the rear of the aircraft. The sky tilted behind the
opening, then swerved as the Starlifter went through yet
another manoeuvre.

'This is where we say fare ye weel – For auld lang syne,
Bond. Now git ye doon that ramp and practise flying wi'out
wings.'

'You'll have to shoot me down it,' Bond shouted. He was
not going without some show of a fight. Letting go of the
spar, he aimed himself at Caber just as the Starlifter dipped
lower, the tail coming up at a precarious angle. Bond
lurched forward, almost losing his balance, going down out
of control towards Caber. In this heart-stopping moment
Bond saw the smile broaden on the man's face, his gun
hand coming up to point the Python straight at 007's chest.

Again the deck jerked under them and Bond staggered to
one side as the aircraft dipped and the door to the hatchway
slid open. For a second, Bond thought it was the movement
of the aircraft. Then, still pushed forward by the angle of
descent, he saw Lavender, the dirk from the dead guard's
stocking firmly in her hand, raised to strike.

Caber tried to turn and bring the revolver to bear, but
the instability of the deck combined with the unexpected
assault gave him no chance. Almost with a sense of dread,
Bond saw the dirk flash down – Lavender's left hand joining her right over the hilt as she plunged it with all her
strength into Caber's throat. Even with the noise of rushing
air, the buffeting and roar of engines, Caber's gurgling rasp
of terror echoed around the vast hold. The revolver fell to
the deck as he scrabbled at his throat, from which the blood
pumped out and down his jersey. Then Caber spun around,
still clamping hands to his neck, fell, and began to roll like a
piece of freight broken loose in a ship's hold.

Bond reached the door, making a grab for the man as the
aircraft once more changed its attitude, the nose coming up
and the engines changing pitch in a surge of power as it
started to gain altitude. Bond grasped Caber, but he could
not hold the heavy man, who slipped away, rolling towards

the point where the deck dipped into the long-angled ramp. Lavender turned her head away, hanging on to Bond, as Caber tumbled like a stuffed effigy, trailing blood, towards the ramp, hesitating fractionally as he began to fall. He must be almost dead already, Bond thought; but the horrible gargle of blood from the dirk-slit throat turned into a bubbling scream of terror as Caber slid down the ramp – a chilling and hideous sustained note.

As he reached the far end of the ramp, the big man's body seemed to correct itself, the gore-streaked face looking up towards Bond, arms outstretched, fingers clawing at the metal. For a second their eyes locked, and even though Caber's already held the glaze of death, they also contained a deep, dark hatred reaching out from what would soon be his grave. Then Murik's giant lieutenant slid over the edge, out of sight, into the air beneath the Starlifter.

'I killed him.' Lavender was near to a state of shock.

'An obvious statement, Dilly darling,' Bond still had to shout through the noise. 'What matters to me is that you saved my life.' He reached up to the big knife-switch, grasping the wooden handle and pulling it up, into the 'off' position.

The hydraulic whine began again, and the ramp started to move. Then, as Bond turned, he saw Lavender looking towards the closing gap, her eyes widening and lips parted. In the space still visible, a pair of Dassault Super Mirages could be seen hurtling in towards the Starlifter. As they watched, Bond and Lavender saw the bright flashes at the nose of each aircraft. The Mirage jets had passed, in a clap of air, with the crack and thunder of engines, before the Starlifter felt any effect from the short bursts of fire.

There followed a series of massive thuds, small explosions and the rip of metal. The deck under their feet began a long wave-like dance and the Starlifter appeared to be poised, hanging in the air. Then the engines roared again, and the deck steadied.

Bond's nose twitched at the acrid smell of smoke.

Pushing Lavender to one side, he slid open the hatchway to be met by a billow of smoke. Two or three of the small-calibre shells from the Mirages had passed through the roof, slamming into the main console, from which the flames flicked upwards, while smoke belched out in a deadly choking cloud.

Bond yelled at Lavender to keep out of the way. Already, during the tension in the rear hold, his subconscious had taken in the fact of two large fire extinguishers clipped into racks on either side of the sliding hatchway. He grabbed one of the heavy red cylinders, smashed the activating plunger against the nearest metal spar, slid back the door and pointed the jet of foam into the control room.

Coughing and spluttering from the fumes, Bond returned for the second cylinder. It took both the extinguishers at full pressure before the fire was out, leaving only eye-watering, throat-cloying fumes and smoke to eddy around the cabin.

Keeping Lavender close on the hold side of the door, Bond waited for the smoke to clear. He was now conscious of the Starlifter settling into a more natural flying pattern. Then came the heavy grind and thump as its landing gear locked into place. The one short burst of fire from the French fighters had done the trick, he thought. The international symbol for an aircraft's surrender was the lowering of its landing gear.

Inside the control cabin, the air was less foul, leaving only a sting in the nostrils. Lavender went straight towards one of the oval windows and, sliding up the blind, reported that they seemed to be losing height. 'There're a pair of fighter aircraft on this side,' she called.

Bond made for the other window. Below, the coastline was coming up, and they were in a long wide turn. On his side as well two Mirages kept station. He peered down, looking for landmarks until he saw the familiar shape of the Canigou. The fighters remained in place, lowering their undercarriages and flaps. They were making an escorted final approach to Perpignan.

Bond looked around. The bodies of the two technicians had been thrown across the cabin, but of Anton Murik there was no sign. Lavender said that, perhaps, when he came round, the Laird of Murcaldy had gone forward to give instructions to his crew. But when they landed at Perpignan and the police, together with M's envoys, came aboard, Murik had disappeared.

In the briefing that followed, one of the Mirage pilots reported seeing a man fall from the rear ramp: undoubtedly Caber. Another thought that a crew member may have baled out, but in the general mêlée he could not be certain.

The jets had come in fast and to start with the Starlifter had only taken evasive action, refusing to comply with their orders. It was only as a last resort that two of the fighters had fired one short burst each. It was after this show of strength that the Starlifter had surrendered. It was also after the firing that the jet pilot thought there might have been a parachute descent into the sea, but, he maintained, it was difficult to be sure. A lot of smoke was coming from the rear of the transport for a while, and there was light, scattered cloud.

'If he did jump,' one of M's officers said, 'there wouldn't be much chance of survival in the sea.'

In the aircraft back to London, Lavender voiced the view that she would never be convinced of her guardian's death until she had actually seen his body.

It was, then, with a certain number of unanswered questions, that Bond reported to M that evening at the Regent's Park headquarters.

22

WARLOCK'S CASTLE

'YOU RAN IT a bit too close for comfort, 007.' M sat at his desk, facing Bond.

'For whose comfort, sir?' James Bond was weary after the long debriefing, which had begun almost as soon as he had arrived back in London during the late afternoon. Since then Bond had gone over the story from the very beginning a number of times, and suffered the constant interruptions and cross-questioning that were par for the course. The lengthy conversation had been taken down on tape, and Bill Tanner joined Bond and M, while one of the senior female officers looked after Lavender—and, no doubt, grilled her as well, thought Bond.

'Even then you let him get away.' M sounded irritated.

'Too close for whose comfort, sir?' Bond repeated.

M waved the question to one side. 'Everybody's. What concerns me now is the whereabouts of Anton Murik, so-called Laird of Murcaldy.'

The white 'phone bleeped on M's desk. Following a brief exchange, M turned to his Chief-of-Staff. 'There's a signal in from Perpignan. Bring it up, will you?'

Tanner left, returning a few seconds later. The news at least solved part of the mystery. M read it over twice before passing it to Bond. The French authorities had now been over the Starlifter from stem to stern. Among the extra fitments aboard, they had discovered a small hold, accessible from under one of the tables in the canteen section. It was large enough to conceal one man and was kitted out with sufficient rations and other necessities for a few days. There were signs that it had been used; and the exit, through movable plates on the underside of the fuselage, had been opened.

'That settles it,' M snapped, picking up his 'phone. 'Better get this report typed up and signed, Bond. I'll have to alert Duggan and Ross. The fellow's still at large.'

Bond held up a hand as though appealing for M to put down the 'phone. 'With respect, sir, can I ask some questions? Then, maybe, make a couple of requests?'

Slowly M put down the telephone. 'Ask away. I can promise nothing, but be quick about it.'

'The requests will be determined by the answers to questions . . .'

'Get on with it then, 007. We haven't got all night.'

'Are Duggan's and Ross's men still prowling around Murik Castle?'

'Moved out this afternoon. They'd been over the castle and Murcaldy village with the proverbial toothcomb.' M began to fiddle with his pipe.

'Did they find anything?'

'Made a number of arrests, from what I gather. A baker called MacKenzie; some of the brawnier lads in the village. Took away a number of small arms and a few automatic weapons. Gather they've left the Laird's collection of antique weapons intact. All the modern stuff's been brought back to London.'

'Did they find papers? Legal documents, mainly concerning Miss Peacock? Possibly some convertible stocks, shares, that kind of thing? Well-hidden?'

'Haven't a clue, 007. Hidden documents? Melodramatic stuff, that.'

'Can you find out, sir? Find out without mentioning when my report'll be going to Sir Richard Duggan and Special Branch?'

M raised his eyebrows. 'This had better be good, 007.' He stabbed at the telephone. Within minutes, Bond and Bill Tanner were listening to one side of a conversation, punctuated by long pauses, between M and Sir Richard. At last M put down the 'phone, shaking his head. 'They took away all stray papers. But no legal documents concerning Miss Peacock. There were a couple of safes. Duggan says they'll be going over the castle again in a day or so.'

'And, in the meantime, it's unguarded?'

M nodded. 'Now the requests, eh, Bond?'

Bond swallowed. 'Sir, can you hold my report for about forty-eight hours? Particularly the facts about the Aldan Aerospace Flying Club – the place we took off from en route for Perpignan.'

'Why?'

'Because I don't want Special Branch thumping around there. If Anton Murik's escaped by hiding in the Starlifter, I believe he'll be on his way back to that flying club now. He has a lot of contacts, and his helicopter's there.'

'Then we should have Special Branch waiting for him . . .'

'No, sir. There are legal documents hidden at the castle, and – as I've said – probably some mad money as a back-up. Anton Murik will be heading for the castle. He'll know the time's come to destroy the evidence of Miss Peacock's claim to the title and estates of Murcaldy. I want him caught in the act, alive if possible.'

'Then we should send in Duggan's men with Special Branch.'

'Sir, he should be mine.' Bond's voice was like the cutting edge of a sabre.

'You're asking me to bend the rules, 007. That's Duggan's territory, and I've no right . . .' He trailed into silent thought. 'What exactly were you thinking of?'

'That the Chief-of-Staff comes with me, sir. That you give us forty-eight hours' freedom, and the use of a helicopter.'

'Helicopter?'

'To get us up there quickly. Oh yes, and just before we go in, I'd like some kind of overflight.'

'Overflight,' M came near to shouting. 'Overflight? Who

do you think I am, 007? President of the United States?
What do you mean, overflight?'

Bond tried to look sheepish. Bill Tanner was grinning.
'Well, sir, haven't we got a couple of old Chipmunks, fitted
with infra-red, and the odd Gazelle helicopter? Aren't they
under your command?'

M gave a heavy cough, as though clearing his throat.

'If the Chief-of-Staff and I went up in the helicopter,
we'd need an overflight about five minutes before landing.
Just to make certain the coast is clear, that Murik hasn't
arrived first.'

M fiddled with his pipe.

'Just for safety, sir.'

'You sure you wouldn't like a squadron of fighter-
bombers to strafe the place?'

Bond grinned. 'I don't think that'll be necessary, sir.'

There was an even longer pause before M spoke. 'On one
condition, Bond – providing the Chief-of-Staff agrees to
this foolhardiness.' He looked towards Bill Tanner, who
nodded. 'You do *not* go armed. In all conscience I cannot, at
this stage, allow you to move into Duggan's area of operations carrying arms.'

'You did say the Laird's collection of antique weapons
had been left intact, sir?'

M nodded, with a sly smile. 'I know nothing about any of
this, James. But good luck.' Then, sarcastically, he added,
'nothing else?'

'Well . . .' Bond looked away. 'I wonder if Sir Richard's
people could be persuaded to let us have the keys to the
castle for a while? P.D.Q., sir. Just so that I can recover
clothes left there, or some such excuse.'

M sighed, made a grumbling noise, and reached for the
telephone again.

It was almost four o'clock in the morning when the Gazelle
helicopter carrying James Bond and Bill Tanner reached
Glen Murcaldy.

Bond had already been through the landing pattern with
the young pilot. He wanted to be put down on the track
near to the point where the Saab had gone into the large
ditch. Most of all, he was concerned that the Gazelle should
be kept well out of sight, though he had armed himself with
two sets of hand-held flares – a red and a green – to call up
the chopper if there was trouble.

Exactly five minutes before reaching touchdown, they
heard the code word 'Excelsior' through their headphones.
The Chipmunk had overflown the glen and castle, giving
them the all clear. There was no sign of any vehicle or other
helicopter in the vicinity.

The rotor blades of the Gazelle had not stopped turning
by the time Bond and Tanner were making their way
through the gorse and bracken towards the grim mass of
Murik Castle below. The early morning air was chill and
clear, while the scents brought vivid memories back into
Bond's head – of his first sight of the castle and of its deceptive interior, of the attempted escape, Murik's control room
with its array of weapons, the East Guest Room and its
luxurious décor, and the more unpleasant dankness of the
twin torture chambers.

They carried no weapons, as instructed, though Bill
Tanner had, rightly, managed to get hold of a pair of
powerful torches. M had experienced difficulty with the
keys, managing only to obtain those to the rear tradesmen's
entrance, which, Duggan told him, was the only door left
for access, the rest having been left with the electronic locks
on.

It took over half an hour for the pair to get as far as the
Great Lawn. Bond, silently making signals, took Tanner
alongside the rear of the castle, the old keep rising above
them like a dark brooding warning against the skyline. If
Bond was right it would be from the helicopter pad behind
the keep that Anton Murik would make his final visit to his
castle; Warlock's Castle, as Bond now thought of it.

In spite of the place only having been empty for a short

time, the air smelled musty and damp once they got inside the small tradesmen's door. Again, recent memories stirred. It was only a few days ago that Bond had been led through this very door and into MacKenzie's van, at the start of the long journey which had ended with a deadly rendezvous over the Mediterranean.

Now he had to find his way down to the Laird's control room and collection of weapons; for Bond was certainly not going to face Anton Murik without some kind of defence. For a while they blundered around by torchlight, until Bond finally led the way down to the long weapon-adorned room in the cellars. Even Bill Tanner gasped as they swung the torches around the walls replete with swords, thrusting weapons, pistols, muskets and rifles.

'Must be worth a fortune by itself,' whispered Tanner.

Bond nodded. They had, for some unaccountable reason, whispered throughout the journey down from the tradesmen's entrance, as though Murik and his henchmen might come upon them unawares at any moment. Outside dawn would just be breaking, streaking the sky. If Murik was going to make his dash for freedom he would either arrive soon, or they would still be waiting for him to come under the cover of nightfall. Bond was running his torch over the weapons when Tanner suddenly clutched at his arm. They stood, motionless, ears straining for a moment, then relaxed.

'Nothing,' said Tanner. Then, just as suddenly, he silenced Bond once more.

This time they could both hear the noise: from a long way off, up through the brick, stone and earth, the faint buzz of an engine.

'He's arrived.' Bond grabbed at the first thing he could lay hands on: a sporting crossbow, heavily decorated, but refurbished, with a thick taut cord bound securely to a metal bow, the well-oiled mechanism including a *cranequin* to pull back and latch the cord into place. Taking this and three sharp bolts which were arranged next to it, Bond motioned Tanner out of the room.

'Up to the hall,' he whispered. 'The light's not in his favour. He'll want to get hold of the stuff and be away fast. Pray God he'll take it all with him, and we can catch the bastard outside.'

There would be more chance in the open. Bond was sure of that. As they reached the hall, the noise of the descending helicopter became louder. It would be the little Bell Ranger, hovering and fluttering down behind the keep. Standing in the shadows, Bond strained his ears. If the pilot kept his engines running, 007 knew his theory would be right – that Murik planned to remain in the castle for only a short time, leaving quickly with whatever documents he had cached there. But if the engine was stopped, they would have to take him inside the building.

Somewhere towards the back of the house, there was the scratch and squeak of a door. Murik was entering the same way that Bond and the Chief-of-Staff had come, by the tradesmen's entrance. Thank heaven for Tanner, whose wisdom had cautioned the locking of the door behind them. There was a click and then the sound of footsteps moving surely, as a man will move in complete darkness when he knows his house with the deep intimacy of years. The steps were short and quick: unmistakable to Bond. Murik – Warlock – was home again.

From far away outside came the gentle buzz of the Bell Ranger's engine, which meant the pilot was almost certainly waiting, seated in his cockpit. Bond signalled with the crossbow, and they set off silently in the direction of the door through which the Laird had returned. Outside it was almost fully light now, with only faint traces of cloud, pink from the reflected rising sun. The noise of the helicopter engine was loud, coming from behind the keep, to which Bond now pointed. Side by side, Tanner and Bond sought the edge of the old stone tower, black and bruised with age, to shelter behind one angled corner, from which they had a view of the castle's rear.

Bond bent to the task of turning the heavy *cranequin*, panting at each twist of the wheel, as the steel bow drew back and its thick cord finally clicked into place. Raising the weapon skywards for safety, Bond slid one of the bolts into place. He had no idea of its accuracy, though there was no doubt of it being a lethal weapon.

The seven or eight minutes' wait seemed like a couple of hours. Then, with surprising suddenness, they heard footsteps fast on the gravel. Bond stepped from the cover, lifting the crossbow to his shoulder. Anton Murik was running hard, to their right, heading for the far side of the keep. In the left hand he held a thick and bulky oilskin package, while in his right he clutched at something Bond could not quite see. Squinting down the primitive crossbow sights, Bond shouted, 'Far enough, Murik. It's over now.'

The Laird of Murcaldy hardly paused, seeming to turn slightly towards Bond's voice, his right hand rising. There was a sharp crack followed by a high-pitched screaming hiss. A long spurt of fire streaked from Murik's hand, leaving a comet trail behind it, passing so close between Bond and Tanner that they felt the heat from the projectile which hit the side of the keep with the thud of a sledge-hammer. A whole block of the old stone cracked and splattered away, sending great shards flying. Tanner gave a little cry, clutching his cheek, where a section of sharp stone sliced through.

Bond knew immediately what Murik was using: a collector's item now, from the early 1950s, the M.B.A. Gyrojet Rocket pistol. This hand-held launcher fired high velocity mini-rockets, propelling payloads of heat-resistant steel like bright polished chrome. The 13mm. bullets, with their rocket propellant, were capable of penetrating thick steel plates. Bond had handled one, and recalled wondering what they would do to a man. He did not think twice about their efficiency. The Gyrojet pistol contained a magazine holding five rockets. He had a one-shot crossbow and no margin for error.

Bond did not hesitate. Before Murik — still running — could hurl another rocket from his Gyrojet, he squeezed the trigger of the crossbow. The mechanism slammed forward, its power taking Bond by surprise. The solid noise of the mechanism drowned any hiss the bolt might have made through the air and was, in its turn, blotted out by Murik's cry as the heavy bolt speared the upper part of his chest.

Murik continued to run, as both Bond and Tanner started after him. Then he staggered and the Gyrojet pistol dropped on to the gravel. Swaying and weaving, Murik doggedly ran on, whimpering with pain, still clutching at the oilskin package. He had by now almost reached the rising ground behind the keep, above the helicopter pad.

Bond ran hard, pausing only to sweep up the Gyrojet, and check that there was a rocket in place. Grunting with pain and anguish, Anton Murik was gasping his way up the bank as Bond shouted to him for the second time. 'Stop. Stop, Anton. I don't want to kill you; but I'll fire if you don't stop now.'

Murik continued, as though he could hear nothing, and, as he reached the top of the mound, Bond and Tanner heard the noise of the helicopter engine rise as lift power was applied. The target was outlined against the now red morning sky: Murik teetering on top of the mound, ready to make a last dash down the other side to the Bell Ranger lying just out of sight.

Bond shouted 'Stop' once more. But for Murik there was no turning back. Carefully Bond levelled the Gyrojet pistol and squeezed the trigger. There was a crack from the primer, then he felt the butt push back into his hand as the rocket left the barrel, gathering speed with a shower of flame — a long trace of fire getting faster and faster until it struck Murik's back, with over a thousand foot-pounds of energy behind it.

Only then did Bond know what such a projectile did to a man. It was as though someone had taken a blowlamp to the rear of a cardboard cut-out target; for the centre of

Murik's back disintegrated. For a second, Bond could have sworn that he was able to see right through the gaping hole in the man, as he was lifted from his feet, rising into the air before falling forwards out of sight.

Tanner was beside Bond, his face streaked scarlet with blood, as they paced each other up the bank. Below, the helicopter pilot was revving his motor for takeoff. One glance towards Bond and the levelled Gyrojet pistol changed his mind. The pilot shut down the engine and slowly climbed from the cockpit, placing his hands over his head.

Bond handed the weapon to Bill Tanner and descended towards the mangled remains of Anton Murik, lying just inside the pad. He hardly looked at the body. What he wanted lay a short way off – a heavy, thick oilskin package, which he picked up with care, tucking it under his arm before turning to walk slowly up the rise towards the old keep. There Bond stood for a good two minutes, taking a final long look at the castle. Warlock's Castle.

23

QUITE A LADY

JAMES BOND STOOD on the station platform, looking up into Lavender Peacock's bright eyes. It had been one of the best summers in a life which held memories of many long and eventful holiday months. Though he felt a tinge of sadness, Bond knew that all good things must end sometime. Now, the moment had come.

The oilskin packet, recovered at Murik's death, contained a whole folio of interesting items, many of which would take months to unravel. Most important of all was the irrefutable documentation concerning Murik's real parenthood and Lavender Peacock's claim to the estates and title. These also proved her real name to be Lavender Murik, Peacock being a name assumed, quite illegally, by her father before he returned to make the claim which had ended in death.

Bond had been allowed to extract these documents, and M saw to it that they were placed in the hands of the best possible solicitors in Scotland. He was optimistic that there would be a quick ruling on the matter. In a few months Lavender would gain her inheritance.

In the meantime, Bond had been given a long leave to recuperate; though Bill Tanner had stayed on duty, his cheek decorated with sticking plaster for over a month.

A few days after his return from Murcaldy, Bond had left with Lavender, by car, for the French Riviera. To begin with, things had gone according to plan. Thinking it would be a great treat, Bond had taken the girl to the best hotels; but she was unsettled, and did not like the fuss.

On one occasion, while staying at the Negresco in Nice,

Lavender wakened Bond in the night, crying out and screaming in the clutches of a nightmare. Later she told him she had dreamed of them both trapped in the Starlifter, which was on fire. James Bond gently cradled her in his arms, soothed her as one comforts a child, and held her close until the sun came up. Then they sat and breakfasted on the balcony, watching the early strollers along the Promenade des Anglais and the white triangles of yacht sails against the Mediterranean.

After a few days of this, they decided on more simple pleasures — motoring into the mountains, staying in small villages far away from the crowded resorts; or at little-known seaside places, basking in the sun, lazing, eating, talking and loving.

Bond explained the new responsibilities that would soon be thrust upon her, and Lavender slowly became more serious and withdrawn. She was still fun to be with, but, as the weeks passed Bond noticed she was spending more time writing letters, making telephone calls, sending and receiving cables. Then one morning, out of the blue, she announced that they must return to England.

So it turned out that, a week after their return to London, Lavender visited a solicitor in Gray's Inn — acting for a firm in Edinburgh — to be told that the Scottish courts had upheld her claim to the Murik estates and title. There was even an imposing document from the Lord Lyon King of Arms, stating that she had inherited the title Lady Murik of Murcaldy.

Two days later, Lavender visited Bond with the news that she had managed to obtain a place at one of the major agricultural colleges, where she was going to study estate management. In fact, she would be leaving on the sleeper that night, to tie up matters in Edinburgh.

'I want to get the place running properly again,' she told him. 'It needs a new broom and a blast of cold air blowing through it. I think that's what my father would have wanted — for me to give the estate, and the title, its good name again.'

Bond, due back from leave the following day, would not have tried to stop her. She was right, and he felt proud of having had some part in what looked like a glowing future. He took her out to dinner, then drove to collect her things and get her to the station.

'You'll come and stay, James, won't you? When I've got it all going again, I mean.' She leaned down out of the train window, the last-minute bustle going on around them.

'You try and stop me,' he said with a smile. 'Just try. But you might have to hold my hand at night — to lay the ghosts.'

'The ghosts? Really? It'll be a pleasure, James.' Lady Murik leaned forward and kissed him hard on the mouth, just as the whistle blew and the train started to move. 'Goodbye, James. See you again soon. Goodbye, my dear James.'

'Yes, Dilly, you'll see me again soon.' He stepped back, raising a hand.

Quite a Lady, thought James Bond, as the train snaked from the platform. Quite a Lady.

JOHN GARDNER

NEVER SEND FLOWERS

An Italian General. An English MP. A Russian novelist. An American Spymaster.

In different corners of the world four high-profile figures are assassinated in less than a week.

Nobody links the deaths but one thing is certain: each of them has been stalked, sought out and killed with care and preparation.

Then comes the fifth death in Switzerland and a macabre and sinister connection. A single blood-tipped rose sent to each funeral.

Enter James Bond and Flicka von Grosse, a gorgeous Swiss intelligence officer, to fit the pieces together. A perilous assignment which starts with the mysterious actor David Dragonpol and leads them to Athens, Milan and on to EuroDisney . . . and an explosive climax.

'All the classic ingredients are there for gourmet Bond lovers'

Birmingham Post

HODDER AND STOUGHTON PAPERBACKS